Sleep When I'm Dead

by

Johnny Barnes

authorHOUSE

1663 Liberty Drive, Suite 200
Bloomington, Indiana 47403
(800) 839-8640
www.authorhouse.com

This book is a work of fiction. Places, events, and situations in this story are purely fictional and any resemblance to actual persons, living or dead, is coincidental.

© 2004 Johnny Barnes
All Rights Reserved.

No part of this book may be reproduced, stored in a retrieval system, or transmitted by any means without the written permission of the author.

First published by AuthorHouse 04/05/04

ISBN: 1-4184-1835-8 (e)
ISBN: 1-4184-1836-6(sc)

Printed in the United States of America
Bloomington, Indiana

This book is printed on acid-free paper.

Table of Contents

Chapter 1
Under The Knife 1

Chapter 2
We Get Paid Either Way 23

Chapter 3
#1 With a Bullet: The One Shot Deal 35

Chapter 4
Zen Again 39

Chapter 5
Cold Black Knight 49

Chapter 6
Room for Interrogation 55

Chapter 7
Black Jack 61

Chapter 8
The Man in the Mirror 64

Chapter 9
Johnny's Jazz and Blues Club 70

Chapter 10
Call Central Casting 77

Chapter 11
The Heart of the Matter 81

Chapter 12
Boston Beat 95

Chapter 13
Trial Run 106

Chapter 14
The Big House 111

Chapter 15
One Foot in the Grave 117

Chapter 16
God Strike Me Dead 122

Chapter 17
   The True Story 134
Chapter 18
   Dead In the Water 136
Chapter 19
   A Creeping Horror 139
Chapter 20
   Body In the Box 157
Chapter 21
   Case In Point 160
Chapter 22
   Diamonds In the Night 168
Chapter 23
   Dead Stop 177
Chapter 24
   Fade To Black 185
Chapter 25
   Voice In the Night 188
Chapter 26
   The Soul Brothers 196
Chapter 27
   The Long and The Short 205
Chapter 28
   Who's Your Daddy? 210
Chapter 29
   Plan 9 From Outer Space 217
Chapter 30
   You Can't Stop the Rain 226
Chapter 31
   Dead Wood 230
Chapter 32
   Cut To the Chase 236
Chapter 33
   The Scales of Justice 241

It's Just That Crazy Time

THAT TIME WHEN YOU JUST WANT TO SAY WHAT'S ON YOUR MIND… you're NOT HUNGRY… YOU DON'T NEED anything to drink… you JUST want to say WHAT'S ON YOUR MIND… TIRED OF BEATING AROUND THE BUSH… you wanna get to the point, cut to the chase… YOU'RE IN THE MOOD, TO SAY IT… STRAIGHT OUT… on the line… lay It OUT for comment… NO MORE coddling TO THE MAINSTREAM, CONTEMPORARY BELIEF OR ACCEPTED PERSPECTIVE… BUT TO TELL IT LIKE IT IS… you WANT TO GET IT OUT AND HIT THE NAIL ON THE HEAD, CLEAR UP THE MISCONCEPTIONS…

YOU WANT TO SAY WHAT'S ON YOUR MIND… and you're not afraid… You don't care what anybody thinks… Spit it out! STRAIGHT OUT.

BUT YOU'RE NOT SURE *WHAT THAT IS*.

You know the drill. Some of it is true. Some of it is lies. You don't know where the truth ends and the lies start. But if there are hopes, there are fears. If dreams can come true, so can nightmares… And then there's those that dwell on the darkside. Those who are so scarred and bludgeoned by life, they can't stand the light of day, but seek the cover of night, the shadow world. They use it, abuse it, give to it, take from it, and travel through it. And there are those who serve and protect it. But… it's JUST THAT CRAZY TIME.

Chapter 1

Under The Knife

It was a cold black night in Boston.

It was one of those chilling New England nights when the sub-zero temperatures and the twenty-knot winds drove the wind chill factor down below the twenty below mark. The kind of chill that penetrated through layers of clothes and into the flesh to the bone. The sky was clear and the stars twinkled from a million miles away.

It was a magical season in Boston. The Christmas lights were everywhere. Along the Fenway, in front of the State House, across Kenmore Square, out to Brighton, and into the Back Bay. Even the Hancock skyscraper was alive with lights. In front of the fifty-floor Prudential, the colored lights on the big Christmas tree from Canada blinked and glowed, crowned by an angel holding a star. The whole town seemed completely lit up. All the trees on the Boston Commons were draped with red, green, blue, gold, and silver lights. Newbury and Boylston streets were buzzing with shoppers and holiday traffic, just as it was downtown and in the North End. Christmas lights were strung down the center mall of Commonwealth Ave. and the Esplanade along the Charles River.

The bars and restaurants were filling, glowing, and bursting with Christmas cheer.

Maybe the murders, muggings, and rapes would stop.

On this night, in a Chinatown detective agency, crime moved its sinister black hand. Bucky pulled out the six-inch double-edged boot knife from behind his back, came up behind Jack, reached around, and held the long knife to his throat. Both men stood motionless, silhouetted by the hallway light coming through the office doorway in Jack Kelly's American Detective Agency. The blade was barely cutting the skin but Jack didn't move. Jack's right arm was held back, twisted up against his shoulder blades. He felt the blade's pressure against his throat and wondered if it were dull or rusty. Jack could feel his heart pounding, hear the breath in his chest hissing and travel up the secret channels to his eardrums, releasing the pressure. His hands were wet. Sweat was popping out on his forehead. Time slowed and then became suspended.

"Get that goddamned blade off my neck!" Jack spoke in a voice made hoarse by the pressure of the knife to his throat.

Justin Jones Buxton-Smythe IV stood very close behind Jack. He began talking into his ear, but Jack didn't listen to the words. Kelly could see Buxton-Smythe's short spiked blond hair out of the corner of his eye. Jack knew when Buxton-Smythe stopped talking he'd likely slit his throat. Jack tried to listen for any inflection in his voice. Some slight indication that he was about to make the cut, but Justin J. Buxton-Smythe IV, "Bucky" to his friends, kept talking. He was getting it all out. Jack knew that the criminally insane followed a pattern for only so long before they veered to the left. The knife was slowly cutting deeper and deeper as Jack's muscles tightened and the intensity in Buxton-Smythe's voice grew.

A thousand thoughts flashed through Jack Kelly's mind in rapid succession. Like maybe he should retire when he gets the chance. He should be selecting colors from a pallet while painting on a sandy beach somewhere. Maybe he should have stuck with the blues band, that big record deal was just around the corner. Maybe he could write cheap, sleazy, big-city crime novels, spitting them out like a welfare mother in a trailer park spits out kids. Or he should have pushed for that cushy paralegal investigator job. Maybe even get a law degree and become a practicing attorney... No, he wasn't that desperate.

His life was flashing, rolling along like a filmstrip, in front of his mind's eye.

The blade was slowly pressing into the flesh on Jack Kelly's throat, right below the Adam's Apple, slowly cutting the skin through its layers. It was a sharp pain and Jack guessed the blade was probably very, very sharp. He felt his warm blood trickling down the center of his chest.

Kelly flashed on the night, as a young patrol officer, he was dispatched to what the voice on the patrol car radio said was a disturbance at a residence. As he pulled the cruiser up to the single-family house the dispatcher updated with "Possible attempted suicide." Another cruiser pulled up in front and Jack made his way cautiously through the front door and into the dark house with his flashlight and gun drawn, not knowing what he would find, or what would come out of the darkness. The two light switches he tried were unresponsive and the glowing beams of their flashlights bounced off the walls in the musty house. There were no answers given to Jack's loud announcement, "Police! We need to talk to you."

Then, as he entered a dark parlor in the back of the house, there in front of him, with the eerie flicker of the television set blaring away, sat a pale man on a couch with his neck and throat slit wide open in a bizarre smile from ear to ear. An Exacto knife was clutched in his blood soaked hand. His eyes looked straight ahead in the direction of the television.

Jack shook involuntarily as he walked between the dead man and the flickering television set. He prayed the guy would not look up and say, "Hey! Down in front! I'm watching 'Cops!'"

Blood still oozed down the front of the dead man's shirt. Blood had filled up in the waistband of his pants, in his lap, pooled up again on the couch, down his legs and onto the floor. Pints and pints of blood. An array of other blades, a steak knife, a bread knife, a big, heavy vegetable cutter and a meat cleaver lay arranged and spread neatly on the coffee table in front of the dead man. But the box cutter, the Exacto knife in the deceased man's bloody hand, seemed to have done the job. No one is truly creative committing suicide. They blow their brains out, jump off a bridge, hang themselves, overdose, or slash and bleed out. Its all been done before. Where's the creativity? Where's the artistic statement?

Buxton-Smythe whispered in Jack's ear, "I saw you with her. She was laughing, and flirting, and I saw you put your hand on Lindsey's leg."

"Then you saw her slap me." Jack said, "She's a walking Bermuda Triangle. She's trouble. I was just doing my job. You hired me!"

"Yeah, I think she was coming on to you. She wants you," Buxton-Smythe said and pushed a little harder on the knife.

As the thin trickle of blood ran down the center of Jack's chest he began to detach himself from the thoughts that raced through his mind. He began to focus on a defense. And a route of attack… His throat could be slashed at any moment, but Jack wanted to have the plan, the move, altogether before striking… And strike he did.

"Buxton-Smythe… ah… Justin, think about what you're doing." Jack managed to whisper.

Buxton-Smythe answered with a demented giggle, tensed up and began to whisper in Kelly's ear again. "Oh, I have, I have…"

"Well think about this. Its maybe, three years or less for assault with a weapon but you could get twenty if you slice me. And you'll get life if I die."

"Got all the answers, detective? You ought to write a book."

"Jack Kelly *lives* the life, Sonny."

"Don't you call me Sonny! Because you don't know who my father is, do you, cop? You don't remember pushing him off the roof of Mass General Hospital, you bastard?"

"Thaddeus Reno?" Jack whispered.

"And my mother was a Provost. Does that ring a bell, dick?"

"I didn't know that the Provost Brothers were related to The Fat Man. I thought they were just the muscle-headed goons Reno hired to do his dirty work. Are you another brother, Bucky?"

"I am a cousin to the Provost Boys. I am the son of Thaddeus Reno. And stop calling him fat. It was a disease."

"Yes. Its called the 'Too Lazy To Stop Eating and Exercise Disease.'"

"He gave me everything a son could ask for. The best schools in England. A great apartment in New York. All expenses paid. And a new Porsche every three years."

"But where is the love… Ahgg!" Jack moaned as the knife cut a little deeper into his neck. "Hey, Porsche Boy, how come your last name isn't Reno?"

"Mr. Reno adopted me. My mother's previous marriage was to my natural father Reginald Buxton-Smythe and her family name was Provost."

Kelly's leg was starting to tremble slightly from the tension.

A state police defensive tactics instructor, who taught physical restraint and control at the police academy used to tell Jack when someone tried to strike or grab him, they were *giving* you their hands or arms. It was an "offering," a "gift from Allah." It was something to break, grab, pull, or strike back at. He would also say in a situation like this one, that Jack should "change the assailant's channel." The instructor was telling the recruits to do something to stun the offender and shake him up. Take him out of his game for just one moment.

Jack's thought's raced over an array of defensive and offensive strikes he could make. It was time to take charge and change Bucky's channel. He had to block the knife and hurt him. He needed to get the knife out of Buxton-Smythe's hand. And quickly.

Jack knew what he had to do. Divide Bucky's attention. Justin J. Buxton-Smythe IV stood directly behind Jack and his right hand held the knife pressed up against Kelly's neck. His left held Kelly's right arm twisted behind his back. Jack had formulated his plan as Buxton-Smythe kept whispering and with syncopated movement swung his left fist and slammed into the sack at the vortex of Buxton-Smythe's legs. His balls. This definitely drew Bucky's attention as he leaned forward, grabbed his testicles, and released Jack's arm. Simultaneously Kelly's right hand slid up between the hand holding the knife blade and his throat.

Buxton-Smythe reacted instinctively to the shot to his nuts and gasped for air in mid-sentence. Jack pushed the blade away from his throat, twisting and holding Buxton's wrist at arm's length. Jack turned to Bucky and gave him the palm of his left hand to the nose, driving it upward. Bucky was shocked and in pain. Jack pivoted to the right and grabbed a good strong two-handed hold on the sweet little baby finger of the hand holding the knife, and bent it upward and back. Jack stood up on his toes to achieve the ultimate torque.

The finger snapped like a dry twig with a loud crack. Jack blew out the air in his own lungs in a moment of freedom as the knife landed with a clank on the floor. Bucky howled, wide-eyed, staring at the finger which was pointing in an entirely wrong direction. One strong side kick to the midsection, a kick to the back of the knee, and Buxton-Smythe was kneeling on the ground. Jack added a straight right hand to the jaw. Buxton-Smythe's will to continue was completely gone. He was done for the day.

Justin J. Buxton-Smythe IV lay whimpering on the floor like a two-year-old. Now he seemed small to Jack. He sat on the floor sobbing and sniffling. The skinny, yet well dressed, spoiled rich boy. He looked more like he belonged on a tennis court or a golf course than holding a knife to a man's throat. Jack watched him carefully and picked up the knife from the floor. He put the knife in the top drawer of his desk and took out his .45 caliber Colt Combat Commander. Jack chambered a round and shoved the gun down the back waistband of his pants. He searched for a set of handcuffs in another drawer of his desk.

"Why can't I work with professionals?" Jack wondered out loud.

He found the cuffs and approached Buxton-Smythe who was still whimpering loudly holding his finger up and kicking on the floor.

"Shut up Bucky! You're under citizen's arrest. I'm going to put these cuffs on you the hard way or the easy way. I'll call for a rescue unit as soon as the cuffs are on."

"Go ahead! Just… go ahead and call," Buxton-Smythe cried like a scared kid. It never ceased to amaze Kelly how many so-called tough guys ended up in tears.

"It's all fun and games until someone snaps a pinky."

Buxton-Smythe felt the inside of his mouth by rubbing his cheek on his shoulder and said, "You loosened my tooth! I don't have a dental plan."

"Here's a dental plan. Chew on the other side of your mouth."

Buxton-Smythe's baby finger and hand were swelling up like a grapefruit so Jack had him put his hands out in the front and put the handcuffs on. He then sat Bucky up in the middle of the floor. Jack dialed 911 and told the police dispatcher that Justin J. Buxton-Smythe IV had just been apprehended attempting to slit private investigator Jack Kelly's throat at the American Detective Agency on the fourth floor of 129 Kingston Street, Boston. He is furthermore being detained, at this time, awaiting the arrival of the Boston Police. And please send a medical unit for a broken finger and a minor laceration, to wit; a knife wound to the throat.

This defeated intruder, Justin Buxton-Smythe, was the boyfriend of a young woman who had allegedly driven him to the apparent brink of insanity. But it wasn't that far a trip. And Bucky was right about his fiancée cheating. Just before she met Buxton-Smythe the football team retired her jersey. Jack had found out quite quickly that she was "seeing" at least two other guys and seemed to have an "Open For Business" sign hanging around her neck. Let us just say that Mr. Buxton-Smythe was less than thrilled with the results of Jack Kelly's investigation on the object of his affection, his near-fatal attraction. Oh well. Kill the messenger.

But Bucky had an ulterior motive. Buxton-Smythe had hatched a plan to seek his family's revenge on Kelly for the death of his father, Thaddeus Reno, and Kelly's testifying against cousin Bob Provost. He also wanted to get rid of a girlfriend, collect insurance money, and at the same time, to not have to pay the private detective's bill.

"You hired me to follow your fiancée around. It's an old story. You told me you had to know if while you were slippin' out, someone else was slippin' in. You set this up. But you stacked the deck! You set me up!" Jack said as he wiped some blood from his neck with his hand.

Bucky began to deny it and Jack slapped him across the face. Jack had never once slapped, punched, kicked or otherwise physically caused pain to a handcuffed man while a police officer. Kelly had used force only when necessary to restrain and control a prisoner or prevent him from hurting himself or another. But now he was freelance, completely independent, and in the private sector. And this bastard was getting a slap.

"You had me follow and get close to Lindsey. You said you wanted to see if she would remain faithful during your engagement. You said that if she couldn't be true to you now she wouldn't be true after marriage. That's the problem with you rich guys. You don't know who to trust."

"I'll tell them you and Lindsey planned to kill me." Bucky said.

"Hey, Porsche Boy, you got your version, and I've got the truth. 'Get close,' you said. 'Test her. Be her friend. See how far she'll go.'"

Jack slapped him again and went on. He was starting to enjoy that.

"It was like shootin' fish in a barrel. I could have gotten her into bed the first night. You underestimate my charm and charisma." Jack went on after a slight laugh, glancing at his profile reflected in the hall mirror and sucking in his stomach. "Sure she succumbed to my charm, but she's O.K. Underneath it all she's got a kind of class that you'll never know. Well, I didn't really get underneath it all, but she's a good and decent person with wholesome values," Jack thought about it and added, "For the most part."

Jack Kelly was a professional and walked the thin line between seeing how far Buxton-Smythe's fiancée would go and actually going there, with her. The line was not always clear and Kelly had crossed it before. Jack would like to think of a bright future, in a land where good people live peacefully, in a time when science and technology leads us into a fantastic era of health and wealth, enjoying the arts, sports, and creativity.

But Kelly was always suspicious. He was always searching. His eyes falling into the shadows to detect trouble on its way.

He didn't want to believe it but maybe we were all just waiting… As our world revolves slowly back towards the center of the galaxy… towards the inevitable black hole that will slowly suck us in… slowly at first… then drifting faster and faster as worlds collide, rushing to their doom.

Jack Kelly wondered just how far he'd go. He wondered if a private detective should be reduced to the level of testing some guys' girlfriend, fiancée, or wife, to see if she'd cheat on him. Maybe that's why Jack got so pissed off. The fact that he'd gone from the Boston Police Homicide Unit's Cold Case Squad to being a high profile private investigator only to be eventually reduced to working with the underbelly of the criminal justice profession. At least lately, it seemed. Kelly now had to take just about every case that came down the Mass. Pike and he found himself in a gray area more than once.

He'd wondered about that before. Can this be an honorable profession? The cops have very strict rules and procedures and are given power and authority but the private investigator has only the arrest powers of an ordinary citizen. He had to wheel and deal. Shimmy and shake. Juke and jive. Pretext is the name of the game. He can use trickery and deceit. Even untruths. As long as it wasn't illegal it was in bounds. And if it was illegal, well... Sometimes it was... oh well.

Kelly wondered how far he'd go, how cheap he was, when he watched a bartender to see if he or she were stealing. Jack didn't really like those jobs, sitting hour after hour, night after night, drinking on the client's tab, listing all of the drinks and tips. But the realization would come to Jack. He was easy to please and was happy to drink for free and write a report for a day's pay for watching the bartender out of the corner of one eye. With the other eye he could watch the game or check out some ladies at the bar. Yeah, it's a cheap thrill. It's what Jack Kelly does. He's a detective. A cheap detective.

He had done his share of security. Spotting at bars. Loss prevention at a department store. Watching a building all night. Bodyguard work for some shady, repulsive, rich, or famous personalities. He had run license plates for a borderline Mafioso. Jack would never do any enforcement or wet work. But he would follow some racketeer's girlfriend while the gangster was with his wife. Or vice versa.

But things had gone wrong this time. He had almost gotten his throat slit. Jack was getting soft. He should have seen this coming. He was played for a fool and almost got killed. Jack got played, on his own turf, and in his world. That's what got to him.

And he had started to fall for the girl. Another big surprise. Jack was always falling, and it didn't take long. He was a step away from asking Lindsey, the girl with the raccoon eyes, for a date. Many men suffered from that male disease, 'Fuggetaboutit,' the male virus that lets a man forget that he already had a girlfriend.

He thought about it all as he stood by the fourth floor window looking down for the Boston Police.

Jack didn't notice the black Cadillac parked in the Handicap Zone across Kingston Street with Bucky's cousin "Bob" Provost at the wheel.

He began to remember the things Bucky said before he attempted to cut Jack's throat. He thought about slapping Buxton-Smythe again. Jack stood right in front of him, looked down, and pointed his index finger, and thrust it straight out at Bucky's chest like he was emptying the contents of his forty-five.

"You knew... You *know* I'm good at what I do! And you had me document every contact I had with Lindsey. You were smiling every time I gave you a report and a bill. The bigger my bill, the bigger your smile. 'No problem Jackie,' you'd say. Yeah, you don't have to pay a dead man. You were setting me up. Your lawyer would present the case when it went to court. Oh yeah! The investigators do all the attorney's dirty work. Then there's a show starring the lawyer. The trial. And on personal injury cases the lawyers sometimes collect expenses and take one third of all the money you get. Just for a few court appearances."

"Call my lawyer! I get a phone call, right? My family pays him a lot of money. Lindon Chase," Bucky whined, nodding his head.

"Let me tell you how the conversation would go," Jack continued. "You ask what his cheapest rates were. He'd say, '$50.00 for three questions.' You'd say, 'Isn't that a little steep?' and the lawyer would say, 'Yes, and what was your third question?'"

"What...? Oh... that's a joke, right?" Bucky groaned, either from the joke or the pain in his swollen, broken pinky.

Kelly continued the scenario, "In court that lawyer, Chase, he'll make his money. He will tell the judge a tale of how the private eye stole your girl when he was just supposed to be her bodyguard. And how he ended up stealing her affection and then was killed as he tried to force himself on your beloved betrothed.

"And then the reckless detective is killed by the rich boy. Justin Boy saves the day as the Bad Private Eye attacks and kills his screaming fiancée. A short story by Justin Jones Provost Buxton-Smythe the fuckin' Fourth,"

Jack slapped him full across the face. Harder than the last. Justin wished his cousin "Bob" Provost would burst in through the doors, he was supposed to be down on the street, waiting for Bucky. He even hoped the cops would get there. He strained to hear a siren in the distance.

"You knew. You set me up. You had another agenda. Revenge for the death of your father, Thaddeus Reno. And after me, you were going to kill Lindsey Saint for the big money you've been putting down with the insurance company. Oh yeah. I knew about that, too. Like you don't have enough money already. You were going to kill her. Maybe right here after you got me. Or right down on the street in front of my office in her car, maybe with my gun. Just roll up all the windows in her airtight Mercedes Benz and pop one into her skull. Yes, you were going to kill her. I can see it in your eyes. She was the only other player who could tell the cops what really happened."

Buxton-Smythe played his last card.

"She's not as sweet as you think, Kelly."

"Be careful. I'm a human lie detector."

"She used to smoke weed a few years back, had a drinking problem, and she danced topless one summer when she was under age!"

"Gee, a menace to society. I'd put those things in the plus column."

"Let's do the bitch. Shoot her in the head. Or have her come up, I'll put a pillow over her face and whack her. It's not too late

Jackie, I've got $250,000 from the insurance coming. We'll split it. What do you say, Jackie?"

"I say don't call me Jackie."

"Sorry, Mr. Kelly."

"Bucky, you tell the cops the whole story. The true story, or you'll be spending many, many years of your life pickin' up soap for Bubba."

"It will never stick in court, Kelly. I told you, I've got attorney Lindon Chase."

"Oh, it will stick, Bucky. The state has a new mandatory five day waiting period to buy a judge."

Suddenly Lindsey Saint was in the doorway. She had come upstairs from her car parked down on the street. Lindsey was tall and thin with long stringy blond hair and wore thick, black make-up under her eyes and black or dark purple lipstick. Maybe the beatnik look was back in, but she reminded Kelly of a small mouth bass. The last time Kelly saw a mouth like that there was a fishhook in it. She had heard the last few minutes of the conversation, Buxton-Smythe's confessions, and his threats.

Lindsey Saint let him have it with both barrels. Verbally speaking.

"You son of a bitch! You were not going to marry me? You were going to do away with me?" She choked on the words and her body shook as she got louder. "Kill me, Bucky? Shoot me in the head? You are a son of a bitch. I hate you. Waiting to marry you was like a death sentence. I'd rather die. You dirtbag fucking son-of-a-bitch! You screaming fucking asshole."

Even Kelly took a moment to blush. He was also wondering what was taking the cops so long. He walked over to the bay windows and looked down on the street.

"I feel free now!" Lindsey finally sighed, throwing up her hands.

A sinister smile appeared on Lindsey's face as she took the engagement ring from her finger and moved closer to Buxton-Smythe who was sitting in the middle of the floor where Kelly had put him. A pathetic, sniffling loser.

"Why don't you just take this ring back? I don't want the reminder."

She tried to shove it through Buxton-Smythe's lips. Her fingers were jammed into his mouth. Lindsey Saint was not taking the break up or Bucky's attempt to murder her very well. She tried to hold his head still and shove the ring down into his mouth. She was repeatedly yelling for him to "Take it!"

Jack hated to lose control. Especially in his own office. He instinctively jumped forward to protect his prisoner. He got within an arm's length of Buxton-Smythe and stopped. Lindsey's fingers were inside Buxton-Smythe's mouth and he was gagging as she shoved the ring deep down into his throat. Jack wanted to protect his prisoner but this lady had some scores to settle. Jack growled at him, "Don't you bite her, Bucky!"

Jack hovered over Bucky and made his hands into fists. He flexed and tensed his muscles in a threatening display of body language as he intensely stared at Buxton-Smythe. Jack regretted his brutish insensibility... he's usually a sensitive guy. But hey, what the hell.

Buxton-Smythe just stared at Jack and let Lindsey shove the diamond ring deep into his throat. He choked and gagged a couple of times, then Bucky swallowed the ring.

Lindsey and Jack stood over the pathetic, whimpering rich pretty boy and pitied him. He was nothing. A loser. But Jack knew that Buxton-Smythe would retrieve that ring... eventually.

Jack looked out the window and saw two fire engines, two ambulance-type rescue units, and three cruisers wind their way past the Chinese restaurants and pull up in front of his four-story office building. He wondered why police dispatchers conspired with the fire department to put on such a great show of overkill. "Jesus Christ, they sent a half-a-million bucks worth of Boston taxpayers equipment to save you, Bucky. The Army, Navy, Air Force, and Marines can't be far behind," Jack said, checking the sky for choppers.

Jack heard the squawk of radios and the sound of footsteps coming up the stairs and approaching the outer office doors. Jack opened them to see Sergeant Donavan of the Boston Police Patrol Division, Detective Lt. Jessica Paris from Homicide, and three uniformed officers. Donavan was from the old school. He was a big, white-haired, Irish beat patrolman that had spent his career on the street. Jesse Paris was a pretty, wide-eyed young detective, who looked more like a college girl than a cop.

"Come in Sgt. Donavan. I've got a felony arrest for you here. A bad boy who tried to slit my throat." And looking at Jessica he added, "Sorry Lieutenant. There's no need for a homicide detective this afternoon."

As the cops entered, Kelly swept out his arm and pointed to Buxton-Smythe like a television spokes-model showing a game show contestant a brand new refrigerator.

"Meet Justin Jones Buxton-Smythe IV, Sarge. He is the adopted son of Thaddeus Reno, the gargantuan 650 pound waste management executive that fell off the 8th floor fire escape at Mass General last year."

"You pushed him, son-of-a-bitch!" Bucky screamed in pain.

"Bucky, hired me to cover Lindsey Saint, here, his fiancée."

Jack explained the situation in as plain a fashion as he could, further pointing out, as if it could be anyone else, the thin, almost lanky, heavily made-up, big lipped girl with the stringy blond hair and dark eyes, Lindsey Saint.

"Yeah, she was cheating on him," Jack said matter-of-factly.

Lindsey stamped her foot loudly on the floor. But she *was* no saint and she knew it. The patrolmen looked at her askance with a trace of amusement.

"I thought that was your M. O., Kelly?" Detective Lieutenant Jesse Paris quipped, referring to the relationship she and Jack Kelly shared a few years back.

One of the patrol officers made a sound like a cat hissing as Kelly continued, undaunted, "Lieutenant, don't you have someone's ass to kiss? Or have you done that already, today?"

"1500 hours, Jack. That's when I meet my boss and do the ass kissing. Promptly at 1500. He doesn't like it when I'm early or late."

"Listen, Sgt. Donavan. Buxton was setting us both up. His girlfriend and me. He had been taking huge insurance policies out on Lindsey and he was going to say I attempted to rape and kill her and then he killed me in the act. But who could possibly believe I would force myself on a lady?" Jack glanced over at Jessica Paris.

The old sergeant had finally caught his breath, coughed in disbelief, and responded with his usual eloquence.

"Sounds like a load of horseshit, Jack." Donavan closely examined Buxton-Smythe up and down and then added, "So what have you done to this poor man?"

"Come on Sarge, I saw my life flash before my eyes. Just start him with *assault with a deadly weapon, criminal restraint*, and let the DA figure the *attempted murder* tomorrow." Jack said sarcastically as he bent his head back to expose the slash in his neck. Buxton-Smythe whimpered, raised his cuffed hands upward, and held his broken finger up to Donavan.

Donavan turned to Lt. Jessica Paris. "Jesse, did I ever tell you how Jack Kelly's grandfahder saved me sainted father's life?"

"Yes, Sarge." Paris answered, but Donavan began telling the story anyway.

"Yeah, he saved me dad's life. You see, Jack's grandfahder was choking the life out of me fahder down at Carson's Beach just for smilin' at his lady friend. Kelly's grandfahder was holding me fahder's head under water. And then Jack's granpa figured, what the hell, and let him go, thereby savin' his life." The three uniformed cops chuckled.

Lt. Paris commented on the 'vintage' furnishings of Kelly's office by saying, "Haven't you bought anything new since 1968?"

"I like new things," Jack said, "when they get older."

Donavan pulled out his radio from his belt holder and said forcefully in his finest command voice but with a bit of a brogue, "Ten-three, Dispatch. Scene is secure. Send the medical in." An inaudible crackle squawked from the patrolmen's radios and the sound of footsteps could be heard ascending the stairs.

Sgt. Donavan told Jack that it had been a quiet night. "Just another floater bobbin' near the fishin' boats down by Atlantic Ave. And the new kid, Hodge, he's a bit of a chowdahead. Anyway, Hodge brings in a hooker, and he has to pat-down search her, before putting her in the cell, there being no matron available. Outside the cell he tells her to assume the position, and she goes into the cell, lays down on her back, lifts her skirt, and spreads her legs." Donavan and the three uniforms were grinning from proverbial ear-to-ear.

Then Donavan says, "You know, Kelly, why a hooker is smarter than a crack dealer?" Donavan looked over at the other cops. "Because, Kelly, she can *wash* her crack and sell it again and again."

Jack groaned as memories flooded into his mind. First, he remembered his grandfather. A motorcycle cop for 32 years.

Jack remembered Grandpa Kelly yelling for Jack to stay off of his big chrome Harley-Davidson motorcycle with the big blue emergency lights. Grandpa Kelly with his shiny badge, handcuffs, and uniform buttons. The smell of his black leather jacket and the gun oil. The sound of his jangling keys and the slap of his nightstick on the kitchen chair.

Jack also thought of one of his last high-profile cases. The incredible case of The Fatman, Thaddeus Reno. One of Boston's more prolific serial killers, who left his bodies scattered over the waterfront tied to piers, light poles, in a rail car, and floating in the harbor. And to top it off, Reno tried to hang it all on Jack Kelly. That's an old story. Another case that hadn't quite played out.

"I guess you heard about the guy last week, held up a liquor store with a sawed- off shotgun?" Donavan explained, "He was on his lunch break from a local construction site. He was wearing his hard hat. It had 'Billy Jones' written on the side. We went to his house and arrested him." Donavan continued.

"Oh yeah, Jack. You wouldn't believe it. We arrested a guy for having sex with one of the deer in the petting zoo on the Common." Donavan added.

"No." Jack said in disbelief.

"Yeah, we listed him under John Doe." Donavan cracked as the three uniforms broke up laughing.

Donavan was a true throwback. To say he was old fashioned was an understatement. He was an old style guy, a square, a straight shooter, reciting clichés. A real mug.

In less than a New York minute the EMT units were all over poor Bucky with his broken digit. They applied a splint. Taped it up. Set up a shoulder sling. To hell with Kelly. He only had a slit throat. The squeaky wheel gets the grease. The medics were so concerned with the prisoner's handcuffs constricting his comfort zone they looked right at Jack Kelly and asked him twice to take the handcuffs off without realizing that there was blood on Kelly's throat. Each time Jack shook his head from side-to-side.

Donavan finally pointed at Jack and yelled, "Take care of this detective! And leave that piece of horse-shit to himself until *this* man is cared for."

When the EMTs finished their work on both Jack and Bucky, Kelly filled in some of the blank spots for Donavan as the whole circus began moving out. First the EMT's packed up their kits, leaving all the used and bloody bandages and rubber gloves laying in the middle of Kelly's office floor. Then Donavan got Buxton-Smythe up on his feet for the three uniforms to begin the transport. He ordered a rookie patrol officer to put his own handcuffs on Buxton-Smythe and the young cop gave Kelly back his set.

"Kelly, I remember when you were a rookie. You were a decent cop, compared to most. But is this what you've resorted to. Violating citizen's rights, trampling on the constitution, and breaking bones to perform your 'interrogations.'"

Sgt. Donavan shook his head from side-to-side.

As Buxton-Smythe was escorted out he reached up with his finger in a long splint wrapped in gauze as an offering of proof of Kelly's unjust brutality and said, "He's trampling on my rights, officer sir."

"Shut the fuck up, scumbag. Nobody's talking to you." Donavan shouted, being the champion of the constitution that he is.

"Hey, I got rights." Buxton-Smythe protested.

"You've got the right to shut the fuck up! Keep him movin' for Christ's sake!" Donavan insisted.

"Donavan, can I give you five bucks to slap the son-of-a-bitch across the face just before you put him into the cell." Jack offered.

"Don't insult me Kelly… I'll do it for nothin'."

"And don't forget, *assault with a deadly weapon* is still a class B felony, when you write the bail slip. And Sarge, no contact with me or Lindsey Saint as a bail condition… if he makes bail." Jack added, handing Donavan Buxton-Smythe's knife from the top drawer.

"Kelly," Sgt. Donavan said to Jack, "always remember you are unique."

Kelly nodded and Donavan added, "Just like everybody else. Come in to Area A at zero eight hundred hours and we'll do the paperwork," the old cop said laughing as they shuffled out the door and down the stairs.

Lieutenant Paris looked Jack up and down and said, "I see you still dress in black, Jack."

"Until they make something darker." Kelly said.

As Jessica Paris straggled out the office door after Donavan and headed down the stairs, Jack yelled to her, "Sorry I didn't have a nice juicy homicide for you! Maybe next time."

Lindsey and Jack were face to face, alone in the office. Jack poured himself a half glass of Johnny Walker Black and she nodded that she'd take one too.

"I'm sorry, Jack," Lindsey said and shook her head from side to side. "I didn't know that Justin was insane."

"I know, Lindsey. Apparently you were no more to him than an amusement park ride with an insurance policy. We were victims of a reverse sting. Just thank your lucky stars, young lady, that he didn't kill both of us. It would have ruined your whole day." Jack was slipping right back into his old familiar character.

"I guess I'm going to miss out on his money, too," Lindsey said, gratefully accepting the Scotch.

Their eyes met and they laughed, a little nervously.

"Besides the ring you jammed down his throat, I liked that line you fed Bucky," Jack said and then mimicked Lindsey's high-pitched voice, "Being with you... It's been like a death sentence!" They grinned and nodded their heads in unison.

"I'm sorry, Jack." Lindsey stopped and looked at Jack sincerely.

"You know, I could have fallen for you." Jack said.

They clinked glasses and looked into each other's eyes.

Chapter 2

We Get Paid Either Way

Well that's another case closed.

The next morning Jack realized Bucky had been paying most of Kelly's fees for the last three weeks. Jack still had two checks from Justin Buxton-Smythe IV that he hadn't cashed. The reports and statements at the PD would have to wait while Jack cashed the paychecks. He dressed, went to his office desk, scooped up the checks, and headed straight for Buxton-Smythe's bank to cash them in for dead presidents. A bird in the hand.

Jack Kelly didn't see the long black Cadillac following quietly behind him.

He got his white Crown Victoria, he affectionately referred to as "Mighty Whitey," out of the garage on nearby Lincoln St. and drove from Chinatown onto the Central Artery. Boston's Big Dig project was near completion but Kelly drove around it and through the heart of downtown Boston passing by the waterfront. He thought about the case that had ended when Sgt. Donavan carted Justin Jones Buxton-Smythe IV out the door of his office and off to a jail cell. He thought about the case, to resolve it.

He would take what could be learned and let it settle into his subconscious… And drive the checks to the bank.

Jack Kelly was closing out the case. He was thinking about how he would spend the cash from the last sizable checks from the rich boy when he passed by where the old Boston Garden had been and the new Fleet Center was and turned onto Storrow Drive West.

The black Caddy followed.

As Kelly passed Mass.General Hospital, he looked up to the eighth floor of the main building and thought about the wrestling match he had with a 650 pound man on a collapsing fire escape on the eighth floor. Bolts had popped. The fire escape had dropped. Jack had almost gotten tossed from the eighth floor. But it was the Fatman, Thaddeus Reno, that took the fall, and the Provost Brothers, that were indicted for murder.

Kelly almost had his throat slit yesterday but these violent episodes were the exception not the rule. Jack remembered almost fondly, the drudgery and long hours of surveillance, just watching for a subject to exit a building or waiting for a car to take off. There were long hours and days of surveillance or research, day after day, in many cases, but it was basically safe work. Jack longed for some downtime.

His next stop was the Charles Circle Branch Bank where Bucky kept his money. Kelly made it to the bank, cashed the checks, and was about to pull into the Charles Circle Sunoco gas station for a full tank when he noticed "Bob" go by in the old black Cadillac limousine that looked familiar. "Bob" was an ex-marine, Special Forces, fringe CIA wannabe-turned-mercenary and bodyguard long on brutality and short on finesse. He was an independent contractor. A kite… if he slipped up, the string was cut and he was on his own. He's a large brute with short blond hair cut in a flat top, clean-shaven, and with tiny pockmarks on his face.

"Bob" was no more than a thug. His last name was Provost. One of three or four Provost brothers. Jack didn't know exactly which one he was. Ricardo or Ray, he thought maybe. The Provost Brothers started their criminal careers in East Boston as grave robbers. They would enter crypts or dig up graves and pry-open the caskets. They stole jewelry from the decomposing corpses. They pulled rings from fingers, bracelets from wrists, necklaces and earrings right off the decaying bodies of the dearly departed. If they had trouble, say, getting a ring off of a bony finger, a jewel encrusted bracelet off a wrist, or a diamond earring from a dried up, decomposing ear, well, they carried box cutters, wire cutters, bolt cutters, and a hack saw.

Nowadays, they did "wet work," the Mob's euphemism which refers to the blood spilling and physical intimidation of strong-arm enforcement. Mostly, money collection and contract hits. The three enforcers had dealt with Kelly on a case Jack referred to as the Dead Men Talk Case. Bob had been an enforcer for multiple murderer Thaddeus Reno. While on this case, last year, Bob had ransacked Jack's office, stalked and threatened him. All in search of a mysterious ledger. Jack had testified in the accessory to murder case against Bob, and his brothers.

Jack knew that Bob had jumped bail while awaiting sentencing and there was a large bounty of cash-money, probably close to five figures, payable for his return, from Bob's bail bondsman. Jack began a semi-loose tail, pulling in behind Bob's car on Storrow Drive West. He got on his cell phone and started a trail of inquiry that would lead to Izzy Feilds, a gruff old cigar smoking bail bondsman. Jack got him on the phone and asked him, "What's it worth to you to pick up your quail?"

"Which one, Kelly?" the gruff old bail bondsman asked.

"The Provost brother that threw my accountant, Joe Panetta, out of his third floor Beacon Hill apartment window and then shot him. The accessory to The Fatman Reno multiple murders. He failed to appear in court, he jumped bail. I think it was a six-figure bail, wasn't it?"

Jack thought he could hear the cigar dropping out of Izzy's mouth and landing on the desk.

"You got Provost, Kelly?" the bondsman cackled excitedly in his coarse voice and then launched into a coughing spell lasting nearly a minute.

"Are you done?" Jack asked.

"Kelly, there are warrants out for Provost and you have a duty to turn him in to the cops immediately!"

"Nice try, Izzy. I'm not a cop anymore. I have a duty to do jack-shit. But, maybe it isn't him. He looked a little hinky. I'm probably being overly suspicious again. Bad habit. Maybe its just some punk that looks like the bonehead that beat you for that six-figure bail. See ya Izzy. Sorry to waste your time."

"Jack, Jack! Don't hang up! I got the money. Just hook him up. You there, Jack?"

"Go ahead, Izzy."

"If he gets cuffed and stuffed, hooked and booked, you get the 10 percent. I need him back, Jack. Just tell me. You can get him?" Izzy followed this query with a thirty-second cough punctuated with a throat clearing spit.

"I think I can locate him with some exhaustive investigative research utilizing the wealth of training and my years of research and experience, Izzy."

"Uh, huh... so... you're looking at him, right now, aren't you, Jack?"

"I think I'm behind him on Storrow Drive. See you soon, Izzy."

Sleep When I'm Dead

Bob's big black Cadillac cruised along Storrow Drive West and took the Harvard Square Bridge exit by the Charles River into Cambridge. Jack spoke to himself, affecting a hard-line Irish brogue.

"In fahkin' Cambridge weah I pahks my cah, theahs only queeahs, lefty commies, and cahledge kids."

Jack looked back at the sun setting over the river and a van loaded with Asian kitchen help crossed in front of his car and stopped. Jack lost sight of Bob's big black Caddy as it headed into Harvard Square. Jack floored the big white Ford and skid around the corner onto Winthrop St. by Brattle and pulled up in front of The House of Blues.

Bob's Caddy was nowhere to be seen. Jack cruised forward slowly, looking up and down every alley and street. Just as he pulled around the corner of Brattle St. Jack looked in the rearview mirror and saw Bob walking right up behind his car. Jack stopped his car and tried to look busy, moving objects around in the front seat, keeping his head down, only glancing indirectly in Bob's direction. Jack held his breath and hoped Bob didn't know or recognize his car.

Bob walked past and Jack pulled his car to the side of the street on Brattle and parked. It wasn't a legal space but the big bounty for Provost would cover the twenty-five dollar ticket. And then some.

Bob walked on toward the Harvard Coop Bookstore and Jack followed on foot from a block back. Bob cut through a walkway between the buildings as Jack shadowed him. The large thug crossed Brattle St. by the Brattle Street Theater and Bogey's Bar and Grill. Jack held up just a bit to avoid a confrontation in the alley and decided to try and take Bob down on the street at the next opportunity. Jack ran across Brattle Street and was ready to draw his weapon if needed as he rounded the corner.

Bob was nowhere in sight. Jack looked both ways. Nothing. No Bob. Jack felt a sinking feeling in the pit of his stomach and spoke out loud.

"Come on! Where are you? Where's my big fish?"

It was the middle of the day. Jack took a few steps down the walkway by the old movie house, looking for Bob in every direction. He poked his head into several shops. No Bob. Jack walked down the stairs to the bar under the theater. Bogey's. Jack shielded his eyes from the reflection of the sun and held his face to the glass, peering in. He couldn't locate the tall fugitive with his short blond crew cut and pock marked face. Jack made up his mind as he scanned the patrons. He would take Bob down as soon as he saw him. No more waiting for the right moment.

But it was too late. Bob was looking to take out Jack, instead. As Jack Kelly turned he was sucker-punched across the side of the face. He collapsed in a heap against the door of Bogey's. Bob stood over him and revealed the snub nose Saturday Night Special he was holding in his hand.

Bob Provost had the drop on him and Jack knew it.

"You are under arrest," Jack managed to sputter, blood coming from his lip, as he slumped by the door at the bottom of the stairwell.

Bob smirked in disbelief and stated, "You don't seem to understand, comedian. I've got the gun and you have the bump on the head. Your show's been canceled. So say goodnight to the folks and you won't be back next week."

"I guess you're the boss, Bob. But I suggest you surrender and hand over that tiny, inadequate, girly gun, Bobby Boy… Bobby Baby." Jack couldn't resist needling the thug.

"Shut your mouth! Your ass is mine now. It's a small world aye, Kelly?"

"I wouldn't want to paint it."

Bob leveled the gun to Jack's stomach and began to tense up.

Bang! The door to Bogey's flew open striking the stairs with a slap, almost knocking the gun from Bob's hand. Bob slid his gun hand down and concealed it behind his leg.

"Is that you, Jack?" Willie Crawford, a local musician, said as he stepped out of Bogey's. His voice trailed off as Willie realized that he saw the gun in Bob's hand and saw Jack on the ground in the doorway disheveled and bleeding.

Willie understood immediately and jammed Bob in the throat with a closed fist then pinned his arms back. Bob was stronger and was gaining ground when Jack got up and ripped the gun out of Bob's hand. The gun clattered up and across the cobblestone sidewalk. Bob shoved Kelly so hard against the door of Bogey's that the bottom wooden panel broke inwards. Kelly was down again.

"Run, Jack!" Willie screamed as he held Bob as long as he could.

Bob was quickly overpowering Willie and he began to move up the stairs to either get his gun, run, or both. He shook off Willie and scrambled out of the stairway as Jack got to his feet, shook the fog out of his head, and regained his balance. Jack drew his Colt Combat Commander .45 caliber semi-automatic from his shoulder holster and he and The Musician stood back against the stairs. Jack Kelly knew that if Bob came into view with a gun in his hand and that gun pointed, in any way, in his direction, Jack would start shooting. And he would not stop until it was over. One way or the other.

"So, I see its business as usual, Jack? How are you?" Willie said.

"If I get shot dead my headache probably won't bother me."

"You know when I get a bad headache, I go right home and have my wife give me a good blow job. I recommend you try it." Willie said.

"Sure. Is your wife home now?" Jack said, trying to peer out from the basement stairway.

"I've got some good ideas, Jack. I can tell what's going to be hot."

"You said the new 'Power Time' CD by the Essentials was going to make #1."

"I don't remember them."

"Precisely." Jack said.

A few moments had gone by and Bob did not appear. Jack cautiously peered out from the strategic corner in the stairwell that he had backed himself into. No Bob. He realized Bob was on the run again.

"See ya." Kelly said and bolted like a rabbit.

Jack changed directions as he holstered his gun. He was operating on instinct. Bob had a thirty-second head start and if he was moving quickly he was already out of reach. Jack gambled. He ran around the corner and went inside the Brattle Theater's lobby. Looking out, he scanned the streets with his eyes, bought a ticket while he watched, and then went inside the theater.

Kelly saw only fifteen or twenty patrons scattered about the small movie house. The screen was blaring away in the darkness showing short trailers of the semi-obscure films that the Brattle offered. The screen was filled with a loud trailer from "The Day The Earth Stood Still." On the screen a giant robotic alien walked down a ramp from a spaceship as a spaceman-from-another-world, actor Michael Rennie, held his hand up making a peace sign and announced 'Nikto Klato Barrabus.'

Jack casually, yet cautiously, surveyed the room and its patrons. He wasn't sure he wanted to find Bob. He would be relieved if this were over. Kelly was long on courage but short on crazy. But it's just that crazy time.

The sound system shouted. "See! The Horror! Feel! The Fright! The Day The Earth Stood Still," with a weird sci-fi soundtrack. Then clips from the Orson Welles classics "A Touch of Evil" and "Citizen Kane" began. Orson's classic camera angles, looking up at a looming, greasy, sinister character with a Panama hat and a filthy looking cigar hanging out of his unshaven face. Jack moved toward a dark corner where he could sit and look around while his eyes adjusted.

Jack remembered the Brattle Theatre was an old New England 250-seat hall nestled between department stores. It hosted plays in the late 1800's until the 1940's with distinguished theatre group players like T. S. Eliot. There were classic plays from Othello and Hamlet to Chekhov. For a brief period the Brattle was a gym for the Cambridge Police Department. Then in the 1950's it converted to cinema. The Brattle always featured independent, unusual, and unique films through the decades.

A young Harvard student-type got up to leave and tripped over his seat. Jack wondered why the Harvard kids were so academically bright but some had a hard time crossing the street.

Jack instinctively ducked as an onscreen shot was fired.

Jack Kelly was experiencing mixed emotions. He couldn't believe he lost Bob Provost. He was excited at the prospect of collecting upward of $10,000 for finding Provost but he would rather be the hunter and not the hunted. Who was chasing whom?

Jack thought of these things as he ducked behind a seat in the next-to-the-last row in the cinema. Bob was bold. He probably knew he was going to get life in prison as soon as he was picked up. Yeah, with a murder rap hanging over his head he won't see the outside again until he's an old man. Why not risk it all? What does he have to lose? They can't tack on another couple of years on top of life in prison? Jack remembered he was dealing with an ex-military special-assignment operative.

Kelly was slumped down near the back row from where he could see the exits and most of the seats. Another "Coming Attraction" began and the screen and sound system exploded in gunfire. It was a scene from the remake of *Scarface*, with Al Pacino as Tony Montana, yelling "Say hello to my little friend!" and unleashing a barrage of gunfire, ripping up a Miami apartment and killing everyone in it.

Jack's eyes darted from left to right. He began to feel uneasy as he realized he hadn't physically checked the balcony. After sitting through clips from Lon Chaney's *The Wolfman,* Boris Karloff's *Frankenstein,* the Marx Brother's *A Night at the Opera,* a brighter film print of a cut from Elia Kazan's O*n The Waterfront,* with Marlon Brando and Karl Malden, came on. Jack decided to take a closer look at the twenty or thirty theatergoers. He wanted to eliminate as many patrons as he could from his search before giving it up altogether. On the screen a beaten and bloodied Brando walked along the docks, heading back to work, longshoremen falling in behind him.

A couple in the second row caught Jack's attention when the girl got up, took a swing at the guy sitting next to her, and moved five seats down. She looked disgusted. Jack imagined the guy had tried to cop a feel and his amorous advances were soundly rejected. Jack really took notice of the guy's singular profile in the flashing lights of the screen. It could be Bob, he thought. The male looked around, cautiously got up and shuffled out to the aisle. It was a dark movie house and the bright lights from the screen stuck in Jack's eyes as the dark form walked up the aisle toward him.

It *was* Bob. He strolled through the movie house, turned towards Jack then drew his gun and came at Jack shooting. As the muzzle flashed and the loud cracks of the firearm filled his ears, Jack scrambled down the aisle in the opposite direction, keeping low and drawing his own weapon. Kelly returned fire and Bob hit the ground. Jack bolted for the stage as the stunned theatergoers screamed and ran for the exits. The smell of gunpowder was strong as a smoke cloud began to form in the air.

Jack hit the stage on his belly, sliding under the screen as Bob got off another shot from a crouched position. A movie clip from *The Maltese Falcon* was running and Kelly heard Bogart's voice talking about "The stuff that dreams were made of."

But this was no dream. A nightmare maybe, but no dream.

Jack ran out the back door of the Brattle Street Theater at the same time Bob went out the front. Adrenaline was pumping through Jack like a five-alarm fire signal. Kelly felt the rush and flashed on what a soldier in Vietnam or Iraq must have felt like when a quiet sunset turned into an enemy firefight.

Kelly blended quickly into the unsuspecting street traffic of happy holiday shoppers in Harvard Square. It was beginning to look a lot like Christmas. His car was illegally parked and Jack felt obligated to move it right away. He was on the way into the Boston PD anyway, it will be just one more lengthy report to fill out and explain. The Cambridge cops could come over there. He'll make a day of it. The paperwork was adding up quicker than Jack could write. Kelly hated the paperwork.

Jack eased Mighty Whitey across the bridge over the river Charles and headed into Boston. He sighed, de-cocked his automatic, and counted the one bullet left in the Colt .45. Then he set the radio dial to an old rock station, WZLX. Jack sang out loud. "Your lovin' give me such a thrill. But your lovin' don't pay my bills. I want some money. That's what I want. Money

Johnny Barnes

Honey! I got some money Honey. I'm gonna fill my tank and buy me some wine."

Chapter 3

#1 With a Bullet: The One Shot Deal

Jack finally pulled up to the Charles Circle Sunoco's Full Service pumps. He intended to let the professional attendant service this fine 1984 Ford Crown Victoria. Jack didn't want to get out of the car and it's just a few pennies more for full service, anyway. Why not? He had just gotten paid. He had cashed in the last two checks he had gotten from Bucky. Jack settled in his seat, found some classical on the old Ford's radio, and was idly staring out onto the cold Charles River. Jack began rolling his window down far enough to tell the attendant to fill it up and check the oil, please.

The translucent liquid spilled in waves across the windshield distorting his view of the river. Jack expected to see the gas station attendant run a squeegee across the windshield. But that wasn't happening and Jack couldn't see.

The first indication of something wrong was the strong odor of the gasoline. It was heavy in the air. A few drops splashed into the car through the partly open window and the strong odor of gas hit Jack like a slap in the face. Kelly heard someone behind his car yelling, "That's gas you're pumpin'!" and realized that the liquid flowing across his windshield was not windshield washer fluid but gasoline. Jack rolled up the window and quickly turned the key shutting the engine off. He looked out through the windshield and through the waves of gasoline flowing over the car. Jack Kelly could see the blurry form of Bob Provost.

He looked like a crazed porn star shooting the money shot. Bob whipped out the nozzle and sprayed all over the hood, windshield, and roof of Mighty Whitey. It was gushing. Jack could hear the dripping, splashing, the spraying, and the flood of gas. He could see the vague form of Bob. And he knew Bob hated him. Jack had humiliated him more than once. In fact all four times they had met, Kelly had humiliated him mercilessly. Bob was taking it all too personally.

Jack remembered every pockmark and crevice on the big dummy's face.

Kelly is about five foot ten and a half and a solid 180 pounds, but Bob is about six-four and two-fifty. Kelly could see Bob's flattop military haircut through the sheets and waves of gasoline. And Jack could see the pink plastic lighter in Bob's left hand as he stopped pouring the gas, dropped the pump handle onto the ground, his face displaying a sick-looking grin. Bob kept smiling and moved toward Kelly's car, flicking the lighter as he walked.

The gas fumes were beginning to get to Jack. The car provided temporary protection from the gasoline but would ultimately become a death trap of unspeakable horror. A coffin of flames. He knew he had to get out instantly.

Jack threw open the driver's side door of the car and stepped out as quickly as he could but the still draining gas poured onto the back of his coat. The smell was devastating and getting stronger. Jack tried to hold his breath. Bob had stepped forward to the front bumper and stopped to within an arms reach of Kelly's Crown Vic. Jack saw him extend the lighter to within inches of the gas-soaked car and flick the flame on. Jack stood by the open door of his car and looked into Bob's eyes. Bob looked up at Jack, grinning.

In a second, Jack pulled his .45 from its shoulder holster and shot Bob in the center of his forehead. Bob's head went back about a foot as he stood straight up. The light began to fade from Bob's eyes as the grin evaporated. Blood gushed out from the hole in the center of his forehead. But the flame in his hand burned on as Bob began falling forward. He fell onto the car, bounced off the hood, and then fell onto the ground by the bumper. As his body hit the ground his arm extended and the lighter touched the gas soaked car. Flames shot up, the hot blue and yellow waves rolling over the car's hood, sides, and spreading across the roof. The wave of flame spread out in every direction, enveloping the white Ford. The flames traveled along the tiny streams in the rain gutters then they reached out for the gas on the collar of Jack's coat and made the jump.

Before Jack could move more than two steps away from the fully engulfed car, flames danced across and up the back of Jack's coat and into his hair. Fire was the thing Jack feared the most. He didn't want to go like that. Not fire. Maybe a little bullet hole. Drowning in water wouldn't be so bad. A nice looking clean corpse. Well, ok. A little bloated and there would be some discoloration. But relatively clean. No burnt, smashed, traumatized, or ripped open flesh or internal parts. If Jack could pick the method of his demise he'd probably pick the basketball court. Just blow out a valve and drop dead on the hardwood. Or on the blacktop at a park basketball court. Gentle breezes blowing up his basketball shorts. A faint smile on his face. Sleep. The deep sleep. The big sleep. The dead sleep.

Jack holstered the gun and struggled with the burning coat as he moved away from the burning car. The gas had soaked through the coat and onto the backside of his pants. Jack felt the heat on the back of his head. His red hair was burning! Jack ripped off the coat and rubbed the back of his head as he ran across Storrow Drive. As soon as he got the fire in his hair out and tried to work on another area, the fire would travel up the back of his gas soaked shirt again. He tried to stop, drop, and roll, but it wasn't working. And he had to get away from the gas bomb that used to be his ride.

The river was another fifteen feet away. He was a blur as he took off. Kelly scrambled to the edge of the Charles, hopped up on the cement railing, and jumped off the side of the Longfellow Bridge into the river just as an explosion from his white Crown Vic filled the air above it with smoke and flames.

Chapter 4

Zen Again

Jack dropped the twelve feet and splashed into the chilly December Charles River water. Hitting the water from 12 feet up was instant relief from the heat and flames burning Jack's back and head. The Standells made the Charles River famous in song when they called it "Dirty Water." Jack loved that dirty water.

He dragged himself up on the riverbank and pulled himself up onto the walkway of the Longfellow Bridge. People had been walking from various places along the bridge and surrounding streets but most people had stopped and were watching Jack.

Talk about a bad haircut. Kelly's reddish hair was burnt down to a quarter of an inch in the back and on one side. The rest was it's usual two inches in length, a longer red shock in the front. His gray dress shirt was hanging out on one side, his soaking wet dark blue pants drooping as he stood there, shivering. Water dripped from his blue tie and drained from his shoes and the shoulder holster containing his Colt .45.

Jack staggered back toward the gas station. He heard the sound of sirens growing louder. The scene was blanketed with the thick smoke that hung in the air. All traffic in the busy Charles Circle had stopped.

Jack walked up to what was once his car. It was his symbol of truth, the work ethic, and basic American engineering. Mighty Whitey was completely consumed now. The roar of the flames, the black smoke, and the smell of burnt rubber and gasoline cut through the clear cold Boston air.

The Ford was Jack's dependable old workhorse. It was the squad car he drove when he was a young patrol cop, the cruiser he bought at the police auction and had repainted white. Jack often found himself talking to that car. He considered Mighty Whitey an old friend.

The fire department's hook and ladder truck roared up, parked in the middle of the street, and within a half a minute hit the blazing car with a solid blast of water. The white steam and smoke billowed and spilled out in all directions. Soon the fire was out. It was no longer Mighty Whitey. The car was a black, soaking frame of smoldering junk. Kelly would have to call it Boston Blackie. It was burnt… and still smoking. It was toast. Jack realized that he should have gotten that extra fire and theft package at his local insurance company.

Jack Kelly had picked up what was left of his coat from the pavement and stood shivering slightly in the middle of thirty-five or maybe fifty people looking at his car when the patrol officers walked up to him. The singed and burnt red hair, ash-smudged face, soaked clothes, and burnt brown corduroy jacket, indicated that Jack Kelly was the guy to talk to. His shoulder holster and gun were still dripping. The backside of his pants were burnt and his hands were black. He had the appearance of a madman.

The black-and-whites began pulling in around the perimeter. A young, stocky, wide-eyed and dark complected rookie walked up and asked Jack, "What happened to you, man?" His mouth was wide open, as he looked Jack up and down and from side to side.

Jack replied after a few long and awkward moments.

"Car's burnt." Jack slowly raised his arm and finger up to point at the car's burnt frame.

"How did that happen?" asked the young cop.

"He did it." Jack again slowly raised his arm and pointed to the feet sticking out from behind the front bumper of the car.

The rookie zone-officer's eyes widened as he realized that he had more than a vehicle catching on fire. He had a dead man here, maybe a murder. He whipped the radio up out of its holster faster than Billy the Kid and radioed for the EMT's to come in, the on-call Medical Examiner, and a supervisor. He gave the ten-code for a man down, a 10-48. Code K. Dead. He kept one eye on Kelly as another officer stood just off at an angle behind him. Both had their hands on the butt of their guns.

By the time Sergeant Donavan arrived the patrol officer had asked Jack his name, DOB, asked why Jack had a gun, and the $64 question. How did that man die?

"Shot him in the head," was Kelly's answer.

The EMT's had moved Bob from the front bumper and the fire fighters had buried Jack's car under a ton and half of water. The area had been cordoned off with yellow crime scene tape. The EMT's attempted CPR twice before finally realizing that Bob was stone cold dead and had been since the bullet entered the center of his brain. "He's flat," the young EMT pronounced as they finished trying to bring back the dead, and their attention finally turned to Jack.

Old Sgt. Donavan arrived and had taken charge of the crime scene. In a matter of minutes, through delegation, he had called for homicide detectives, the forensics unit, a photo-tech, checked the ETA on the Medical Examiner, had notified the staff on-call, and ordered coffee and donuts. Then he strode up to Jack Kelly and spoke slowly.

"Chaos, disorder, destruction, and death. I guess your work here is done, Kelly." Donavan said and added, "Why is it always in my zone?" He pulled off his squared hat and scratched his head. When Jack didn't look up, Donavan got serious.

"All right Jack Kelly, let's have it and it better be good. Keep the horseshit to a minimum. This is the second time I've seen you in the last twenty-four hours and I'm still wondering about your last story. You were supposed to be in the station this mornin,' long before now, to explain the Criminal Threatening with a Weapon case from last night. And your car's registration was given out after shots fired at the Brattle Theater one and one half-hour ago! So give it to me straight." Donavan demanded as he relieved Jack of his gun.

"He tried to roast me. I shot him."

"That's it?"

"That's it." Jack said, coughing.

"Well, do you know him or do you have this effect on everybody?"

Detective Lieutenant Jessica Paris, just arriving and being told Sgt. Donavan was interviewing the shooter, began making her way through the small crowd surrounding the scene. She had heard the answers to Donavan's questions, but had not realized that the dirty and wet shooter was Kelly. She stepped out from behind Donavan and said forcefully, "You'd better start making your answers make some sense, Mister, or you will find yourself downtown facing a homicide rap. You have the right to remain… Jack?" She said, surprised.

"I have the right to remain Jack? Well, thank you very much. As if I could be anyone else."

"You… you… are filthy and wet. What are you doing here? You did promise me a homicide for the next time we met, didn't you? I mean, what's going on?" Lieutenant Detective Paris said, suddenly becoming quite flustered.

Jack stared into her eyes with a far away look as if remembering something from the deep past.

Donavan's thick Irish brogue cut through the somewhat awkward silence. "Jack, you of course know your esteemed former colleague, homicide detective Paris. She's here in an official capacity, Jack."

Jack mimicked Donavan's accent. "Donavan, I've oft' suspected that yer brogue was part manufactured. I know yor fahdder worked the BPD with my grandfahdder and yer were born in Southie, which was, is, and ever shall be, a part of Narth America. Now leave me alone with this fair lass and I'll confess how that rabid mad-dog crimnal tried to kill me and I saved the Commonwealth a bundle of quid by defending me self, and all of humanity, from the deranged hoodlum. Who, by the way, has several active felony arrest warrants on him. He is a fugitive that's been driving around, unchecked, I might add, committing felonious crimes in *your* sector for at least *your* last two shifts. And I believe you have been working for what is approachin' over twenty 'ours straight, as if you needed the money, in violation of union ahticles and department SOP's."

"Kelly, there are three secrets to life. Money, cash, and money. But I'll leave you for the moment in the capable care of the Boston Police Department's esteemed Homicide Division. But we have another matter pending. A felony Criminal Threatening with a Deadly Weapon. Remember those slice marks on your throat, Kelly?"

"Well, also, Donavan, about that discharge of weapons in the Brattle Street Theater? I'll call The Musician, Willie Crawford, and have him come in, too. He disarmed 'Bob,' the guy lying down over there, when he was about to pull the trigger on me. You can have Cambridge PD sit in. But Bob did all the shooting. Well, most of the shooting. OK, I'll be writing a long report on that one, too."

"Jesus, Kelly. You are a menace to society. Am I gonna have to put a man on you night and day?"

"No, but maybe a woman." Kelly said and turned back to Lt. Paris.

Donavan's attention turned to a rookie spitting on the gas station's sidewalk.

"Young Hodge, there, poor rookie. He's got a dead badge." Donavan said. When an officer is killed, or dies, eventually his badge number finds its way back into the ranks and is re-circulated. Some say its good luck. Most think it's not. Donavan walked away shouting orders to young cops stringing crime scene tape.

"Officer Hodge! I'll stick my foot so far up your ass that your breath will smell like boot polish for a week. Don't spit in my crime scene!"

While Jack shivered in the winter air, medical personnel were holding navy blue blankets all around the dead Bob. The M.E bagged his hands, photographed and prepped him for transport to the morgue.

"Kelly, this might not be the time, but, since I saw you last night, I was thinking we should get together for a drink," Lt. Jessica Paris said after a long pause.

Jack wondered if she was really interested or was just playing him.

"Last thing I heard was that you were engaged to the Mass State Police. Well, one of them anyway. Don't you think your trooper would object?" Jack was still bitter about Jessica dumping him after he resigned from the Cold Case Homicide Unit and then retired from the department altogether.

"That's old news, Jack. I'm not with the trooper anymore. I caught him sneaking 'favors' from a working girl at Centerfolds. The slime ball."

"Investigator, wasn't he?" Jack asked.

"He couldn't find the hole in a doughnut. He was K-9."

"So he used the dog to find the hole in the doughnut. I'm sorry, Jesse. You mean the holier-than-thou trooper got caught with his pants down?"

"I videotaped him, Jack. I didn't believe it so I set up a video camera."

"You still got the tape? Never mind. I don't want to know."

Jack stared at the floor as if thinking about some past experience while Jessica glared at him.

"He's not the one they caught at the Rte. 95 rest stop, is he?"

"No, Jack."

Jack asked her, "Do you know the difference between an elephant and a State Police cruiser?"

When Jesse didn't respond, Jack said, "The elephant has his trunk in the front, and the asshole's in the back."

Jack didn't get much of a smile so he continued.

"Kid asks his dad for a pair of toy six-guns, a toy badge, and that big state trooper hat. The kid gets them for his birthday, puts them on, and says, 'I'm a State Trooper. Got my State Trooper guns, my State Trooper badge, and my State Trooper hat!'"

"The kid and his dad go out to do some errands and drive to a gas station on the highway and while his dad pumps the gas the kid goes to the men's room. Inside the men's room, while the kid is standing at the urinal, a guy comes out of the stall, stands at the urinal next to the kid and stares down at him. The kid looks up at the stranger and says, 'I'm a State Trooper! Got my State Trooper guns, my State Trooper badge, and my State Trooper hat!'"

"The man says, 'Would you like to play with my dick, little state trooper?'"

"The kid says, 'No! Hey! I'm not a real State Trooper.'"

This produced a gush of laughter from Detective Lieutenant Jessica Paris.

"How about you, Jack? Are you single?"

"There's only one of me. Actually I've been looking for some one, really bad. Are you really bad?"

Jack kept up the banter. "You know the difference between a wife and a girlfriend?"

"35 pounds?" Paris answered, taking the wind from Jack's sails. Then she asked Jack, "Do you know the difference between a husband and a boyfriend?"

Jack's blank stare brought the punch line from Jesse.

"35 minutes."

The ice was broken but they both realized that the situation called for at least a minimum of professionalism.

The Lt. said, "We've got some work to do here, Kelly. Lots of paperwork and forms to fill out. Incident reports. Narrative and Utility reports. Use of Deadly Force. Arson report. Interview transcripts. You know the route. You trained me."

"You forgot the swimming with no lifeguard on duty form."

She wasn't your average cop. She was a cultured pearl. Jack remembered how he had a crush on her since the first time he saw her. Jack was still working at Homicide when Jesse walked into his crime scene. It was a gang hit and Jack tripped over the body as he walked toward her, staring. He walked toward her like he was in some kind of trance. He thought she was a reporter and he was going to check her ID until he saw her badge under her tweed sports coat hanging on her tight fitting jeans. She was an evidence tech and was not impressed with Jack's regard of the key piece of evidence. But the body didn't complain. Jack regained his balance and stumbled toward her. She pegged him for a klutz right away. It was an opinion Jessica Paris had of Jack that would stand the test of time.

She was intelligent looking. Not the centerfold type but a sharp college girl that didn't have to exploit every nook and cranny. Jesse had a brightness that twinkled in her deep blue eyes. She was pretty all right. Dark, almost black, hair cut straight across in almost an eighties style shag. On her it looked good. She was all blue eyes, red lips, and a long curvaceous body, but it was her intelligent manner and speech that were her most outstanding characteristics.

Jesse Paris wasn't your ordinary woman. She had gone through many prestigious schools and colleges and traveled extensively. Berkshire Country Day School, Simon's Rock School For Girls, Smith, Harvard Law. She was from a cop family. Her father, Captain Jim Paris, struggled to put his only child through the best schools, and he did. But she became a cop anyway. She wasn't the average Irish or Italian cop with right wing conservative views fueled by alcohol and the cynicism that comes from dealing with the low end of society at its worst, night after night.

It seemed that Jack Kelly never got to first base with her. Maybe it was because each of them had been seeing someone else regularly when their paths had crossed. Each was deeply involved with someone. There was never a time when they worked together when the two of them were free. Free to explore the attraction between them. But they did a little more than just flirt on occasions.

It was rare that in the intense cop world, each of them could find stimulation, both physically and mentally, from each other. There was a very strong attraction between them. They found refuge from the manic world of the Boston Police Department within each other. They had found another similar soul on this crazy planet. It was especially rare in law enforcement circles. Jack and Jesse just couldn't find the time or place to fall in love.

The verbal banter they enjoyed, with its sexual innuendoes, philosophical proficiency, and socio-psychological underpinnings revealed two psyches in tune with the cosmic perspective. They got along well and they were obviously attracted to each other.

She was fresh. Optimistic. Not yet jaded by a system that wears a cop down and overwhelms her by putting repeat offenders back into the general public to prey on the weak again and again with reckless abandon.

"Lets get you looked at by the Meds and get you down to Bowdoin Street."

"I don't suppose I could go by the office and grab a shower and a cup of coffee?"

Sgt. Donavan blurted in from fifteen feet away, "Kelly that's not going to fly again! Not today. You're already late for the last Incident Report. Next you'll want to shave, shower, get a haircut, eat breakfast, and read your horoscope. I know you won't be getting an oil change for that car. By then we'll have us another incident. I'm assigning an officer to escort you directly to headquarters for processing, unless the detective has an objection."

"Good thinking, Sergeant." Paris said smiling at the shivering Jack.

Donavan's last few words shook Jack. Processing? Was Kelly being charged?

Donavan squared off to Jack and added, smiling, "That's right Kelly, processing."

"What's the charge?" Kelly stood up straight.

"Burning without a permit!"

Chapter 5

Cold Black Knight

On the ride to the station in the front seat of Jesse Paris's unmarked Ford Taurus, Jack turned the heater up to full blast and thought about his old friend, the Crown Vic.
"You know that was my old patrol car?"
"Every cop in town knew that car, Jack."
"Donavan didn't have to say that."
"Say what?"
"That I wouldn't be changing the oil in my car today."
"Oh, you poor guy."
"I'm a sensitive, caring, feeling guy."
"Don't, Jack. Tears are welling up in my eyes."
"The experiences I had in that car!" Jack moaned.
"Jesus, Jack. You sound like you had sex in that car." Paris said incredulously and then looked over at Jack who was wearing a sheepish grin. She added, "Oh no! Jack Kelly. You didn't. Did you? You did."
"You should know. Don't you remember?"

Jack remembered the night they had a flat tire down by the waterfront. She blew and he pumped. Then they changed the tire.

"Yeah, well…" Jesse was blushing. "Well at least I worked for the department and was assigned to that car. Well, I was assigned to you, and you were assigned to Mighty Whitey. And I certainly don't want to know who else you had sex with in your car. Or were you alone, Jack?"

"You're never alone when you're schizophrenic. At least that's what the little voices keep telling me. But Jesse, just for old times sake, why don't you pull the car over and you can slide over here and sit on Daddy's lap and we'll pretend we're on a bumpy road."

Jack Kelly also thought about the scrape he was in. It was more like three scrapes. He had been cut by a knife to the throat. Shot at in Harvard Square. And almost roasted and toasted. Jack didn't feel too well at the moment.

"Look at me. I'm still wet. I've got gas on my clothes. My hair is burnt in clumps."

Jessica giggled at the sight.

"Just swing by my office. I live in the back. Let me get out of these wet clothes and brush my teeth. At least let me get my Red Sox baseball cap?" Jack was really trying to sell it.

Jessica laughed again and drove past the Area A police station and on towards Kelly's office.

Lt. Paris parked the car in front of Kelly's Chinatown office and this time they took the elevator up to the fourth floor. Upon entering, Kelly lit a cigar and flipped on a jazz station. He was going to make the best out of this short respite.

"Make yourself at home, Jesse. Should I start some coffee?"

"We've got coffee at the station. Any way you like it."

"I like my coffee, like I like my women, hot, black, and ready for the cream."

"Oh, Jack, that's really old, even for you," Jesse said, shaking her head from side-to-side as she poked around the Guns and Ammo and Guitar Player magazines on a coffee table.

"Don't make me drink that station house shit, Jesse. Unless you're trying to force a confession out of me. Can we drive through Dunkin' Donuts?"

"Sure."

"I'm just going to jump through the shower. I won't even shave… well, just my face."

Jesse smiled back and said, "Do whatever you've got to do. Take all the time you need. I'll give you ten minutes."

Kelly felt good sliding out of the damp, dirty, and burnt clothes. Jack turned on the shower and let it run until it was just the right amount of hot. Steam filled the bathroom. As he stepped in, the shower's hot water pelted against Jack's skin and it felt so relaxing. He imagined all the tension in his body was being splashed from him and washed down the drain. Kelly shouted out, "Oh, yeah!" and as the hot water streamed down his face he imagined it was taking the stress away with it. Thank God for small things, Jack thought. A little personal time. A little space.

"Let's go Kelly!" Lt. Paris yelled and thumped against the bathroom door.

There are two ways of arguing with a woman. And neither one works.

A soaking wet Jack Kelly walked past Jesse with only a thin towel wrapped around his waist.

As they stood there in the warm, streaking sunlight, Jessica said coyly, playing Jack, "Am I being really bad for being here?"

"Not yet." Jack answered and leaned in to steal a kiss.

Of course the phone rang and Jack picked it up.

"Willie? Yes, I'm here. You're talking to me. Yeah I'm all right. It was on the news? What station? They used a file photo? In uniform or plainclothes? Oh good. I hate those old pictures of me in uniform. No. Just some of my hair and clothes got burnt. And Mighty Whitey. It's a total loss." Jack looked over at Paris with his best sad puppy-dog eyes, "Yeah, I ventilated his forehead. I'm on my way to Area A on Bowdoin Street with Lt. Paris."

"Sounds like you're taking the long way, Jack," Willie said wryly.

"You got a gig, Willie?" Jack asked, shifting Willie's focus.

"Well, I've got three different bands I'm working with. But I don't play out as much as we used to. Times have changed, again. You know it ain't wicked fuckin' cool to drink and drive anymore. A lot of musicians are fading outta the business. They'd rather be home in their three-decka drinkin' a Forty, smoking a blunt, and playing in their living rooms, attics, garages, and cellars. Music is being deprived of a bunch of wild, stoned-out, drunken musicians."

"Yeah. Look, would you come in and tell the cops and DA what transpired over in Cambridge? Within the next couple of hours? Yes. OK. I'll see you there. Ask for Lieutenant Paris. Yeah, Jesse. OK. See you there." But The Musician wouldn't let him go and said, "Hey Jack? Wait! Want to hear the Joke-of-the-Day?"

"Look, Willie…" But Jack knew it was quicker to comply and rolled his eyes in resignation at Jesse.

"Yeah, go ahead." Kelly said in resignation.

"A woman gets home, runs into her house, slams the door and shouts, "Honey, pack your bags. I won the lottery."

The husband says, "Wow! That's great! Should I pack for the ocean, or should I pack for the mountains?"

"She says, 'I don't care. Just pack… and get the fuck out.'"

Jack hung up the phone and Jesse asked, "How's Willie? Still living on the edge?"

"He's in a zone of his own."

Jack and Jesse stood quietly in the fourth floor office for a moment. Jack looked at the afternoon sunlight streaming through the windows and his gaze followed a jet leaving Logan International Airport as it climbed up into the hazy midday sky.

He hit the speakerphone button and checked his answering machine.

BEEP. "Jack? You playing poker Monday night? It's at Ed's apartment over The Naked i. Bring beer and cooked shrimp with the red stuff. And lots of money." Jack's blues guitar playing, professional photographer friend, Cooper said. Cooper was a close confidant of Kelly's and they spoke often on the telephone, analyzing, rating, and sizing things up. Coop is brilliant in his own way and quite limited in other ways. He is kind of like a multitasking NY stock exchange agent juggling thirty properties at once along with their time lines but his shoe is untied and he gets hit by a bus while crossing Wall Street.

BEEP. A sweet female voice said, "You need anybody this week Mr. Kelly? If you do, just call me, please. But I do *not* want to bodyguard that Wang executive again. He needs an escort service not a detective agency. If that big Wang ever grabs my ass again I will shoot him myself," Rachel, a female operative that did occasional bodyguard and surveillance work for Jack, said.

BEEP. It was Ed, the bartender at The Naked i. "Jack? There's a meeting of The Regular Rotating Super Secret Monday Night Poker Players. My place this week. Liquor in the front and poke her in the rear. Now that's good advise for anybody… I'll be at the club tonight from 4PM 'til 2AM. Stop by. And if you see that waitress, April, tell her that the bar is closed but my pants will remain open."

Lt. Jessica Paris was looking at Jack standing in the center of the room with nothing on but a towel. Jesse's glances turned to stares. She focused her vision on the towel draped easily on Jack's hips. She attempted to use her telekinetic powers to make the slipping towel, slip completely off. She had never demonstrated this ability before... but maybe this time... She was in total focus. All of her powers began streaming together. Out in front of her. All her efforts were directed and came together, wrapping around Jacks towel and infiltrating it... She attempted, with her mind, to pull the towel down, off Jack's long, thin, yet muscular, legs... Her breathing became deep and fast. The towel looked to Jesse like it would slip down over Jack's slim, smooth hips any second.

When Jack realized she was staring he hung up the phone.

"I... ah... guess I should get going, here." Jack said as he caught her looking him up and down.

"I guess you better put some clothes on first." Jesse said, smiling.

Jack put on his blue Red Sox cap and said, "How's this?"

Chapter 6

Room for Interrogation

After arriving at the Area A police station and being escorted to the stark interrogation room, Jack settled in for a long afternoon. He made a hole in the lid of his large Dunkin' Donuts coffee and got as comfortable as he could in the small bare room with its tiny table and old wooden classroom chairs. Jack periodically looked at the one-way mirror on the wall knowing that someone may be looking in. He adjusted his tie in the mirror and began to stare in, deadpanning. Jack stood up and moved in to within several inches of the one-way mirror. He could no longer help himself and he started mugging ever so slightly, checking his profile, looking for nose hairs, lifting one eyebrow, picking an imaginary particle from his front teeth and making loud sucking and slurping noises.

On the other side of the glass, Paris turned to Donavan saying, "What an infant."

"That's alright. We've got Detective Mulroy going in."

"Mulroy? He's the hardball sex crimes investigator from Steroidville?"

"Sit back and watch the magic, Lieutenant." Donavan said with a mysterious smile.

A very large and muscular interrogator about 28 years old, clean shaven, with short brown military-cut hair came into the interview room, slammed the door shut, and took some papers out of the file folder he was carrying. Jack noticed how well groomed the young man was. Not a nose hair hanging out. Not an errant eyebrow hair independently shooting off toward the ceiling.

The young man stood there and said, "I'm Detective Mulroy, Sport," and he shuffled the papers around, put his foot up on the seat of the chair and leaned over Jack. His hot breath came down and surrounded Jack like a fog but Jack detected no odor. No smell of Italian or Greek food. No smell of cologne, coffee, or mouthwash. Kelly, the old investigator, looked for anything that would help him to start analyzing his interrogator. The young man looked mean and seemed to be either pissed off or suffering from indigestion as he looked down at Jack.

"You did it," he said, nodding his head matter-of-factly.

"No I didn't." Jack responded, just out of principle.

"Yes. Yes you did."

"Nope. Didn't do it."

"You know that I know that you know more than you're saying," the young investigator said.

"Well, I know that you know that I know what you're thinking. 'Cuz I was watching you when you were watching me watch you... you know?" Jack cracked.

Detective Mulroy looked on the verge of getting physical. The vein on the side of his neck bulged and his lips got thin and tight. He dropped his foot from the chair and leaned further over Kelly. Donavan and Paris peered through the one-way glass intently.

"You think this is a joke? I'm gonna make you my pet-of-the-month. If that's how long it takes me to see you go down for this," the young sleuth promised.

"I'm flattered, but I don't think I did it."

"Oh. Now its you 'don't think' you did it?"

Jack Kelly scratched his head and looked reflectively at the door and then glanced at the mirror as the young interrogator continued.

"No? Maybe you're 'bi-polar.' Or maybe it was one of your other personalities. Like the little Boy Scout, the disciplinarian, the sick, dirty little pedophile priest or the whoremaster. That right, Pimp Daddy! Or maybe the nurse came out to administer some medicine or the farmer brought his pigs to market!" The young muscle-bound detective was bearing down on Jack and seemed to get angrier. "The biker or the clown. I know it wasn't *your* fault… Maybe your father left home with the gardener when you were little. Or your uncle took naps with you and showed you how to touch his one-eyed trouser snake… Maybe your mommy loved you too much or not enough. It wasn't *your* fault."

The young cop stood upright with both feet firmly on the ground and looked up into the corner of the ceiling. He seemed to be transported back to a time more pleasant. This time he started out with a soft, whimsical voice. "You saw a pretty little girl, wearing a pretty pink party dress. Someone happy, healthy, and brimming with life, love, and light. And you had to snuff it out!" he screamed at Jack, slapping his hand down on the desk. "You had to crush it, didn't you? You had to put a stop to the fun. You're a poison, choking the life out of everything you touch. You had to spread your filth, didn't you? You're a cancer eating away at all that's good. You had to spread your foul spew." The detective's spit was flying, as his voice grew very loud and more menacing. Jack looked back in confused horror as the overzealous cop escalated, "You are a scumbag and I won't rest until you're locked far away in a deep, dark, hole where no sun shines, and no one can hear *you* scream. Because no one cares!" the detective screamed.

Jack was staring at the investigator in bemused disbelief when Sgt. Donavan opened the door and stuck his head into the room. He was trying hard, but failing to stifle a laugh as he said, "Mulroy! That pervert rapist is in Interview Room 3, two doors down! Jack was a Boston Police detective when you were riding your tricycle to the candy store. This is a homicide investigation. Jack only shot a bad guy in the head, he's no sick fucking pervert. Are you, Jack?"

The small groups of detectives assembled outside the door were smiling and snickering.

"Oh. Sorry, wrong room," the investigator looked a little sheepishly and pointed at Kelly and added, "But I still think you did *something*."

As Mulroy left the room Sgt. Donavan and Lt. Paris came in smiling.

"Very funny, Donavan," Jack said.

"Who says it was my idea?" Donavan said looking at Jesse.

Lt. Paris told Jack that they were going to record the interview and sat down at the tiny table. Both took notes as they questioned Jack.

"Let it be noted that Kelly has waived his right to counsel. So Jack, how can you get into three separate police investigated felony incidents in less than 24 hours?" Donavan asked.

"I get up early."

"How about your previous run-ins with Provost before? Were you seeking revenge?"

"I knew him as Bob. Bob is a bad man. *Was* a bad man. I guess I had reason to seek revenge. He threw an acquaintance of mine out a third floor window. Maybe I did want revenge. Is that so bad? You make it sound so cheap," Jack said sticking out his lower lip and added, "Let's just say I refused to star in his psychodrama."

"I can see why you're no longer a cop, Kelly. You think this is all a game."

"Look, Sarge, have you seen his triple III interstate criminal record? Have you run a C.O.R.I. check? Check with the Sexual Offender Registry. He's got a list of priors going from the ceiling to the floor. Bob Provost must have fallen out of his family tree. He's only been in this state for four years. His first address was the Treatment Center for the Sexually Dangerous at Bridgewater, and then he was transferred to the Ten Block at Walpole State Prison, or Cedar Junction as it's called now. 'A rose by any other name.' He jumped bail on a murder charge. He's a felon in possession of a firearm. Check the serial numbers on that, run them through L.E.A.P.S. if they haven't been filed off. It's probably stolen or been used in the commission of other crimes. He has convictions for strong-arm robbery, kidnapping, attempted murder, gambling, extortion, larceny, multiple assaults and weapons charges. And I believe fishing without a license, mopery in the nighttime with intent to gawk, and perhaps buggery."

Jack got no laughs, so he continued.

"This was a clean shoot. I'm sure you've read all the witness statements from all three incidents before you talked to me. Haven't you?" Jack still received no reaction and continued. "Other than case officer Lt. Paris, the Homicide unit hasn't shown much interest. Nor the Staties. If *they* thought they could get a conviction they'd be on me like a dog in heat trying to climb over each other to make the arrest. The riff-raff I capped was a bad man. A murderer who jumped bail and who tried to shoot me and fry my ass. He is, was, a sick bastard who should have been doing life at Walpole. Too bad the good people of Massachusetts did not execute him before letting him out on bail. This ain't no game Sarge, when you're getting shot at, or gas is pouring down the back of your neck. And he's runnin' around shootin' at people and playing with a lighter. Half the hair on my head is burned off! And think of the environmental issues."

"Alright Kelly! Jeez... I'm just testin' ya to see if you're going to hold up. I know it was clean. I know who you are. You're from the old school. My father worked on the beat with your grandfather. You don't have to browbeat me with the environmental issues. That's hittin' below the belt." Sarge smiled and they both nodded.

"Dam straight." Jesse agreed.

"Sarge, you need to take up a hobby. How about golf?"

"I played golf once. I shot a 68... Then we moved on to the back 9." Donavan laughed at his joke. He loved the old jokes the best.

After nearly three hours of interviews, filling in the details, Sgt. Donavan and Lt. Paris thanked Kelly for coming down.

"Anytime I can shed a little light on the Dark Side."

"Seriously Jack, you know, lettin' the cat outta the bag is a whole lot easier 'n puttin' it back in." Donavan said and Jack nodded even though he had no idea what the Sergeant meant.

Kelly and Sgt. Donavan retrieved Jack's .45 automatic and the license plates from Mighty Whitey from the Property and Evidence Room and the old Sarge told a patrol officer to give Jack a ride back to his office. As he left the Area A station Kelly saw The Musician waiting in the lobby for his interview.

"Who cuts your hair? Stevie Wonder?" the Musician asked Jack.

Chapter 7

Black Jack

Jack Kelly still looked like he was on the losing end of a dogfight, but he decided to have the patrol unit drop him off at The Naked i, the strip joint in Boston's Combat Zone. Ed McGee, Jack's old rock and roll pal, worked there as a bartender and he was always good for some quick mental realignment. And he was much cheaper than a psychiatrist.

Ed was a 5'10" stocky, curly haired Irish-Italian. An athletic 46 year-old and a bona-fide health nut. He ate only low fat, no fat, raw vegetables, fish, Creatine and whey, Gainer's Fuel, and a variety of powders and pills. He exercised 29 out of 30 days a month. He did sit-ups, push ups, 25 miles-a-day on the stationary bike and he lifted weights. He claims exercise and diet will be the religion of the future. One time Jack tried to eat a hot dog at a Celtics game and Ed slapped it out of his hand like Jack had pulled a gun.

Kelly walked into The Naked i and as his eyes adjusted to the dim lights Ed spotted him and began to walk along with Jack on the other side of the bar.

"Did you hear? That Chink neighborhood association is buying out this whole block and The Naked i, the Two O'clock Lounge, and the Caribe are getting shut down. Jack? Man, these places are historic. Soldiers on leave and returning from WW II made this strip of bars flourish. Remember when we were kids, my uncle on the big B-3 Wurlitzer organ with old Charlie Flannery on drums backing up the strippers? And when I was in college, I'd come here and Jay Leno used to do the jokes… bombed out half the time. Remember?" Ed put a shot of Scotch in front of Jack.

"Damn slant eyed neighborhood association." Ed mumbled.

"Its Chinatown, Ed. They don't have your sense of history. And you're not prejudiced. What's with all the derogatory shit?"

"Hey, I accept all denominations. But two of my favorites are twenties and hundreds."

"They just aren't patrons of the arts." Jack said, looking up at the plump and pimply white girl stripper wearing a bathing suit sliding up and down the greasy brass pole in the center of the runway.

"She looks kinda beat, Ed. The standards here are slipping."

"You look kinda beat. What happened to your hair? You got clumps, it looks… What the fuck? Like… burnt. And you smell like, smoke and gasoline, man. What were you doing? One of those crazy stunts the kids try? What the fuck?"

"I got to quit smoking. Give me one of those Garcia Vega cigars, over there, Ed." Jack said pushing a five across the bar. "Can't smoke inside a lot of places. Pretty soon you won't be able to smoke on the sidewalks. Then you won't be able to smoke anywhere! I'll be hiding out like a goddamn criminal sneaking a smoke in a back alley. Blowing smoke out of bathroom windows. Driving out to the wilderness to light up."

"You gotta join a health club, Jack," Ed told him.

"I did. It cost me $800. I didn't lose a pound. Apparently the gimmick is, you've got to go there and do stuff."

While Ed was getting the key for the humidor box, retrieving the aforementioned cigar, and placing it and a fresh book of matches on the bar in front of Kelly, the TV news began covering the shooting at the Charles Circle Sunoco gas station. Jack prepared his cigar, wetting it and making a hole in the end. He struck a match and lit the big Garcia Vega. Ed stared at Kelly impatiently, until the cigar was fully lit and he had exhaled a stream of blue smoke. Then Ed said, "Well?"

Jack pointed over his shoulder at the Channel 4 News. Ed looked up and saw the gas station with yellow crime scene tape around the pump area. He saw the cops, the fire trucks, ambulance, the blackened shell of Jack's burned out Ford, and a dirty black-faced Jack standing next to Paris and Donavan. And he saw the large body of Ray-Ricardo "Bob" Provost lying on the cold cement under a white cotton sheet.

"Holy shit, Jack." Ed said and fumbled under the bar for the remote control, turning up the sound.

"Jesus, Savoir of the Seven Sisters of the Shamrock! Who was that?"

"Remember the big dummy who came in here looking for me last summer, worked for Thaddeus Reno, caused a problem? Cleared off the bar? The big pock marked flat top, Bob, Big Boy Bob, My Boy Bob?"

"Oh, yeah. What happened today?"

"He tried to light me on fire. So I shot him."

"Ah, Marone. Putana, de la Madonna! You OK? You just tell me. What do you need?"

"Another car." Kelly said dejectedly.

Chapter 8

The Man in the Mirror

The next morning, and after a haircut at the little shop on Hanover Street in the Italian North End, Jack got back to the office-apartment. He stared into the mirror. His red hair was a little shorter than he liked it, he looked like a 36-year-old prep-schooler, but it would grow back quickly. After it was cut and clipped the burnt area on the left side and back of his head had blended in well with the rest. Kelly looked closely at his face in the mirror. His finger traced the shallow knife slice across his throat. He talked out loud to himself and didn't care if there was anything wrong with that.

"My name is Jack Kelly. Crowd says, 'Hi, Jack.' I am an addicted killing machine. It has been eight hours since I last killed somebody. Applause." He continued his diatribe to the man in the mirror.

"Little man you've had a busy day. What are you doing tonight, Jack? I don't know. What are *you* doing, Jack? This week is really shaping up. I got my throat cut with a knife. There was an attempt to frame me for murder. I've been pistol-whipped and shot at in Harvard Square. Had gas poured over me. I've been lit on fire and I jumped off the Longfellow Bridge into the Charles River. I shot a man in the head and killed him. The cops would love an excuse to yank my private eye ticket. And at the moment I don't have one client with any goddamned cash money. This week is really shaping up. I need a vacation." Jack sighed and then went on.

"I try to keep out of the news. I don't need my face splashed all over the papers or on the goddamned TV screen. But if this week is any indication… What do I need, a goddamned PR agent? Next chance I get, I'm taking some lucky lady out to dinner or a club and home for some romance. Some hot pants romance. Teased and pleased. Racked and stacked. Stumped and humped. And I'll have a few drinks, too.

In fact I may even get buzzed. So what if I have a drink or two. I'm over 21. I'm a sophisticated cosmopolitan. I can function as a professional American businessman. I can have a couple of drinks to make the transition from a tough business day into the world of the arts. Of relationships, culture. I'm not driving around. I'll be at home with some heartfelt jazz on the entertainment center, some soft lighting and an open book.

Perchance a little romance with a sophisticated young professional woman of independent means. A social life."

A date. Jack thought about just how long it had been since he had a real date.

Jack had gotten so skeptical he ran a criminal records check on any woman showing any interest in him. What he needed was a rendezvous with a sexy and attractive lady. A night of dancing, theater, or even a good movie. She arrives at the door, a flowing, colorful dress. Or a short mini. Her hair just right. All lipstick and eyes. She would smell just right. The mood, the time, all of it is right.

But of course Jack thought of the girl he just lost. There wasn't anything he could do about that. She was a kindergarten teacher. Sweet, innocent, trusting. And a knockout. An Italian-Irish, green-eyed, longhaired, girl-next-door. An American beauty.

She had no problem handling the stress of Jack's lifestyle. The intensity that Jack brought to certain cases was maddening at times, but she always rode it out. It wasn't too much for her.

But it was bad enough. Jack Kelly was constantly preoccupied. Sometimes the goons, thieves, hookers, and cops intruded into their personal relationship. But she could handle it. Until the day she died.

Kelly finished shaving his face and assessed the recent damage. His hair was still visibly burnt and clipped a little too short in the back. He stared into his tired and cynical looking eyes. His eyes were still red, white, and blue. He stepped into the shower, again. Jack wanted to wash the black soot out of his hair until the full chestnut red color shone through again. After getting cleaned up he put on some comfortable clothes and re-heated the take-out Chinese food he had in the fridge and ate it very slowly. Jack put on some Miles Davis and sat on the couch resolved to an evening of solitude until he heard the knock at the door.

"Oh no!" Jack mumbled. He was gun shy from recent events.

A quick look out the peephole in the outer office door revealed the big blue eyes of Jesse Paris looking in. Her black hair fell onto her bare shoulders. She wore a black evening dress, a set of white pearls, high heels and lipstick. She held up a bottle of Remy Martin Cognac.

"Oh yes!" Jack said, opening the door.

She was radiant. Just what the Doctor ordered. Each cloud has its silver lining.

"You're a sight for sore eyes. Did the opera close early? Do come in." Jack said sweeping his arm across the expanse of his cluttered live-in office. Kelly could smell the elegant perfume of the beautiful and sophisticated woman as she walked past.

Jesse said, "Jack, today was so long. It brought back memories. Memories of you and me, in a time when I couldn't really tell you how I was feeling about you."

She wanted him to open up to her. He looked into her eyes and said, "I know what you mean. But I've been there all the time. And I want to be there for you. I still feel a strong connection to you. We've been through a lot of things, together and separately." Jesse raised an eyebrow. "I want to get closer. I need to be closer. Don't hold me off," he said pushing her back towards the couch. "Let me in. Let me all the way in. I want to be in you. All over you. Around you... and inside and out of you. Under you." They were both smiling as Jack moved closer and closer, kissing her, while he attempted to jive her socks off. Jack always seemed to react that way in serious moments. Jesse began to laugh as Jack continued his schtick.

"On top of you. Over, under, around, and through. 'Til I become one with you... And our souls melt together in the night."

They fell on the couch and the ice was broken. After several cognacs and a little more small talk, Jack was admiring her long and smooth legs and thought he could see a glimpse of the milky white inner thigh at the top of Jessica's black mesh stockings and garter belt. He could take it no longer. Jack put his mouth on her mouth and kissed her gently, again and again. He slowly began to release the passion he had held in for so long. His lips fondled and flexed. He kissed. He caressed. His playful tongue touched her lips and darted in and out of her mouth. He drank of her lips. The passion flowed between them. He could sense the overflowing desire she felt for him by the way that her mouth responded to his. His hands moved over her shoulders and back. They moved lovingly. He wanted her. His hands moved expertly over her body. Up and down her thighs. Up along her legs and under her dress, over her thighs and to her waist. He felt her hard nipples through her dress as she pressed against his chest. He seethed with a full-bodied sexuality that he had repressed for too long.

She responded in kind. No, in unison. She wanted him. She had devoted a lot of thought to Kelly lately and she had made up her mind. She wanted him badly. She did not shrink away from Jack. She shifted and pressed her body against him. She was not backing down. Her hunger was as deep and desirous, as was Jack's.

Kelly was quite stiff with desire and had to back away slightly because of the rock-hard erection that stood between them. He was a little embarrassed but he was not going to let that spoil this romantic moment. He began to envelop Jesse in his arms. He held her tightly, and then let her go. Then he moved in even closer and began to play her like a stand-up bass.

She was like clay in his strong hands and he wanted to mold and form every part of her body. His hands pulled her closer. He stroked her back and then held her hips in his hands. He felt the bottom of her bottom and moved to the top of her top. He caressed and rubbed the back of her neck and gently pulled on the hair in the back of her head until she arched her back and her lips parted.

She had been thinking about him. And now she was thinking about going down on him. She blushed a little, but she could not deny her passion and continued her seduction, pushing his shirt up. She knew it was time. Jesse took him in her hands and kissed his lips, neck, and chest and moved down to the groove running down the center of his belly. She pushed Jack back on the couch and slid down and unbuckled his belt and pants. She softly and playfully bit his sides and lower stomach. They both moaned in ecstasy as Jesse went down on him and took him between her lips, her tongue exploring the shape of him as she took him all the way into her mouth, the mouth that wanted him so badly.

After moans of release and ecstasy, Jack began to sit up but Jesse pushed him back onto the couch and he lifted her dress up to her hips as she straddled him. He entered her slowly and soon found the groove and the beat. Jack was getting into a slow rhythmic stroke. She became more and more vocal, breathing heavy at first, then moaning, and finally releasing a series of light screams punctuated by a couple of shouts of, "Oh my God." Jack wondered if anyone in the artist's studio below could hear them, but he would not be able to stop, even if he had to. Jack wet his fingers on his tongue and reached up, fondling her elegant breasts and tweaking her nipples between his thumb and forefinger. He held her breasts firmly in his hands and moaned. Kelly's passion grew to a climax. The tension in Jesse Paris had built until she found release, biting her own knuckle almost to the point that it bled.

They clutched each other tightly as they slowly and finally stopped moving. They had found a moment together in this crazy world where two souls could touch.

"A penny for your thoughts." Jesse whispered as they lay together quietly.

"They're not worth a penny. I'd have to give you change."

"Another satisfied customer." Jesse said blissfully.

"There's plenty more where that came from," Jack answered even though his tank was empty. "I'm good in bed. I can sleep eight to ten hours in a row."

Chapter 9

Johnny's Jazz and Blues Club

Jesse smiled and they both stretched out on the detective agency couch and soon began to drift. Jack's head was nestled into Jesse's shoulder. The soft leather couch felt good as Jack pulled the thick blue comforter over them. Books were scattered around the couch. But Jack hadn't seemed to be able to finish a book in a while. Jack gazed at the cover of an old brown stained paperback, Carter Dickson's "She Died A Lady," until his eyes closed.

Jack slept deeply. He dreamt of the club that he would own some day. Johnny's Jazz and Blues Club. Johnny was Jack's given name although all his friends called him Jack. It would be right in downtown Boston. Not that big, size-wise, but lots of atmosphere. A club that attracted the city's best jazz and blues musicians, and the women, fringe players, and the crowds that showed up when those elements came together.

Jazz and blues. The combination was a life long pursuit for Kelly. Jazz and blues was the backdrop, the tapestry of Jack Kelly's life. He was a natural-born investigator, but his love was music. He played the drums, harmonica, bass, sang, but his main instrument was the guitar. Jack played in high school bands, through college, toured and played the clubs in and around Boston for some years, while a paralegal investigator for his brother's law firm. He knew how clubs worked. He had been in hundreds. He worked security for nightclubs. And at one time Kelly had managed The Channel, one of the biggest live music clubs in Boston.

And he needed a place to play his blues on Monday nights.

Johnny's Jazz and Blues Club. It started as he heard a saxophone wailing deep, dark blues in the distant night. As he walked toward the sound the jazzy sax riffs seemed to divide, multiply, and deepen. Now he could hear the drums. He heard the crack of the snare and the sizzle of the cymbals. The crisp high-hat ticking out the time. The steady thump of the bass drum. And then the bass filled in all the holes. He heard the tinkling of high notes on the piano.

The jazz riffs were solidly building as Jack's dream took him around the corner, closer and closer. He walked through the light rain like it was god's holy water. Through the foggy Boston night and up to the glowing green and purple neon lights. And right through the open door of Johnny's.

Jack walked in like he owned the place. And he did. Everybody was happy to see Jack Kelly. The house was buzzing with cool jazz, soft conversations, clinking glasses and cash flowing into the registers at the bar. Jack took up his seat at the end of the bar, lit a cigar, and ordered an old and rare Cognac from Jimmy the bartender.

Jack enjoyed this serial dream. But then, as is often the case, the rain got heavier, the thunder louder, the lightning flashed with a crack that echoed throughout the canyons of the downtown buildings, and the power went out.

In the morning as the two lovers awoke on the couch together, Jesse said, "Jack, you could never be serious. Everything is fun and games to you."

"I wear immaturity like a shield, baby. I guess I could feel the pain. I guess I could let everything get me down. I guess I could be as bummed out as everyone else, I'll work on it."

"You see? You're not serious. You're making light of it."

"Making light of what? What brought this on?"

"Making light of... things," she said.

"What is this, girl-speak? What are you trying to say?"

"Well... I would just like to talk serious with you once in a while."

"That's my way of dealing with things, Jess. Maybe I've been hurt before. Maybe a woman took my heart and ripped it out of my chest, threw it down and stepped on it, ground it, crushed it, scraped it up, spit on it, and fried it in butter, fat, and lemon and served it up to me for dinner... Sure I've been hurt. Hurt bad. But I'm not bitter." Jack looked at her blank expression out of the corner of his eye to see if she was buying any of this.

Kelly rolled over on top of her and asked if they could talk about that later. He kissed her lips lightly. As Jack pulled his head up, the thin gold chain he wears around his neck swung forward and tapped Jesse lightly on her nose.

"What's with the gold chain? You Italian?"

"Ooh! An ethnic slur. Very funny, Jess. You got Italian in you?"

"No."

"Do you want one? Really, I wear this gold chain to remind me," Jack said as he rolled off of Jesse and a serious look came over his face. He stared at the ceiling as if remembering something from long ago.

"Remind you of what, Jack?" She said, sitting up.

"This gold chain reminds me… I got a place to hang my sunglasses when I walk around naked." Jack said as he jumped up and did some kind of Hootchie-Kootchie dance on the end of the couch.

"Jack, I've got something to talk to you about." Jessica said getting up and putting on one of Kelly's dress shirts.

"All good things must come to an end."

"Seriously, Jack. But it's no joke. It's about a little girl."

"Oh. You want to have a *menage a trois*? I don't know, Jesse. I'm a sheep in wolf's clothing. A little threesome action, hey? I almost had one of those, once. There was me. And all I needed was two girls."

Jesse looked at Jack and emitted a long sigh, shaking her head from side-to-side.

Jack continued with, "Yeah. So you want to have a love triangle?"

"I've got a love triangle for you." Jesse said, smoothing out the front of the big shirt over her panties before continuing.

"Listen. Seriously please, Jack. This little girl, she is eight years old, she has no one to protect her. No parents or relatives. There's a lawyer draining her estate."

"A lawyer? So there's a shark in the water."

"Exactly."

"Even a shark won't eat a lawyer. Professional courtesy. Do you know the difference between a tick and a lawyer? The tick falls off of you after you die. Why did New Jersey get all the toxic waste and New York get all the lawyers? New Jersey got to pick first. What's the difference between a lawyer and a vampire? A vampire only sucks blood at night."

"Jesus, Jack. Isn't your brother a lawyer down the Cape?"

"Yup… Well, so, what's the problem, you're the law. Can't you stop this attorney from raping the estate?"

"There's no direct evidence. I can't get the Bureau Chief to add the case. I can't get any other detectives to put in any time on it. There is no complainant. No obvious crime has been committed. The whole department is, you know, *reactive* instead of *pro*active. The whole business is basically either complaint generated or we get called in after-the-fact. The patrolmen and dicks at the BPD want to take on as little as they can to keep from being overwhelmed. And they still have their hands full with domestic disruptions, murders, accidents, robberies, burglaries, identity thefts, computer crimes, sex crimes, assaults, fights, traffic control at fires, disturbances, and all the other calls for service, and whatever."

It seems they weren't interested in Lt. Jesse Paris's theories on a crime that might or might not happen. The detectives she worked with weren't interested in any outside work that didn't pay. No complainant equals no crime.

"So what have you got?" Jack asked.

"I've got a young girl who is in danger."

Jack Kelly thought if he didn't get something a little more concrete, she'd be adding his name to the list of uninterested. They moved to the small office kitchen and began making breakfast as she continued.

"She is an heir to a fortune, Jack. A large fortune. And she is standing in the way of an overly aggressive attorney. I've spoken with the chauffeur for the little girl and he thinks that the lawyer is making attempts on the girl's life."

"Why is this such a crusade for you, Jess? You deal with man's inhumanity to man on a daily basis."

"Maybe I've got my reasons, Jack. Maybe she reminds me of a little girl who had no one to turn to. A little girl who was at the mercy of conspiring adults, who just wanted to take advantage of her, and who would instill a warped impression of what life was supposed to be about."

"Maybe I think I know who that little girl was, Jesse."

"And the girl's chauffeur is an old family friend." Jesse said, looking away.

Jack could tell it was not the time to play psychiatrist. Instead he asked Jesse what the driver said the girl was in danger from.

"Maybe poison or drugs. He can't prove a thing at this point, hence the lack of police involvement."

Kelly didn't jump in with his usual one-liners. He stared at the ceiling and asked,

"How large a fortune are we talking about?"

"Her family left her a huge fortune. Gold, jewels, stocks and bonds. Good investments. Real estate. Businesses large and small. She's diversified. Insulated. She could live on the interest alone."

It didn't take Kelly long to add up the pros and cons. There was money. Not readily accessible, but, there would be money down the line. But maybe of even more value would be the indebtedness that Lt. Paris would hold to Jack Kelly, for life.

"So what?" Jack said, thinking aloud.

"What?" Jesse asked.

But Jack was thinking. Worse case scenario was that Jack wouldn't get a dime but Paris was the kind of connection that would owe Kelly enough to provide him with information. And information is the life's blood of a private investigator. And she wasn't bad looking either. Maybe it was the way she walked. Or the way her hair fell onto her shoulders. Maybe it was the way she looked in a slit skirt or the way she smiled when she wanted something. The way she moved around his kitchen, reaching up to get things. Bending over to pick things up. Maybe it was the way she smelled like a garden. A garden of earthly delights. Yes, that's what she was, a heavenly garden of earthly delights.

"Could you just meet with the chauffeur and me at the restaurant of your choice, Jack? Will you help me, Jack? Will you help her?"

Finally, Kelly spoke. The moment was his. He looked Jessica Paris straight in the eye. Kelly was interested and had already decided to take the case. Or at least look into it.

"This is where good and evil meet. Ground Zero. Heaven and Hell. You can get hurt here. Or make your bones. I'll help you."

"Is that why you became a cop, Jack? Are you a white knight, Jack? Why are you in this law enforcement and investigation business?"

"Let's just say I'm a blue knight. You know me. I'm a crime fighter. I'm thrilled to live out my childhood fantasies of battling good over evil."

"Is that it? Is that why you're a detective?"

"No, I just like the big flashlight."

Chapter 10

Call Central Casting

Later that day Jack called The Musician.
"How was your interview?"
"I just told them what I saw, Jack. Took about twenty-five minutes and I was outta' there."
"Yeah, I don't see any problems. I think they realize that I did what I had to do."
"It was righteous, Jack. Are you OK?"
"I guess so. I'm fine, actually. I'm all set with what I had to do. That guy was a piece of shit. He was a bad man. I think I did everyone a favor." Jack said, and then he went silent, wondering if Bob had a mother.
"You sure you're OK?"
"Yeah, thanks Willie. I had some company last night, and she kind of verified, or validated me, so to speak."
"Who? What? You got laid?"
"I had a romantic experience, Willie. Why do you got to reduce everything to its lowest level?"
"Don't evade me, Jack… The waitress at The Rack again?"
"No."

"The Stripper?"

"No! Look, I don't kiss and tell. Discretion is the better part of valor, and all that shit. OK?"

"You slut! You whore!" Willie charged.

"I didn't get any money." Jack defended.

"So don't tell me," The Musician said, sounding hurt.

"It was Jessica Paris."

"No! Did you fill her aching void? I know she worked with you, before, and you two… but… So what happened with you and her the first time?"

"I guess we flew too close to the sun on wings of love and passion…. We crashed and burned."

"She dumped you, huh?"

"Yeah. For a goddamned state trooper."

"You gotta be kiddin'. So that's what you meant by being validated. Not as a man, but as an innocent man. You birddog. How did that happen? Were you rubbing her leg with your foot while she was grilling you in Interrogation?"

"She just showed up here, late last night. Dressed to kill."

"Was she killer? All killer and no filler? Was she good?"

"I don't answer that kind of question, Willie. But I will tell you that she moaned so long and so loud that when we finished the whole neighborhood had a cigarette."

"You dog!"

"By the way, she gave me a case." Jack mentioned.

"A case of what?" Willie said. Jack had momentarily forgotten that anything he says to the Musician could be immediately misconstrued.

"It may not pay, at least for a while, but I want you to help me out on it. Can you put in some time on spec?"

"What's it about, Jack? I'm supposed to go into the studio with an old school hotshot producer, Jimmy Miller, who worked with the Stones, Steve Winwood, and Clapton. Why don't you come along? You can play some guitar and maybe sing one of the songs. You got a great voice, man. I couldn't sing if I had Elvis stuck in my throat. But you could have made money with that guitar."

"I did. I sold it."

The Musician sighed, as Jack continued, "Look, Willie. It's about a kid. A little girl that might get quietly erased, if someone doesn't check this out."

"I'm there." It was the response Jack wanted to hear.

The Musician was a regular guy and then some. He was drop-dead cool. Women fell for him so easy. When he wanted them to be, his pick-up lines could be as smooth as the Boston Symphony Orchestra's string section playing Mozart.

The Musician is of mostly Italian extraction. He lives in a triple-decker in Southie with a bunch of kids, a dog, and a beautiful Irish-American wife. She is a saint, too. She loves him unconditionally, even though Willie would say the craziest things in front of her. The first time Kelly met Willie's wife, Mrs. Mary-Lou Crawford, Willie introduced her to Jack saying she had answered his add in the Personals. Willie told Jack the add read; 'HARD DRINKING, CIGAR SMOKING LAY-ABOUT WOMANIZER, SEEKS PRETTY, SEXY WOMAN TO CUT LAWN, GENERAL MAINTENANCE, AND LIGHT ENGINE REPAIR. MUST HAVE OWN TOOLS. BRING GASOLINE AND BEER.'"

"But seriously," Willie said looking at Mary-Lou, "the best way to my wife's heart… saw through the breastplate."

Willie would look at her, look back at Jack, and say, "When I first met her, I called her my little Buttercup. I should have called her my little Suction Cup. But that was then. Now I haven't had sex in so long I find myself getting excited watching my car getting a lube job up on the rack at Sears."

"Willie Ellis Crawford!" she'd exclaim, but this would only egg him on.

"Now, you know baby, I listen to every word you say!" The musician would say and then look at Jack and add, "I listen to every word she says. As long as it's during the commercials or time outs."

She'd get mad and he would just say something like, "But, I love that sweet cherry pie," give her a little squeeze and she would melt.

"We made love once and she got pregnant. Right Honey? I got some powerful spooge. One little splatter of baby batter. The proverbial first shot out of the gun, huh, Honey? Unless there was a second gunman on the grassy knoll."

The Musician did a variety of odd jobs. PI work with Kelly and a couple of Jack's associates. He played in at least three bands and did recording studio work. He hustled musical equipment. He was a fringe gambler, betting on almost any game. He says he gets inside information and claims he's ahead, but he's either even or slightly behind. The Musician was known to put certain people together for a small fee. He will drive a truck for money or a friend. He was always available to go out sailing or fishing. He was always around. He's the guy who says, "Yeah, I'll go with you."

He knew when to smooth somebody out. And he knew when to keep his mouth shut. Maybe his belt didn't go through all the loops but he was no criminal. He had a clean record. Not even a parking ticket. He could walk the line. He was straight from Central Casting. Right on the edge of crime.

Chapter 11

The Heart of the Matter

The next day Jack Kelly drove the two miles from his Chinatown office to Anthony's Pier 4 restaurant on the waterfront. Jack got there early and took a table with a water view by the kitchen. Working boats passed in and out of Boston Harbor, even on this cold December day. He had already eaten half-a-dozen shrimp and drank a Sam Adams when Jesse walked into the restaurant and over to his table with the chauffeur.

"Hi Jack. This is Ric George, the gentleman who I spoke to you about. He has been employed as a chauffeur and mechanic with the Stanton family for… most of his life, as his father was, too." Jesse made the introductions as the two sat down.

The three ordered lunch, made small talk about the restaurant, the impending snow storm, the New England Patriots, the Celtics, Red Sox, and what its like being a chauffeur, a cop, and a PI. The chauffeur, Ric George, was a short stocky man, about 5'5" tall, 64 to 69 years old, with a mop of white hair. He was of Scottish decent and still had more than a trace of an accent.

Kelly wanted to dispense with formalities and steer the conversation closer to the subject-at-hand and said, "As for credentials, if you need to see them, I have my business card with me, although Al Capone's business card said he was a used furniture dealer. And I am still a member in good standing in the Mickey Mouse Club."

Jack got a polite laugh from the crowd of two.

Jack Kelly was no friend to small talk and as they got nearer to the end of the meal the questions drifted towards the subject-at-hand, circling like a bird of prey. When Lieutenant Jessica Paris took her last bite of swordfish and had washed it down with a white wine, Jack and the chauffeur made eye contact and Jack said, "Tell me about it."

"This could take a while, pour yourself a drink and smoke 'em if you got' em," the driver responded with his fine Scottish brogue.

The chauffeur told the story of how two people fell in love. The little girl's parents. The father was Reginald Stanton. He was a young sailing instructor at the New Bedford Yacht Club in Padanaram, South Dartmouth, and *she* was the only Rothchild heir, of the publishing house Rothchilds. She was taking sailing lessons each summer. She grew before his eyes and flourished. She was a rare beauty. With a king-size crush on her sailing instructor.

The child's mother summered in Padanaram. Living on her family yacht at the yacht club and in and around Cape Cod and the Islands. It was Back Bay Boston for the private school year. From Copley High to Radcliffe. The year she graduated, the sailing instructor asked for her hand and they married. They settled down in the mansion in Belmont. There wasn't much of a call for sailing instructors during the frigid winters in Boston but he didn't have to work with the kind of money she had. He had locked himself in by marriage.

The Rothchild family had made money the old fashioned way. The fortune had grown through solid deals and sound investments. The money diversified and grew some more as it had through many generations of the Bostonian Rothchilds. The Stantons inherited all of it. They gave a lot to charity and rarely spent it on themselves. The family creed was, "A bargain, is a profit in waiting." Whenever a large purchase was made the family would end up making a profit. Some of the land and houses they bought tripled in value. The frugal nature of the family not only guaranteed that the fortune would stay intact but served to increase the wealth in leaps and bounds. It soon passed the point where investments were growing at a rate that money was coming in faster than it could be spent.

The chauffeur told the story of how the little girl, Suzanne Stanton, was born a year later, with the proverbial silver spoon in her mouth. She had the best of everything. And loving and caring parents to boot. There were nannies, tutors, maids, chauffeurs, cooks, doctors, even lawyers, at her fingertips.

Jack Kelly shook his head from side to side and had to interrupt.

"Look, I started out with nothing. And I still have most of it left. Tell me she's not spoiled." Jack said, to the blank stares of Jesse and the chauffeur.

"She's not," they said in unison.

"She's the sweetest little girl, Mr. Kelly. An absolute angel." The chauffeur said.

"She wears a halo and everything, Jack." Jesse said slowly and a little loudly, as if she were talking to a five-year-old. Jack wondered why women talked to him, from time to time, like he was a child.

"Sorry. Sarcasm is just one of the services we offer at Jack Kelly's American Detective Agency." Jack apologized and the Chauffeur continued.

"Her parents died under suspicious circumstances," Ric George said, glancing over at Jesse as if seeking approval, "Since then her grandfather also died, less than a year ago, she has been slowly isolated by The Lawyer. Her grandfather had told me that I would be named in his will, as the guardian of little Suzanne and the executor of the estate but that will, never surfaced. The Lawyer has assumed almost total control. It has gotten progressively worse. Now that it's the winter holiday season she's not even going to school. I'm worried that he will make his move before the end of winter. I know he's tried already. He's going to do away with that child. I feel it. Don't think I'm crazy. I'm just the chauffeur, sir, but I'm not a fool!"

He seemed a little crazy, but not a fool.

"Did you know, Mr. George, that St. Patrick drove the snakes from Ireland?"

"Yes, Mr. Kelly."

"And the snakes came to America, and the very next year, they founded the American Bar Association." As no one disagreed, Jack went on, "Did you know Lieutenant, when I was young I thought about law school and passing the Massachusetts Bar exam?"

"Just when I thought you couldn't sink any lower, Jack." Jesse replied.

Kelly returned his attention to Mr. George, "Take it easy, man. You don't have to reach into my chest and pull out my heart. I made up my mind to help the minute Jesse, I mean Lieutenant Paris, asked me."

Lt. Paris headed for the Ladies room and Mr. George told Jack a story. "One time, back in the day, in Glasgow, Scotland, an attorney died in a pub and needed burying. There was a funeral director present and he told the owner of the bar he could bury a lawyer for a penny. So the pub owner gives him a full five-pound note, and says, 'Fine, bury as many as you can.'"

"You know, Jack, in some parts of Northern Scotland its still legal to hunt and trap lawyers using money as bait. Not at night, though. And not within 200 yards of a courthouse, car accident, or an ambulance. And not from a moving vehicle unless properly licensed."

Kelly liked the old man.

"I don't have much money but I can give you fifty percent of my small salary. Would that be OK, for a start, Mr. Kelly?"

Kelly assured Mr. George that fifty percent was a noble offer and it would be sufficient to look into the matter. Jack told himself that he would take the poor man's money just to make sure The Chauffeur was sincere. And like the shrinks say, "If you don't pay, you won't get better."

Kelly wanted to make arrangements for Mr. George to meet him at his office tomorrow so he could get more of the details, but The Chauffeur pleaded to meet with him tonight. The urgency in the old Scotsman's voice led Jack to believe that the driver was sincerely worried about his charge and it was time to get down to brass tacks and talk business, get down to cases, get to the meat. It was time to get to the heart of the matter.

As the Lt. returned the waitress asked Jack if he wanted a wet-nap. He said yes and Lt. Paris said, "Is that like a wet dream, only shorter?"

Lunch was over.

Jack Kelly returned to his office. The living arrangement was somewhat unofficial because of the status of the building's zoning laws. A tiny outer office with hooks for raincoats had just room enough for a desk and three wooden chairs and it led to the inner office doors. Kelly liked the creaky old wooden doors and floors, even if his buddies called it alternately a firetrap or a rattrap. The office itself had a living area off to the immediate left. Jack would pull a screen across when he conducted business. On the immediate right was a kitchen overlooking the alley. The smell from the Chinatown restaurants, through the sometimes-open window, disguised Jack's pathetic attempt at cooking. He ate out a lot.

The bedroom was all the way in the back past the office, straight-ahead. In the office were file cabinets with a TV on top, a bookshelf, and a card table with case files laying on it. Cabinets with equipment like binoculars, cameras, tape recorders, and the like covered the wall to the left. A row of bay windows covered the right with a long fake leather couch underneath. He had a huge solid oak desk and a leather chair that could lean all the way back and was good for napping, if only Jack could take a nap without getting a headache. In the back was a big, ornate, bathroom door and on the wall behind Kelly's desk was an oil painting that Kelly had done while still a schoolboy, of a distant globular galaxy, M32, with a wall safe behind it.

Jack sat at the big desk and cleaned his gun. He pulled out the clip. No bullets left in there. He racked back the slide twice, pointed the gun downward, and pulled the trigger three times. No bullets in there. He looked into the barrel. No bullets in there. There had been six gone from the magazine in the Brattle Street Cinema. And the last one in the chamber went to Bob's head.

He dismantled the gun and wondered if the water of the Charles River would rust the old Colt 1911 Combat Commander. He wondered if he should get one of those newer semi-autos with more bullets. The kind of newer weapon with staggered magazines that hold fifteen rounds. Double-action only. Maybe he needed more firepower. A fifty-caliber Desert Eagle with bullets the size of your thumb. Get a nice laser sight. Put a red dot right on the target.

He dropped the parts of the weapon onto a newspaper spread out on the desktop. There were still tiny beads of moisture lining the internal grooves and walls of the gun. Jack wiped it down, then threaded a patch onto a rod, sprayed on some Breakfree gun oil and slid it repeatedly through the barrel. Jack Kelly loved the smell of the gun oil.

He thought about the case. He wondered what the inherent appeal of it was and why it wasn't ringing his bell. He ran the rod repeatedly through the barrel of the gun as he searched for motivation. There was a knock on the office door.

By now it was 9:30 at night and perfectly acceptable to offer Ric George a drink. "We got Dewar's Scotch, Hennesey Cognac, Skyy Vodka, red French Beaujolais wine, a good Rhode Island Red table wine, and this week's special, I think, is a couple frosty Guinness Stout in the fridge."

"No thanks." The Chauffeur said as he sat across from Jack, placing his traditional chauffeur's hat on the arm of the chair.

"Tea?"

"No thanks, Mr. Kelly."

"I was just cleaning my gun, it got submerged in the Charles River day before yesterday, and this is the first chance I've had to clean it. I'll just put it back together while we talk, if you don't mind."

"I saw that in the paper, Mr. Kelly. I wouldn't do your job for all the tea in China."

"Well, let's get to it then. Why do you feel the girl is in immediate harm?" Jack said as he tried to picture all the tea in China piled up on a barge headed for his office.

"Well, what's her name? I'm sorry, I never got that," Jack apologized.

"Stanton, Suzanne Stanton."

"What kind of immediate danger is Suzanne Stanton in?"

"Well, sir," The Chauffeur cleared his throat and continued, "this lawyer, his name is Chase, Mr. Kelly, Lindon B. Chase. I think… I believe he has tried to poison her, has drugged her, has been trying to drive her out of her senses, and I think he is trying to kill her, possibly by staging an accident. He wants to take control of the estate. The very, very large Stanton estate."

"Well… that… that says it all. Yes. This much I have gathered. And… what brought you to these conclusions, sir? What evidence do you have?"

"I told you this afternoon that her parents died under suspicious circumstances. And I'm sure she has been drugged or poisoned. Attorney Chase has his own doctor look after her. It's not right that only his doctor looks at her."

"This is a conspiracy involving members of the medical community?" Jack asked just to try to rattle the complainant.

"Hear me out, Mr. Kelly."

"Call me Jack. I keep thinking my fathers in the room when you say Mr. Kelly."

"It's the lawyer, Mr.… Jack."

"Just Jack."

"Lindon B. Chase. This lawyer. He impressed me at first, before Mr. and Mrs. Stanton perished in the Senrab, off of the Islands. That was their sailboat, the Senrab. A wooden 48 foot Concordia yawl. Something made a hole in the hull, under the port bow waterline. It was suspicious. They often sailed the Elizabeth Islands off Cape Cod. Cuttyhunk, Martha's Vineyard, Nantucket. This lawyer, Chase, stepped in immediately. He helped out with the estate. Then it started to seem like he wanted control over everything. Soon after the parents drowned, he was acting like *he* had inherited the estate, not little Suzanne."

"I can tell you if a lawyer is lying?" Kelly interjected.

"How?"

"His mouth is moving." Jack said, his mouth forming a big grin and his eyes widening. He got no laugh and told himself he was just trying to depth-find the Chauffeur's comedic profile, as he cleared his throat and asked Ric George how long he had known Lt. Jesse Paris, but what he really wanted to know was *how* he knew her.

"I've known little Jesse since she was about three years old. I was a close friend of her father. Watched her grow up. And her dad would be proud of her now."

Jack thought that the information was a bit sparse but he listened as Ric George continued.

"This lawyer, Lindon Chase, is as crooked as the letter S. After you shake hands with him, you ought to count your fingers." Ric George continued, "He is trying to institutionalize Suzanne. Or at least trying to drive her around the bend. I think he has given her drugs. Mind altering drugs. She has had some bad experiences. It's been like an old movie from the Fifties, '*Shock Corridor,*' He wanted her to think she was going crazy, and go along willingly. The doctor would come over and sedate her one-day and speed her up with 'vitamin' shots the next. I think he wants to declare her unstable or not responsible, *non compos mentis*, or whatever the legal term is."

"Nuts."

"Maybe even poison or chemically imbalance her. Maybe LSD or Quaaludes, Thorazine, some new psycho drugs I can't even pronounce. Or amphetamines, I don't know. He continuously manipulates her psyche. Total control. He had her sickly and totally dependent on him and his doctor friend. They're going to succeed in driving her mad one of these days. And that day may be coming sooner than any of us think!" The Chauffeur could barely keep himself from rising from the chair.

Jack was impressed with the sincerity and concern the driver had but some things were not adding up. "Why would a physician risk his license and future standing in the community? What could possibly motivate him to join in a conspiracy of this caliber?"

"Well, the Lawyer, well, how should I say this… eh, is light on his feet." Mr. George said.

"Light on his feet? You mean, he's not a manly sort of man?"

"He might be a, eh, what we used to call a fairy."

"You mean if he's not gay, he's on the waiting list?" Jack asked.

"Yes."

"Being a homosexual does not qualify a person for criminal activity." Jack stated matter-of-factly.

"And the doctor, is his, ah… they ah… at times, when they think no ones around they ah… get together," the old chauffeur said, biting his lower lip and looking downward.

"You mean Chase is getting his squash steamed by the doctor? He's traveling on the Hershey Highway? Is it deliveries in the rear for the good doctor?" Jack asked.

Ric George nodded and said he wasn't quite sure just what the couple did. He and Kelly sat in silence for a moment. Things weren't as simple as they seemed. There was a powerful manipulative attorney with big money involved. There are definitely sharks in the water.

"Mr. Kelly… Jack, the family fortune is very, very large."

"Like a couple of million." Jack threw out the figure as nonchalantly as he could.

"Much more."

"Twelve, twenty million," Jack said not believing the figure himself.

"Total assets of over 80 million, I believe."

Jack could not realistically conceive of a fortune so large. His tiny mind could not begin to assimilate what it would be like to posses a family fortune of such magnitude. Jack began to realize the extreme motivation that this kind of money could inspire. Especially in a lawyer. The Chauffeur continued.

"Two weeks ago I was working on the Bentley in the garage and I wanted to call the auto part store to see if they had the part I needed. I picked up the garage extension. It is separate line connected to the phone in the pool house and I heard Chase talking to another man. First thing I heard was 'Fire.' And Chase said 'I don't want to burn the house down.' The other man said, 'How about a car fire, they could drive off the road and a gasoline fire? We'll get 'em both.'

"Who talks about an accident that *could* happen? I couldn't hang up. And this guy was talking about a space heater that could 'fall' in the child's bath. They hung up soon after. I don't know who the other man was, but I heard the Lawyer. They didn't say whom they were talking about but I am afraid it's little Suzanne. I'm afraid they'll mix up the medications they give her and she'll have an overdose or something and the attending physician will be the Doctor. And the Lawyer, he's got a couple of goons, two or three brothers, I think, who do his dirty work. I'm an old man and if something happens to me… She's got nobody, Jack, she has been isolated, doesn't go to school, or leave the grounds, and she's getting sicker and…"

"Hold on there, driver. Take a breath."

The old Chauffeur was animated and breathing hard.

"I will look into this, Mr. George. But I'm going to need proof. This lawyer knows the law. The guy is a professional."

"That's what the cops said. 'Proof.'"

"Look." Jack protested, but the man got insistent.

"When she's dead, will that be proof enough?"

"Look. The cops need some evidence, or at least reasonable suspicion, some probable cause or it won't hold up in court. Without some more tangible proof they can't do a thing. But this *is* private investigator territory. I don't need a thing but a client who will pay me to conduct a legal investigation. I'm going to start putting some time in. And from what you've told me, I want to help." Jack reached out and pressed the old man's hand. "She's lucky she has you, sir." Jack told him and he meant it. The old man had a tear in his eye.

"You love that girl, don't you Mr. George."

The old man could take it no longer. He began sobbing uncontrollably.

"Jack. You're a good man. I just know it. I've got to tell you. I am Suzanne Stanton's true father. Her mother and I had an affair for years. I didn't want her to be called illegitimate. Only the family knew."

"Wow!" was all Jack could manage to say.

"I'll take that Guinness now, Jack." The old man said, blowing his nose.

The kid was lucky she had this loyal, trustworthy, caring chauffeur. And he was her biological father. The pieces to the puzzle were making more and more sense. Jack instructed him on how to document some of these suspicious events. How to record phone conversations with a phone jack and a micro-cassette recorder and use a video camera. But Jack would contact another lawyer and see what's involved in legally removing Chase from the estate and installing a more suitable advocate, although Jack suspected that whoever installed Chase signed estate documents over in an ironclad executor situation for the Lawyer.

"Why doesn't the Lawyer get rid of you? And why don't you just come forward as the child's rightful father? We'll have a paternity test done. We can petition the court, get you custody, and we'll fire Chase."

"I don't want her to be illegitimate, Mr. Kelly."

"But you don't want her to be dead, either."

"I'll consider coming forward in the near future, but for now, I've never really confronted Chase, although I believe he suspects that I know something improper is afoot. If he thinks that I would go directly to the police if I were fired, he'd be right. When I overheard that conversation, the other man said something about 'gettin' rid of' them both.'"

The Driver reached into his pocket and dropped a wallet size photo on the desk in front of Jack. The young girl looked so sweet and innocent. Tiny blonde curls cascaded down the sides of a smooth and angelic face, framing her wide, bright blue eyes. She looked to be about seven or eight years old in the picture, a little older than Jack had envisioned her. Suzanne had a sweet, trusting, and happy smile. A bell rang and a light went on inside Jack Kelly's head. He got a chill and swallowed. This was the face of the case. The part that was missing.

Jack surmised from what Ric George told him that the Lawyer and his goons had little opposition to their plans. No interceding family member, friend, or social worker. It seemed that no others suspected the attorney's scheme to gain total control of the family fortune. This may be a good opportunity for an investigator to gather info and evidence. Maybe this matter would be something Jack could do something about.

Jack regarded his foe. A lawyer firmly entrenched in the estate of this little girl, and he was very, very calculating, powerful, and influential. Jack realized the Chauffeur was looking at him as he scratched his chin in contemplation.

"They plan to do her evil, Mr. Kelly."

Jack gave him his summation.

"'Everybody's got a plan. Until they get hit,'" Jack said looking the Chauffeur directly in the eye and confidently smiling. "Heavy Weight Champion of The World George Foreman said that."

"This is the lawyer other lawyers hire when they need one." Ric George added, "A cold, calculating, cutthroat."

The Chauffeur had gotten to Jack. He had told Jack Kelly, that he, the faithful family servant, had been having an affair with little Suzanne Stanton's mother, off and on, for many, many years and that he was the little girl's biological father.

After the Chauffeur left, Kelly called The Musician and asked him to stop by the Boston Public Library and make copies of everything he could find on Attorney Lindon B. Chase. Then they planned to conduct some surveillance on the counselor in the morning.

Chapter 12

Boston Beat

Jack got a rare good night's sleep and was ready to roll when Willie Crawford came by in the late morning. A gentle snow began to fall as Jack crossed Kingston Street to Willie's van. The van was mostly used for hauling amplifiers and drums to recording studios and gigs. Jack had gotten the attorney's address over the phone from Information and they proceeded out Comm. Ave. in The Musician's beat-up old blue Ford Econoline van.

The Musician was a lanky fellow, almost six-foot, on the thin side, with long, dark, shoulder-length hair. He was actually older than Jack, but looked the perennial teenager. He wore the typical jeans, sneakers, T-shirt, Boston Red Sox cap, and black leather jacket unless otherwise specified. Willie Ellis Crawford played the bass and real good bass players were hard to find. The Musician was in demand for studio gigs, live dates, and could fill in with almost any band, in any style of music. But he loved the private investigator work and Jack used him often. His casual, cool looks made him great for undercover work; he could go almost anywhere, on any street and not make anybody suspicious.

As the Musician drove through Kenmore Square they both looked over at The Rat, a nightclub that had spawned a generation of rough edged rock and roll. Bands like Barry and The Remains, The Barbarians, The J. Geils Band, The Cars, and the bands that inspired them. It was a wild scene for bands like The Nervous Eaters, The Atlantics, The Neighborhoods, The Legendary Night Crawlers, The Back Bay Beat, The JB Group, The Boom Boom Band, Farrenheit, The Lyers, Mission of Burma, Johanna Wild, ThunderTrain, Johnny and the Zodiac Killers, and the Real Kids. And NYC bands played there, too. The Talking Heads, Mink DeVille, Television, The Ramones, Dead Boys, and Blondie. Even some of the English and Irish bands played there. The Police, Thin Lizzy, Elvis Costello, The Damned... There were just too many bands to mention.

"I heard its gonna close?" The Musician said as they passed Boston University and the Paradise nightclub.

"The Rat?"

"Yeah. Some Japanese guys from NYC bought it and are gonna make a huge three story restaurant. It's the end of an era."

"It's the end of an ear ache," Jack sighed.

They arrived at the corner of Comm. Ave. and Harvard Ave. and after a bit Willie Crawford found a parking space diagonally across the corner from the six-floor office building housing the law office of Lindon B. Chase, Esquire. This week's New England snowstorm was getting heavier by the minute and the sidewalks and streets were turning white. The people moving through the intersection were walking a little more briskly. Jack got out of the car and walked into the office building. He read the directory in the lobby, saw that Chase's office was on the third floor, and walked back to the car. He checked all the third floor windows with binoculars trying to locate window lettering marking the law offices.

"Did you know there's window lettering on the third floor of a building in Harvard Square advertising for the firm Dewey, Hookem, and Cheatem?" Jack said to The Musician.

"You mean Dewey, Cheatim, and Howe. Yeah, that's the office of those two guys that do 'Car Talk' on National Public Radio."

"They must have lifted that from the Marx Brothers."

"Three Stooges," The Musician corrected, and asked, "Want to hear the Joke-of-the-Day?"

"I wish I knew what this 'mouthpiece' looked like," said Jack.

"I got his picture here in the clippings somewhere."

"Good work, Willie. I love working with a professional."

Kelly put down the binos and began to thumb through the copies of six or seven articles Willie had gathered from the microtext files at the Boston Public Library concerning the Lawyer. Willie began the stakeout with his trademark ramblings.

"Want to hear the Joke-of-the-Day?"

"OK, Willie."

"A woman accompanied her husband to the doctor's office. After his checkup, the doctor called the wife into his office alone. He said, 'Your husband is suffering from a very severe disease, combined with horrible stress. If you don't do the following, your husband will surely die.'"

"'Each morning, fix him a healthy breakfast. Be pleasant, and make sure he is in a good mood. For lunch make him a nutritious meal. For dinner prepare an especially nice meal for him. Don't burden him with chores, as he probably had a hard day. Don't discuss your problems with him, it will only make his stress worse. And most importantly, make love with your husband several times a week and satisfy his every whim. If you can do this for just the next 10 months to a year, I think your husband will regain his health completely.'"

"On the way home, the husband asked his wife, 'What did the doctor say to you?'"

"She looked at him and replied, 'He told me you're going to die.'"

Jack groaned.

Young women, wanting to get their exercise in, before the snowstorm hit, jogged by on the flattened snow in front of the van. Both men exhaled in unison, both lost in some brief fantasy.

"I used to jog a lot more," Jack said, lost in yet another fantasy.

"I'd jog but I'd spill my drink." Willie said.

"I'm glad I stayed in shape. I take the stairs up the four flights to my office, most of the time, even though there's an elevator. The old wooden stairs creak and crackle as I pound out the 100 steps," Jack said with pride, "I guess most guys find it ideal to jog along a country road along a river or lake, but give me the city. I love jogging right out of the office through Chinatown, into the downtown area, and into the Fanuiel Hall Market section. Past the rows of vegetable and fish stands, the vendors shouting, up and down the street, 'Nice oranges, here!' and "Buy some meat?" and 'Fresh fish, here.' Then under the Central Artery, into the North End, right down Hanover Street. I can smell the Pizza and Lasagna cooking, the Rigatoni and the spices in the Chicken Parmesan. I'd jog along past the Aquarium. Then into Government Center with it's towering office buildings. Around and up to Beacon Hill and down onto the Esplanade, the Hatch Shell concert area, the sailboat docks along the Charles River to Kenmore. Through the Fens, up by the Berklee School of Music, and back down Boylston St. to the Pru…"

"Alright! You're making me tired," The Musician said and attempted to elevate the conversation to a more lofty area.

"I think about things. If moths like to go towards the light, then why do they only come out at night?"

"Well, ah… are you sure they only come out at night?"

"How come everyone knows about the Secret Service?"

Jack just looked at The Musician blankly as he went on.

"I didn't want to be just anybody. I wanted to be J.F.K. I wanted to be John Lennon, Mohammed Ali, Keith Richards, and Elvis. I wanted to be Jesus. Ghandi, the Buddha. And I wanted to see God."

"How did we get into this?" Jack remarked.

"Jack? Do you realize the ramifications here? Don't you get it Jack? We're just actors here. This is life's one act play."

"Don't get heavy on me."

"Come on Jack. Don't tell me you don't search for the inner meaning. It's all around you, Jack. We are one and we are all together."

"What's that from? The Sgt. Pepper album? You know you sound like a broken goddamned record, sometimes. How much acid did you take in the Sixties? Did Sidney Gottlieb and those CIA shrinks dose you with LSD during the Cold War to test their brainwashing techniques?"

"Jack fuckin' Kelly I know you. I've known you since you were the kid who moved here from New Bedford to Southie. I've worked for you and with you. Worked out with you. Played the blues with you. Gotten stinkin' drunk with you. And you made me take those Tae Kwon Do lessons."

"Why do you always bring that up?"

"Listen. What I'm trying to say is, I know you are a deep thinker. I know you're tapped into the cosmos. What were you raised?"

"As a male, unlike you, who wore dresses and lipstick."

"Fuck off. You know what I'm talking about."

"Episcopalian." Jack confessed.

"Oh… that's like Catholic-Lite, right? And you're a closet Zen Buddhist. All our deeds follow us from afar and what we have been makes us what we are. You're the Zen Cop."

"You know what they say about Zen. That and a buck will get you a cup of coffee." Jack went on. "The Zen Buddhist says there is no use in worrying about a problem that can be solved. And if a problem cannot be solved, there is no use worrying about it."

The Musician sat silently.

"So what is it you're trying to say?" Jack wondered.

"I'm talking about the Big Picture."

"That's what you're trying to say?"

"Life's like a movie."

After a long pause Jack threw in the towel and said, "Well, why didn't you just say so?"

Finally there was a moment of silence. People were scrambling to get home from the workweek. Jack decided not to make this a long surveillance. Action or no action, he would cut this one short, even though it was three o'clock on a snowy Friday afternoon in December. It was prime time.

"My seven-year-old daughter says to me this morning, 'Daddy. For Christmas I want big boobs and a belly ring.'" Willie Ellis Crawford said staring at the brake pedal.

Jack did not say a word but still The Musician continued.

"She is a good little girl, though. She was drawing on a paper last week. I asked her what she was drawing. She says 'I'm drawing God, daddy.' I told her nobody knows what God looks like, honey. She says 'Well, you will in a minute.'"

Jack held his silence. The Musician continued on, "And my boys a pip. Last night I put him to bed early and he asks me for a glass of water. I tell him he had his chance for water. He says 'Dad I'm thirsty, can I have some water?' I tell him no. He whines, 'Dad I'm thirsty, get me some water!' I tell him if he doesn't be quiet I'm going to spank him. He says to me, 'Dad? On the way in to spank me, can you bring some water?'"

Kelly was unmoved.

"Jesus Christ, Jack. I know you think about things!"

"I'm thinking no more coffee for you… Yeah. I'm thinking about the dead bugs under the snow that are still in the grill of that red BMW parked in front of us. So what?"

"You're looking at it but what are you thinking?"

"I'm thinking about it from the standpoint of a forensic entomologist. An insect can detect a newly dead body odor two miles away. Some bugs rest at night. The geographic area where a bug comes from can be pinpointed, to a degree. A suspect can, theoretically, be linked to a crime scene by the bugs found in the grill of his car."

"See? That's what I'm talking about! You know this shit and you're always thinking about it. You're always on the case."

"*You're* on drugs." Jack countered.

"My body is a temple."

"Well, there's been a lot of people praying at your altar. Why don't you bop over to that Cumberland Farms and get me a Pepsi and a newspaper. The Boston Herald."

"OK, I took a purple Xanax. I been saying 'No' to drugs… unfortunately drugs aren't taking 'No' for an answer."

"You're soft."

"I exercise. First I get out of bed, take two or three deep breaths… and that's about it."

"That's great, Willie."

"And I take vitamins every evening. I wash them down with a six-pack. I have the body of a twenty-year old. I keep it in the trunk of my car."

Jack just looked aside at The Musician with a look of mock disgust, as Willie continued, "Oh, you're no angel, Jack."

Jack looked indignant and responded with, "Yeah, that's right. Sometimes I like to smoke, swear, and spit. Maybe watch a boxing match and yell and pound my fist on the table. Yeah, sometimes I like to light a big, stanky cigar, crack open a six-pack of beer and spill some on my sweatshirt. I yell at the goddamn referees. I'm a guy. Guilty as charged," Jack said and continued, "I also have a sensitive, caring, nurturing, loving, spiritual side. In fact, I'd like to reveal it to you now, Willie." The Musician looked at him askance as Jack continued.

"I know it doesn't show from the outside. I look to you and everyone else to be a man's man. The complete male from head to toe. The Alpha Male. But, since we're being so honest and revealing. This isn't easy, but I've been living a lie. I've got a confession to make." Jack said, as The Musician's eyes got wider and he looked at Jack in horror. Jack continued.

"I'm a lesbian. There, I've said it. I'm glad I told you. I feel a great weight has been lifted from my shoulders. A dark cloud has passed and now the sun is streaking through."

Undaunted, Willie resumed his oration, mistaking Jack for someone who cared, and ignoring Jack's frivolous confession.

"What about the theory that states if ever someone discovers exactly what the universe is for and why its here it will instantly disappear and be replaced by something even more amazing. In fact I think it's already happened."

"Lay off sniffing the glue."

"I think about things. I think about all the undiscovered songs. Songs of inspiration. Songs of the people. Of the culture and history. The thousands of songs that are written by 'undiscovered' musicians. The sheer tonnage of musical ideas lost in this country alone on a nightly basis and it's enough to make you weep."

Jack looked at Willie in disbelief.

"All this from a guy who thinks a Hunter's Orange vest goes with camouflage pants," Kelly cracked.

"I think about the songwriters in the days of Brahms, Handel, Mozart, and Beethoven. How did they have their songs recognized and preserved? What about the songs never recorded? Where are they now?"

"They wrote them on sheet music. You're getting heavy, again."

"Are they lost forever? What about the songs never written down? Jimi Hendrix lived in Handel's old apartment in London. Maybe one night he wrote a song of beautiful composition. A classic and magical song. And forgot to write or record it."

"More likely he passed out from the drugs and alcohol."

"I can imagine he turned up his amp and was distorting, twisting, and feeding back," The Musician started playing air guitar as he sat behind the wheel of the van. He simulated the sounds of a distorted and amplified guitar. "And the neighbors downstairs bang on the ceiling, yelling 'Keep the bloody noise down, bloke!' and when Handel was writing the Messiah, the neighbors bang on the ceiling, yelling 'Keep the bloody noise down!' I think about these things."

"You're scaring me! Get out of the car."

A pretty college girl of unique structure and build walked by the front of Willie's van and Jack felt compelled to remark, "Nice ass."

"Wow, tighter than a snare drum. Look at her." The Musician said as his jaw slacked, his eyes opened wide, and he gazed unabashedly at the pretty schoolgirl. "Why don't we just follow *her*?"

"Lead me not into temptation. I can find my own way. Besides, she's not your type. She's not inflatable."

"She is Gluteus to the Maximus. I'd use her underwear for a coffee filter."

"Get out of the car."

"I been chokin' my chicken in the shower for so long I'm surprised a baby hasn't crawled out of the shower drain and called me daddy."

"That's it. Get out of the car!"

"That's why I'm the Captain of the Chicken Chokers, Wildman of the Weasel Waxers, the King Kong of the Monkey Spankers."

"Jesus Christ, save me! Don't do this to me." Jack pleaded, and added, "If you were my kid I'd punish you."

"If I was your kid that would be punishment enough," The Musician countered.

"Why must you reduce everything to sex?" Jack asked.

"I've got a theory…"

"OK, Nostradamus. What's your theory?"

"My theory is that its' all about pussy. The world revolves around pussy. Yes, Jack, its pussy that rules the world."

"What about money?"

"Money to buy pussy. But its pussy that makes the world go 'round."

"But you need faith." Jack offered.

"Faith that you're gonna get some pussy." Willie said, making the sign of the cross.

"I thought it was love that made the world go 'round?"

"Yes. Love of pussy. It's pussy that rules the world."

"Get out of the car."

The Musician said he'd get Jack a Pepsi and a Boston Herald. He got out of the car and followed a coed up the street to the corner store. Jack had located the photo of Lindon Chase in the paper and had been alternately looking at it and looking back at the office building.

Jack didn't expect to see the Lawyer come conveniently strolling out of the building. But that's what happened. The Lawyer walked out of the building, down the sidewalk, and right past Jack sitting in the blue van. Chase and Willie walked right past each other and Willie got back in the driver's seat and handed Jack the Pepsi.

"No Heralds. Do you think they still sell Tab?"

"Never mind that, my observant operative. You just crossed paths with the Lawyer."

"Huh?"

"He just walked right past you."

Chapter 13

Trial Run

"Where?" Willie twisted around looking in every direction then looked back at Jack, who hadn't taken his eyes off the subject. Willie followed Kelly's gaze to a small, frail man walking diagonally across the intersection and into The Wine Cellar.

The Lawyer looked pretty much like his picture in the paper. A dark suit, white shirt, dark tie, all wrapped around the small frail frame of the 60-year-old shyster. His hair was gray, almost white, and combed across his head to compensate for a thinning top. Surrounding his pale complexion were dark facial features and a relatively long and pointed nose. He walked with a quick shuffle, taking small steps, and he carried his hands up high over his stomach.

He came out of the wine store and waited for the next Green Line. The trolley was already coming down the hill, screeching and rattling along the tracks.

"You drive, I'll watch." Jack said as they both settled into their seats. Jack put the clippings back in the folder, put the folder under the seat, and added, "We're going to have to be careful with this bird, it's a litigious society and this guys a lawyer."

Sleep When I'm Dead

"He's heading back into town, I'm going to get over into the other lane." The Musician said swinging the old blue van onto Harvard Ave. and then back onto Comm. Ave heading back into town.

Lindon Chase got on the trolley and it rolled down the winding avenue towards the heart of Boston. Jack could see Chase sitting in the crowded trolley as the snow got thicker and blew at an angle. At Brighton Ave., the next stop, more people crowded in. Jack saw a woman standing over the Lawyer and he imagined the woman was wondering why Chase wasn't offering her his seat.

"Is that him sitting about halfway?" Willie asked.

"Watch your driving, I'll watch him… Yeah, that's him."

"What are we going to do when the trolley goes underground and turns into the subway at Kenmore Square?"

"Follow it down the hole!"

"OK."

"I'm kidding. I don't know. Jesus, that's a new one. I guess, as we get nearer Kenmore, we'll move ahead of it, you'll drop me off and I'll jump on the trolley at the Kenmore station."

Before that could happen the Lawyer disembarked at Boston University.

"Let's stop in at BU and ask Billie Bulger where his mobster brother Whitey is," The Musician said. "We'll collect that One Million Dollar reward and call it a day."

The Lawyer walked across the street to a small parking lot and soon pulled out in a big brand new cream-colored Mercedes-Benz and headed back outbound on Comm. Ave.

Willie had mirrored every move and they swung in behind and two cars back as Chase crossed over the BU Bridge and started heading outbound on Memorial Drive. Kelly took the binoculars out and wrote down the registration plate number on the big tan

Mercedes. It was Mass. Vanity plate, C-I-V-I-L. Willie continued his running monologue, again.

"I think about creating an audio-synthesized landscape at the edge of light. I would design it with airbrush whispers, floating on a cloud at the center of perception. Hypnotic and sensually thick layers of lush synthesizers in ethereal atmospheres of warm textures winding through a cyberspace vortex and sent careening through space. I would create the slow rhythmic throbs of a sound painting. Haunting soundscapes drifting through a blue cosmos of light. I want to construct and orchestrate flowing compositions of sonic mood merging."

"*What* are you on? Should you be driving?"

"Where is the passion? The beauty? Where is the truth?"

"There are times when I don't think I know you, at all. I don't know who you are. You need to go back to the hospital for more observation. Get out of the car."

"I'm driving."

"I don't care anymore. I've lost my will to live."

"Well, it's my car."

"Oh, yeah."

The cream colored Mercedes drove along the river slowly through the drifting snow. Four or five inches had accumulated but it was dry and fluffy.

Jack turned to the musician who was smiling at him broadly.

"What are you grinning at? Watch the road."

"I checked through yesterday's paper, while I was in the store. A writer for that rag you read, The Boston Herald, called you a hero for defending yourself and shooting that guy."

"'Heavy is the head that wears the crown.' So, why are *you* so glad they're calling me a hero?"

The Musician said beaming with pride, "Well, it's like this. I'm a musician and an actor… and I'm part of your team. When you shine, I shine. It's like quintessential, man. Like Miles Davis and John Coltrane, baby."

"No good dead goes unpunished." Jack lamented as he kept his gaze on the barely visible Mercedes.

"C'mon Kelly. Just admit it. You're a thinker. A sensitive, hero, thinker."

"Don't piss on me and tell me it's raining. You're trying to polish a sneaker, pal. And I told you, don't get heavy on me."

"What's the matter Jack. Afraid you'll show your human side? Or even your feminine side?"

"I once got in touch with my feminine side… And I got a yeast infection."

"Jack I know you're deep. I'm deep. I thought about it when I got hurt. When I was unloading the drums, amplifiers, and sound system behind the Paradise at 2 O'clock in the morning and got hit by that cab. I was on the ground, barely alive, my guts were hanging out."

"One time I banged my shinbone on the coffee table."

"Goddamn it, Jack!"

"Now you're taking the lords name in vain? Just after telling me how sensitive and deep you were?"

"Goddamn it. You're right. I gotta stop sayin' 'goddamn it.' If there is a God, the Judeo, Christian, even Islam God, I'm gonna pay for that. Every time I said 'goddamn it', I'll have to pay. And I must have said 'goddamn it' quite a bit by now, goddamn it!"

"Now you're scaring me. That was a dangling participle and that's only supposed to happen to older men."

The cream Mercedes sedan wound its way through Cambridge, around Fresh Pond Circle, and out Route 2 West towards, Belmont, Concord, and Walden Pond. Rte. 2 was covered in snow and the old van slipped more than a few times on the big hill heading up into Belmont. Jack looked back down onto the city and wondered if the snow could get much thicker. He looked at Willie. "How much we supposed to get, anyway? I haven't heard the weather. I thought about ten inches, last I heard they said, unless it intensified."

Jack found a weather report on the radio as the Lawyer took an exit at the top of the big hill on Rte. 2 and headed south into Belmont's upscale neighborhoods.

Jack turned up the radio as the news anchor said, "The Nor'Easter has intensified and the storm has been classified as a potential blizzard on this Friday night at rush hour. Two to three inches an hour is now expected for the overnight. Winds of 25 to 35 Miles Per Hour are expected to contribute to the blowing and drifting. Total accumulation should be over 22 to 34 inches. Logan International Airport is closing and a parking ban is in effect."

"Holy shit," The Musician said as they turned a corner onto an affluent Belmont street, "Blowing and drifting… That reminds me. I should call my wife."

Chapter 14

The Big House

"What is going on here? Where the fuck are we?"

"I know where we are," Kelly said, and instructed Willie to park behind another car three houses down from the large, white, mansion. The Lawyer pulled into the driveway and shuffled into the side door of the big house. The winding residential street in Belmont ordinarily overlooked the Charles River flowing toward the Atlantic through Cambridge and on to the shadow of Boston's buildings. Except, at this time, a blinding snow, a white out, limited the visibility to about 100 yards. The fat chunks of snow went from left to right in a strong and steady wind. Jack liked the cover the snow provided. As it turned to dusk there were still cars on the road and some foot traffic as people scrambled to get supplies and headed into shelter. And some were caught unprepared.

"Where?" The Musician asked after a few blessed minutes of silence.

"The little girl's house. The Stanton Mansion."

Jack got out the binoculars, looked around and assessed the neighborhood. He wondered if they would appear to be suspicious to the neighbors but all bets were off in a snowstorm. He pulled the file folder out from under the seat and arranged the clippings while there was still light enough to read. The snow was blowing sideways, sticking, and piling up fast. It was a fat six inches now, but the plows in New England don't come out until there's something substantial to push.

The Musician went on. "So, is this something serious with Jessica Paris?"

"Look. We spent the night together. Just because she saw me naked doesn't mean she has to marry me."

"I thought you would end up marrying that kindergarten teacher."

Kelly thought about the schoolteacher that died in his arms. He had fallen hard and long and he wasn't over her yet. She taught kindergarten and first grade. Jack seemed relatively mature to her after dealing with six-year-olds all day. She fell for him and they planned to get married as soon as Jack got over his fear of commitment. He finally snapped out of his momentary trip down Memory Lane and looked at Willie.

"Does it cost a lot to get married, Willie?"

"Oh yeah. I'm still paying. I never knew what real happiness was until I got married. But by then it was too late… Scientists have discovered a food that diminishes a woman's sex drive by 88%. Its called wedding cake. *Where* is the love?"

"What are you, Dear fucking Abby? I tried love and I got screwed. Or all I got was screwed. And she died, man. There should have been so much more."

"See! Jack Kelly, that's what I'm talking about. You're a deep thinker."

"Yeah. There should be much more… Like foreplay. And I'm about as deep a thinker as my little helmet-headed soldier.

God gave me two heads and only enough blood to run one at a time." Jack wasn't getting any laughs tonight. Tough audience.

The Musician saw an opening and jumped in. "Remember my first wife? Oh, baby! Love brought me to my knees. I asked her, 'Will you tell me when you come?' and she said, 'Why? You won't be there.' She finally left me while I was doin' a weekend gig in Montreal. For a guy with four goddamned rings through his ears and two in his nose."

"Men who have piercings are very desirable to a woman. They obviously can handle pain and they can pick out jewelry."

"And she cleaned me out. She got the ring, I got the finger."

"That's another reason why I've never been married."

"Come on, Jack. You've lived with women for extended periods of time."

"Yeah, but I wasn't married."

Willie continued, "Anyway, we got divorced for religious reasons."

"Huh?"

"Yeah, I'm Catholic, and she's Satan. We went to divorce court. The judge says to my wife, 'I'm gonna give you $1200.00 alimony a month.' So I says 'That's fine Your Honor, I'll throw in a couple of bucks, too!'"

"Get out of the car."

Willie grabbed the door handle and opened the car door.

"Wait!" Kelly said as a familiar black 1999 Cadillac passed their car and pulled up into the driveway behind the Lawyer's Mercedes.

A guy about thirty years old, heavy set guy, almost as wide as he was tall, with a dark beard and wearing a backwards baseball cap, got out of the passenger side and a tall, thin, lanky guy a little older, got out on the driver's side. The tall guy looked familiar to Jack. Slowly the recollection, and the realization, came to him and he said to no one in particular, "'Out of all the gin joints…'"

"What? Are you gonna start doing Bogey?"

"That's Skinny, Billie Provost, he used to drive the Fatman, Thaddeus Reno, the waste management king, around. And, I believe the other wide one is his other brother."

"Other brother?"

"Yeah. You'll remember his older brother 'Bob' I shot in the forehead a couple of days ago."

"Oh, I *remember*."

They watched in silence as two of the remaining Provost brothers pulled a footlocker from the trunk of the car and carried it into the house through the side door.

"You got a phone in your pocket?" Jack asked.

"No, I'm just happy to see you." Willie said checking his pockets and his backpack and asked him, "What do you think they would do if they walked over here?"

"They probably haven't even buried their brother Bob, yet. But he was a bad man and he shouldn't have done what he did. They're probably still a bit disgruntled 'bout me shooting him in the head."

"You packin' heat?" Willie asked.

"If you mean my sexual apparatus, yes. If you, in your quaint little colloquialisms, are referring to a weapon, well… Don't leave home without it." Jack pulled back his navy blue Barracuda jacket to reveal the .45 Colt Combat Commander resting in its black leather shoulder holster. It was an infantile gesture but Jack knew it would find its mark in Willie.

The van was nice and warm as Jack moved the radio dial until he found a local jazz program on WMBR, the MIT college station. He knew the schedule of every jazz show, every jazz feature hour, and the frequency for all of the jazz stations. Jazz, blues, and some classical. Jack used it as therapy. These were the sound that soothed the savage. He found the right station and settled in as the snow piled up on the windows of the old blue van, and on the roadway and the rooftops, trees, the houses and walkways.

Darkness was falling as well as the snow. Jack wondered if he should have done this surveillance alone, as Willie Ellis Crawford continued, "Maybe I'm only happy when I'm hittin' those high notes. Laying out the perfect solo. Playing the right chords with an eloquent phrasing. Going where I've never been before. Pushing the envelope. Finding the groove and getting in it… And I'm also happy when my balls are slapping some groupie's ass."

"I'm shocked and offended." Jack said.

"You know women are more aggressive than men are. Oh, yeah! Even business wise. They have no problem being cold. Women have no compunction about hiring or firing and sealing the deal. They're cold. And sexually, well, they are super beings. It's their game, man. We are infants. We are the marks. The pigeons. They are the predators." Willie said and continued on.

"And you know I heard what you were saying before about being a lesbian. You were creeping me out there for a second. But I guess, from a woman's point of view. Not that I know what a woman's point of view is…'cuz… If I was a woman, not that I would want to be."

The Musician continued, stammering and losing his train of thought, looking wide-eyed at Kelly, "If I was a woman I'd be out patrolling LaGrange and Washington Streets looking for tricks right now."

Jack rolled his eyes and pushed him a little further. "So, if you were a woman would you be attracted to a guy like me?"

"If I were a woman I'd be attracted to any man that could walk, talk, and had more than change in his pocket."

"Get out of the car, you slut."

"Where am I gonna go?"

Chapter 15

One Foot in the Grave

"You're trying to kill her," the old Chauffeur, Ric George, screamed as he slapped the druggist folded paper containing heroin powder from Gino Provosts' hand and knocked Suzanne Stanton's cereal bowl onto the floor. "Not while I'm alive!" Mr. George yelled as Chase and Billie Provost entered the kitchen.

"Then when you're dead!" Gino yelled back as the three grabbed the short and stocky driver. But the diminutive lawyer was not much help. The short yet strong driver deflected Gino's punches. The old chauffeur managed to get the kitchen door partway open and pulled himself loose from the thin brother, Billy. Mr. George ran the twenty feet to the garage and locked the door behind him. But it wasn't a very solid door.

The Chauffeur was in the cranberry colored Mercedes limo and had the door shut as Gino broke the garage's side door open. The chauffeur had left the keys in the limo and he hit the automatic door locks. The engine started and roared as George stomped on the gas. He looked back to see the three men tugging on the door handles. He hit the remote garage door opener and the big door began to slide up.

"I'll see you in Hell!" Mr. George shouted.

As Skinny Provost looked for something to smash the car's window open, Gino Provost realized that the rear driver's side window had been left completely down. He reached in and grabbed the driver by his hair and pulled him backward. The chauffeur screamed in pain as Gino pulled a clump of bloody hair from his scalp. Gino got a hand under George's chin and pulled the man back far enough so that his hands could not reach the gearshift lever to take the car out of park.

"Get that fuckin' car door open!" Gino yelled into the Lawyer's face. Chase reached in past the Chauffeur's head and pulled the door lock up and opened the car door just as the garage door opened completely to the street. Skinny found the garage door controls on the wall and the garage door slowly began to close as the three stood watching the life being choked out of Mr. George. Gino pulled the chauffeur's head back so far, it was partly extended out of the rear window and his throat was being choked on the car doorframe.

"Shut the fucking window on his head." Gino yelled.

"What?" the wimpy Lawyer asked, recoiling at the thought.

Gino strained to hold the struggling driver. "Roll up the power window on his neck! I can't hold him much longer."

The Lawyer looked down and saw the power window buttons on the open door. He pressed the button and the rear window began rolling upward. Gino pulled the Chauffeur back as far as he could, extending the man's whole head out of the window. As the window began to crush the windpipe and neck of the Chauffeur, Gino removed his hands. The driver struggled, turning and kicking his legs, and pounding the window with his fists. He made gurgling and choking sounds as the power window began to skip, its motor unable to push up the window any further. The Chauffeur's eyes looked desperately from side to side as he gasped and struggled. The whites of his eyes got bloody and they almost seemed to pop out. And then they closed and he appeared to stop breathing.

The Lawyer was smiling strangely and looked as if he enjoyed the physical power over another that he had. He continued to hold the power window button down. It was the Lawyer's time for revenge for having been bullied and beaten up throughout his whole life. It was this desire for power over others that had driven him to the law.

Smoke began to exit from within the car door until Skinny Provost finally pushed the Lawyer's hand from the button, saying, "Jesus Christ, Chase!" Skinny leaned in and shut the car's engine off.

"Well, he had to go anyway," Attorney Chase proclaimed. He was still smiling and shallow breathing as if he had just had some quick slam-bang thank-you-sir sex in the back of a roadside rest stop. The Lawyer leaned against the front fender of the red Mercedes and looked to his two hired thugs for approval. They looked back at him with disdain.

The three murderers caught their breath and sucked the cool air into their lungs. They looked at each other wondering what their next step would be and Chase walked back around to the open driver's door. He turned the power on and rolled down the window. The Chauffeur slumped back down into the driver's seat. Chase leaned in and put a finger to Mr. George's neck, feeling the major artery for the slightest weak pulse. Just as he thought he might have detected a faint tap the Chauffeur suddenly sat bolt upright and screamed in the Lawyer's face and Chase fainted falling down onto the garage floor.

"Oh, shit!" Gino said as he and Skinny stepped over the Lawyer and pulled Ric George out of the car. The Chauffeur was still dazed and confused. Gino popped him with two quick overhand rights and Mr. George slumped in their arms.

"Let's drag the old fuck out to the pond." Gino said as the Lawyer began to stir.

Out the garage door and into the back yard the brothers struggled as they hauled the short but heavy chauffeur, each brother taking an arm with his feet dragging in the snow. The Lawyer fell in behind them trying to shake off the pins and needles he felt in his arms and neck.

The exhausted brothers dumped George on the icy edge of the duck pond. "What was that scream? Why did he scream?" Chase said, rubbing the sides of his face and wiping the falling snow from his balding pate.

"I don't fuckin' know." Gino said, "I'll ask him when I get to heaven."

"What if he goes to hell?" Chase quipped.

"Then you can ask him." Gino said.

Gino and Skinny broke the ice on top of the duck pond with the heels of their boots and a stick. Gino looked down at the waking Ric George and then at the Lawyer. "Do it!" he said.

The Chauffeur's face was distorted under the broken ice and water as the Lawyer and the skinny Provost Brother held his head down in the pond behind the mansion. Ric George's eyes were as open as they possibly could be. His mouth was open-wide now, his teeth bared and lips drawn back. Gino held his struggling legs, Skinny pushed down his shoulders, and the Lawyer held his head down under the water. There was a look of panic on his face as George struggled in vain against Chase's determined hold on the back of his head. Ric George had held his breath as long as he could. Struggling and kicking had made him want the air worse than any junkie ever wanted his smack or crack. The

Chauffeur's lungs screamed for air and he fought the desire to give in and pull something into his lungs.

He squirmed but his lungs demanded him to suck in, and the cold water streamed into his mouth, throat, and filled his lungs. As the cold water filled his chest, his eyes stared straight ahead and his face took on a look of strange and silent disbelief. Then he was calm.

A dead body sinks in the water for ten to twenty days, depending on the water temperature. In several days the bloated body's skin color changes from light to darker and turns greenish. The skin blisters and loosens in five or six days. The toe and fingernails begin to separate. The body slowly fills with gas. Then rises to the surface.

In the cold, late December waters of the duck pond behind the Stanton Estate the body of Ric George would be found long before he could float to the surface. There must have been air pockets in the rubber of the old man's shoes because one heel and one shoe stuck out of the water just a few feet from shore where the thin ice had been broken. His head and arms had come to rest on the bottom of the shallow pond.

Chapter 16

God Strike Me Dead

The only movement Jack and Willie had seen in the last two hours at the Belmont mansion had been the garage door going all the way up and right back down again. Later the Provost Brothers walked out of the kitchen doorway carrying the footlocker and deposited it back in the trunk of the Cadillac. It looked a lot heavier than when they brought it in.

"I think we may be going somewhere now."

"Aren't we going to wait for the Lawyer?"

"I think we'll follow the Brothers. We'll follow a hunch."

Skinny brushed the accumulated snow from the Caddy's windows and got into the driver's seat.

"Should I scrape off the windows, Jack?"

"No. Just shut off the engine, duck down, and we'll let them pass by. Then we'll brush off the windows and fly."

The Caddy backed out of the driveway and rolled past Willie's van. As it slid around the corner Willie started the blue Ford Econoline and they jumped out and wiped the snow off the windows in six seconds flat.

"Let's move out!" Jack shouted as they hopped back in.

Willie swung the van around and the rear tires spun furiously but the vehicle hardly moved.

"Easy big fella," Jack reined him in.

The Musician let up on the gas and the tires got some traction from the heavy weight of the old blue van. Jack shut off the radio and rolled down his window part way. Willie tried to push it a little and skidded into a fire hydrant. The Cadillac was no longer in sight.

Willie had done enough moving surveillance with Kelly that he wasn't going to panic. He backed up, slid the heavy van into drive and soon became acclimated to the conditions and they slid back onto the street leading back to Rte. 2.

"We should be gaining on them soon if they went this way." Willie said.

"They did. I've been following their tire tracks. I can't believe the Provosts are working for this guy now. I can't believe I keep running up against these Cretans. Somebody should put the whole family out of their misery."

"Well, you been doing your part, Jack."

Through the blizzard they saw a set of taillights up ahead at the entrance to Rte. 2. They lost sight of them again as they turned on to the four-lane highway that runs back in to Cambridge and Boston. The windshield wipers worked feverishly to maintain visibility. The snow was thick but dry powder. It was up to ten inches but it was all fluff and the blue van got up to fifty heading down the highway into Cambridge.

After a few tense miles of maneuvering down the road the taillights of the big black Caddy came up into view a short ways in front of their car. Willie slowed it down and fell back a little. He could barely see the taillights in the white out.

"That's right. Don't get too close, I don't wanna be made. These Provost Brothers don't seem to like me. You know, this snow is actually great cover."

"Why are we following them?"

"Well, we're following a hunch. It's the hunch that we'll learn more from these guys, going somewhere, than the Lawyer going nowhere. What was the trunk about? Are they taking things out of the house? The Lawyer is probably bleeding everything he can out of the situation. But he obviously, my dear Crawford, utilizes these punks, I more than suspect, to do his dirty work, and it's that dirty work we wish to uncover."

"How do you know that?"

"Its on page 47 of the Private Investigator's Handbook."

"Oh." The Musician said glancing over at Jack.

"Look out for that car!" Kelly yelled.

An abandoned car sat half in and half out of the breakdown lane in a snow bank.

"Jesus Christ Almighty! Can't you get your ass end out of the road?" The Musician yelled out the window.

"Now, do you think you made that poor bastard, stuck in a snowstorm, feel any better?" Kelly commented.

"I don't want him to feel any better I want him to get his ass out of the road."

The Musician began to sing, "I don't care if it rains or freezes, as long as I got my plastic Jesus, riding on the dashboard of my car. I don't care if it's dark and scary, as long as I got my Virgin Mary, riding on the dashboard of my car."

The two cars passed through the Fresh Pond rotary and down Memorial Drive along the Charles River and into Boston. Jack wondered how long they could follow the Caddy before the professional criminals noticed them.

A right by the Museum of Science and they were on the Central Artery heading south through Downtown. The snow intensified and Willie was having trouble seeing.

"Where's my Pepsi?" Jack asked.

"I drank it." The Musician answered.

The Caddy got off at the Broadway exit and drove through the center of Southie. It was nine O'clock on a Friday night but the blinding snowstorm had driven every one indoors as they passed the rows of stores and barrooms. The streets were soon covered by almost a foot of snow. There was not a plow in sight as they quietly passed the rows of triple-decker tenements in Southie and headed out towards Castle Island and Pleasure Bay.

"I don't know if this old boat can go through much more of this before we have to get out and push." The Musician said.

"Well, that's not so bad. You're about six blocks from your house on M Street. But nobody cuts through Southie, it's a peninsula, a dead end. They're headed somewhere right around here. We'll tag along for just a bit longer."

The Caddy went all the way to the end of Broadway, drove half way around the parking spaces surrounding Pleasure Bay and parked in a space near Fort Williams. Ordinarily, they would have a great view of the Bay, the Fort, and the container terminal where the barges loaded with truck containers filled with goods were offloaded. But tonight they could not see anything but white snow blowing sideways. Willie and Jack pulled into a spot behind the only other van parked down there. It was the only place available where they had a chance to see and not be seen.

"I don't like it." Jack said.

"Hey Jack, I think there's a couple doing the wild thing in that red car over there. The windows are all steamed up. I think she's on top of him."

"Watch the Provosts."

"They're just sitting there. What are they doing?" The Musician said.

"I don't like it. They may have made us. They may have called some one to meet them down here. We've got no way out of here. It's a dead end. I don't like it."

Kelly's looked around through the snow for a car entering the area. Then he looked back at the Provost Brothers. He decided the surveillance was over.

"Willie, let's get out of here. Drive through the parking lot with your lights off, real slow."

Willie drove along the parking lot between the beach and the roadway at about five miles-per-hour. The visibility wasn't more than ten feet and The Musician turned the windshield wipers up as fast as they would go. Jack turned on WGBH-FM, the classical station on 89.7, and stuck his head out of the window. Willie wondered what was ahead and slowed down to about three MPH.

"We've got to be close to Broadway by now. Put your lights on and get out on to the roadway, we'll buzz on out of here and call it a night." Jack offered and took a deep breath.

Willie's hand was on the knob and he was about to hit the headlights when a set of car lights coming from a road perpendicular became visible through the snow. A big black Ford Bronco went through the stop sign and passed them, heading out to the Fort. "Gotta love that four wheel drive," The Musician said.

Jack could barely see ten feet in front of the van.

"This must be it," Jack said as Willie switched on the headlights and drove back down Broadway. Soon the streetlights helped guide them back into the residential area.

Jack thought they had dodged a bullet until he looked into the rearview mirror and saw the Cadillac pull up behind them. He put on his seatbelt.

"Willie, the Caddy is behind us but he's probably going home. Why don't we take a left up here and make sure they're not following us?"

The Musician took the left and so did the Caddy. Willie looked at Jack for a sign to take it up to another level. "Easy big fella. These road conditions are bad news. If we skid out and crash they could walk up to us and do whatever they want with no witnesses in this storm. Just maintain and head for the Area D station. I'm betting this Ford van of yours can not be pushed by a Cadillac."

Jack felt pretty sure of his assessment until the second set of headlights appeared close behind the Caddy. The headlights of the big, flat black Bronco.

"That Bronco is in four-wheel-drive, Jack."

"Yeah, but you're one hell-of-a driver!"

The Caddy was a few feet from the rear end of the van as Willie first rounded one corner and then the next. As Willie turned left out onto Broadway a shot rang out and the Caddy accelerated and slammed into the left rear quarter-panel of the van and both cars began to fishtail. The big van regained its control and headed down Broadway as the Caddy slid into a row of parked cars. Jack watched in the rearview as the Caddy tried to back out. The scene with the Caddy shrank and faded to a tiny picture in the rearview mirror. Then the big black Bronco filled the mirror as it pulled in behind them with its high beams on.

"Look Jack. This van is no match for that four-wheel drive Bronco in this snowstorm." The Musician said, "I'm not kidding! God strike me dead."

A shotgun blast blew out the van's rear window and Jack and Willie slumped in their seats and tried to shrink their heads into their bodies like turtles.

"Don't say that!" Jack yelled out and drew his .45. He looked back peering over the seat.

"Shit! Take a right. Start taking turns." Kelly couldn't see into the Bronco as their bright high beams shone directly into the van, blinding Jack. As the blue van took the right-hand turn and slid around the corner the dark Bronco stayed on their tail. Kelly saw the barrel of a shotgun sticking out of the passenger window and felt helplessly outmatched. He looked ahead as they approached the end of the street and Willie slid the big van around the corner, going up on the sidewalk, and nearly missing the street sign.

"Just stay on the street, Willie!"

The Bronco slid too, and clipped the sign as it pulled in behind again. Jack looked back and saw an Asian male about 19 years old in the passenger seat trying to aim the shotgun at them. Blam! Jack saw the muzzle flash as another shot roared out, striking the van's rear quarter panel. The Musician was driving like a pro. He turned to Jack and said, "Why don't you get out? You can do some of that Tae Kwon Do karate bullshit on them."

"Don't start with that, Willie."

"Look at my fuckin' van!"

"Its gonna be your ass if you don't lose these guys."

Willie hit the gas and the van moved past the point of being in control and began to fishtail. The Bronco had dropped back about twenty feet as the next intersection approached. Jack barely noticed the rows of tenements whizzing by.

"Easy, Willie!"

"What do you want? You want me to lose them? I can't see twenty feet in this fucking snowstorm. There's a four-wheel drive tank jammed up my ass and they're shootin' out my windows!"

The van slid around another corner, fishtailed, turned around 180 degrees, hit a parked car broadside, and stalled out in the middle of the street.

Both of the guys were rattled, but took stock and realized that neither one was hurt. Not yet, anyway. They looked at each other and smiled as the radiator hissed and the snow dampened all sound. Then Jack heard the gurgling muffler sound of the Bronco as it slowly pulled up to within five feet in front of them. Jack squinted out into the headlights and had a sinking feeling in the bottom of his gut.

He looked out at the big, flat black Bronco and raised his Colt Combat Commander up and out the window. He crouched as low as he could and got some cover from the doorframe.

"Start this thing."

As Willie turned the key, Kelly wondered what the next move would be. He had probable cause to unload on these guys. They'd been trying to kill him for the last fifteen minutes. But Jack held off as the big Bronco just sat there. Its' engine gurgled and growled.

The van's starter labored and the battery sounded as if it were dying. It turned over slower and slower. "Grrrr, grrrr." The Musician looked out the driver's side window for a place to run as he anticipated the next shotgun blast. Jack stared straight ahead with his finger on the trigger.

The van's motor suddenly started and The Musician eased down on the gas. He put on the lights, switched to high beams, and jammed it in low, swung out to the left and headed slowly down the street.

"What just happened there? Who are they?" The Musician asked.

"I don't know. Hired muscle. I guess they'd rather be behind us 'cause here they come." Jack said as the Bronco sped up to get behind them again.

"Try to find some public place if we can't make it to Area D. Maybe Flanagan's Super Market or The Triple O' Lounge."

Willie took another right and was back on Broadway heading into town. The Bronco took advantage of the empty street and pulled along side then, smacking into the van and knocking it sideways, but the van held its own. The Bronco rammed the van again and Willie retaliated by steering into the Bronco twice as hard. The Bronco didn't budge.

"Pull it back! Slow it down without locking the brakes."

Willie pulled it back and the Bronco rolled past.

"Take this right on A Street."

Willie slowed and took the right onto A Street as the big flat-black Bronco, unable to slow down, continued on down Broadway.

"I saw the brake lights go on. Let's lose these guys." Jack said.

The van sped down A Street in the blinding snowstorm, shut off its lights, and pulled into Southie's Fort Point Channel Post Office parking lot. Willie stuck his head out of the window and rolled into a space in the middle of six other vans.

They sat there in silence for a while. Finally, The Musician spoke.

"Who the fuck is going to pay for the damage to my car, Jack?"

"Don't worry its covered."

"It's covered? Well you're a man of your word Jack, and if you say it's covered, it's covered. But I'm fuckin' freezin' with the rear window shot out. I'll have to duct tape some plastic over it. What am I going to tell the old lady?"

"Tell her you love her and you're glad to be alive. And tell her to never let you work with Jack Kelly again. If Jack Kelly calls your house and so much as asks you to go to the store with him, don't go."

A set of headlights moving slowly down A Street became visible on this dark and snowy night. They were a familiar set of lights accompanied by a familiar sounding exhaust.

"Think you can follow those lights without turning on yours?"

"I can try."

The van moved through the snow that was up past the hubcaps. Willie and Jack both had their heads out the windows as they bounced over a curb and headed down A St. Willie made better time and fell in about 40 yards behind the larger Bronco.

Willie stuck his head inside and yelled, "I think I can see better without the headlights on. Hey, there's the nightclub we played at all the time. The Channel is right over there."

"You mean The Channel *was* right over there. They tore it down last summer."

"Yeah, I know. I got a mental block."

"You have more than a mental block. Slow it down."

The Bronco took a right through an alley, and then another right, over to the area off of Melcher Street that housed a community of artist lofts. Factories gone bust.

As the van followed behind through the alley, in the whiteout, Jack said, "I don't like this. Slow down. Watch out at the end of this alley. Get ready to shove it into reverse and back out."

The van nosed out of the end of the alley and Jack just caught the taillights of the Bronco taking a left a block down.

"Stay right here. That's Binford Street. It's a dead end."

The van sat in silence as the snow came down even heavier. Willie rolled up his window and Jack rolled up his half way, staring at the empty top of the street. Willie found a weather report on the radio. It said heavy snow all night.

It was one o'clock in the morning as Jack stared out into the still raging whiteout.

"I'll go see where they went and we'll call it a night," Jack said and looked at The Musician. The Musician just watched as Jack slid out of the van door and walked into the snowstorm.

Jack walked up the sidewalk along the six-story brick building, then disappeared around the corner. The Musician didn't like it when Jack disappeared from view. He strained his neck and stared intently out into the blizzard. Willie shifted in his seat like a wide-eyed dog whose owner has gone into the Seven-Eleven for a pack of Marlboros and a six-pack of Bud Light.

The Musician had just cleared the remaining broken glass out of the rear window and the snow off the windshield when Jack returned and hopped into the warmer van. As Willie got in, Jack motioned him to drive on and the Ford Econoline slid out onto Melcher Street to Summer and into Boston.

"They went to 44 Binford Street. A big old six-floor factory building that's been broken up into maybe two warehouses sections and four lofts. An old closed down shoe factory, a huge book storage repository for a hundred thousand old books that had no resale value, but someone could not bear to throw away, and a coal distribution company with easy access to the rail yard. It's at the end of a dead end by the railroad tracks. The Bronco is out back and the Provost Brother's Cadillac was parked in front. But for now, this is going nowhere, let's call it a night, Wild Man."

"Good, 'cause I gotta go home anyway and watch ESPN. They're doing a special show titled '*Coed Spread Eagle Aerobics from Hawaii.*'"

Chapter 17

The True Story

Jack finally got to sleep. He had hoped to dream of the nightclub he would run someday, Johnny's Place. But he instead dreamed of his fiancée. She was the beautiful girl that died in his arms. The schoolteacher.

He dreamed of the day that he saw her die in his arms. It was a case of simple arrested breathing. Asthma attack. Quiet, quick, and deadly. All of Jack's training in Rescue Breathing and First Responder CPR couldn't help her. Kelly could only watch helplessly as she slipped away. And then the dream became surreal. She had on the light blue Victoria Secret silk pajamas he had bought her with the matching fuzzy slippers. And the white terrycloth robe. He still felt stunned and couldn't move. He was in shock.

He saw her move from his arms as she stood up. She turned and walked away, toward the foot of the stairs. She began to ascend the grand spiral staircase, up toward the clouds, up into the blue of a warm and sunny sky. Looking back at Jack periodically, she moved up the first flight, looked down at him and continued on. Further up the spiral staircase. Up flight after flight. High above

Jack. Into the clouds and closer to the warm sun. She drifted ever upward until she was almost out of sight.

Jack spoke softly at first.

"I love you."

"I love you," she answered.

Then louder he shouted, "I love you," until he screamed it over and over.

"I love you! I love you!"

But she was gone and Jack sat upright, wiping the sleep and the tears from his eyes.

Chapter 18

Dead In the Water

Jack had slept through most of Saturday morning as the city awoke to the paralysis of a major snowstorm. All the local TV stations ran non-stop coverage of the winter's first major snowstorm. The first of about five or six New England gets every year.

Kelly was still lying in bed watching the coverage when he got a frantic phone call from Lt. Jessica Paris. "I'm at a crime scene, Jack. It's at the Stanton Estate. It's the driver, Ric George. He's… he was floating ass up in the duck pond. The kid who shovels the walk found him."

There was silence.

"Jack?"

"Yeah. Are you on a cell phone?"

"Yes."

"Can I come out there?"

"I'd rather you didn't at this point, Jack. I want to keep your involvement in this case out of my reports for the moment. Politics, Jack."

"OK. Describe the scene to me."

"The body was discovered about an hour or two ago in the pond behind the house. It's pretty gruesome. Face swollen and deep purple, he stinks bad... darkened skin, post mortem lividity, and his neck apparently crushed on one side. Eyes wide open."

"Is there... are his eyes very, very bloodshot?"

"Yes. The whites of his eyes are bloody red."

"Batekial hemorrhages. That means he was choked, strangled, or garroted."

"The M.E. is just entering the scene." Jesse told Jack. In the background Jack could hear the unmistakably annoying voice of Sergeant Cataldo, yelling, "Hey, Dr. Ryan. Can we get a doggie bag or do we have to eat it here?"

"Can I come out?" Kelly asked, pulling the bedcovers over his head.

"I'd rather you didn't, Jack. Sgt. Cataldo and the Belmont Police Department have the scene secured, they are extending us a little professional courtesy, but I'd rather not start inviting my own guests to the party. What's been going on?"

"What am I a suspect?"

"Really, Jack. Don't play that with me. You're a gun-shy paranoid."

"Yeah. You're right. Once bitten twice shy. It was just last year my picture was in the paper with 'SUSPECTED SERIAL KILLER' underneath it. But to answer your question, nothing too much has been going on. Friday night, last night, in the snowstorm we followed the Lawyer out there, to the Belmont estate and the Provost Brothers showed up. We didn't see the chauffeur around. We didn't go in. But I bet they had something to do with it. The Brothers loaded something in a long footlocker and put it in the Caddy. Then we followed the Provosts to Southie and got chased out at gunpoint. That's it." Jack looked down at his feet squirming in the end of his warm bed, and asked, "What was the time of death?"

"The M.E. hasn't got a chance to figure it yet. Everything is covered by two feet of snow. We're just taking photos, documenting any evidence, and securing the scene."

A canine officer walked by with a German Shepard on a leash. The dog growled at Paris.

"What was that?" asked Jack.

"We're running a cadaver sniffing dog through the house, just in case. I guess the dog senses my dislike of dirty, filthy animals."

"You don't like animals, Jessica?"

"I love animals… They're delicious."

"Didn't your personal trooper have a canine? A tracker, wasn't it?"

"Yes. 'The Chicken Slut.' The mutt would do anything for little pieces of chicken. That dog would dance around. She would get on her hind legs and dance and twirl for a piece of chicken."

Jack was licking his lips. He was hungry. And he wondered what *he* would do for little pieces of chicken.

"Who's in charge of the investigation?" he asked.

"Well, I'm trying to get it. But Belmont and Sergeant Cataldo's got the scene."

"What do you want me to do? And why is the body dog there?"

"You've done a lot already by telling me the Provost Brothers and Attorney Chase were here. You can swear to that, right?"

"Yes. Me and The Musician."

"Just one more thing, Jack. The dog just finished going through the house. The good news is no dead girl. The bad news is no girl at all. She's not here. Jack, the girl is missing."

Chapter 19

A Creeping Horror

Jack Kelly's client, chauffeur Ric George, was dead. The girl he was charged to protect was missing and maybe dead. Jack walked out of the bathroom, wiped the shaving cream off his face, and put *Workin' With the Miles Davis Quintet* on the CD player.

Jack knew that if she was alive, little Suzanne Stanton needed help. Kelly, with his flare for the dramatic, drank a shot of Cognac, stared into the big walnut mirror behind his desk, and recited out loud the lines from *The Maltese Falcon*. "When a man's partner is killed, he's supposed to do something about it. It doesn't make any difference what you thought of him. He was your partner and you're supposed to do something about it. And it happens we're in the detective business. Well, when one of your organization gets killed it's bad business to let the killer get away with it. Bad all around. Bad for every detective everywhere.'"

A missing kid. It was just a routine case. It was not like a partner. But it was the same. Jesse had come to Jack asking for help, The Chauffeur asked for help, willing to give half his salary. And God knows the girl needed help. Maybe Jesse had given the case to Jack a day too late. Obviously it was too late for The Chauffeur. It was Mr. George and Suzanne Stanton that had needed protection. The cops were involved now, but Jack still felt obliged to investigate.

He started by taking some time to sit at his desk and go over the case. He needed to assess the information he had, where he was, and what he needed to do. Jack thought about the child he was charged to watch over. Now missing. He had been warned that a certain party wanted to do harm to this child. He should have gotten her out, right then and there. And Jack had failed to protect her. That fair-haired, beautiful child he had seen in the photograph. An heir to a mega-fortune. A child who could not protect herself. That wide-eyed innocent. Now missing.

There had been attempts in the past. They may have been undocumented, but Jack believed that there was definitely something sinister afoot. Jack could only shudder at the thought of what could be happening to the child, as he sat powerless, with no direction. Is she dead somewhere? In an unmarked grave? At the bottom of a river? Under a floor or in a wall? Or is she alive?

When there is abduction, especially of a child, time was not on your side. Every hour that went by could take her further away. Every hour that slips by means the child could be closer to death. Jack didn't want to think about the things that a deranged criminal might do to a young girl. If she sees their faces, she can testify against them. The odds were that she'd be dead before long.

Jack had to believe that she was alive. He tried to picture her held in a boarded- up room. Maybe handcuffed to a radiator or a bedpost. A couple of big muscle headed punks guarding her. Or maybe she was in a cellar. Or a garage. Or in the trunk of a car.

Kelly remembered seeing the Provost Brothers loading the huge steamer, the footlocker, into the trunk of their Caddy. He was thinking they later unloaded it into the warehouse and book repository at Binford Street in Southie, in the snowstorm.

"How could I be so blind?" Jack shouted out into the empty detective agency.

Jack reached for the phone on his desk and knocked the receiver on the floor. He picked it up, got a dial tone, and then realized he didn't remember the number. He read it off the yellow legal pad on the desk and dialed it.

"Boston Police, Fire, and Rescue. Area A," the man answered.

"Lt. Paris around?" Jack asked.

"No sir, she's unavailable."

"You'd better page her then."

"Who is this?"

"Jack Kelly... I was... ah..." Jack never knew quite how to say he used to work for the same company, the BPD, because he knew, sometimes, it no longer counted for much.

"I know who you are, Jack. Sgt. Mike Medved, here. Haven't seen you for a while, Jack. 'Been hearin' 'bout ya though.'"

"Hi Mike. Stuck on the desk? Or are you milking the system for the OT? Do they still call you the Milkman for your ability to make a stolen bicycle case last into three hours overtime?"

"You know I have devoted my life to serving the good people of Boston without regard to my own personal safety. And I'd do it for free."

"Is that why you've made more money than the Chief, three years in a row now, Milkman?"

"How's things in the cushy world of the private investigator. I heard you only take one case at a time."

"No, I drink one case at a time. Where's Jesse, Mike?"

"She's left about fifteen minutes ago saying she was going to get some lunch, take some time off this afternoon, and head for mandatory nighttime firearms qualifications at the range when it gets dark. She may call in, or go straight home. Is this business or pleasure, Jack?" Jack could almost see the smirk on Medved's face.

"I guess you'd better page her, Mike. It's business. And a nasty business it is."

Jack waited… It was excruciating. The seconds seemed to drag… The minutes felt like larger chunks of time. Then it was two hours and no call from Jessica Paris. He wished she had written her home number down for Jack before she left that morning. The morning after they had made love. A wistful smile overtook Jack's face as he remembered just how long they had made love. How her hands explored his body. And how her lips nipped at his chin and neck. How she slid down his chest and put her hands on each buttock cheek and nestled her own cheek on his belly. His belly quivered slightly in expectation of ecstacy. And Jack knew how badly he needed it.

Kelly was not about to call the Precinct, pleading for the Lt. to call him. What the hell was she doing at Firearm Qualifications anyway? This was the major case that she was so passionate about three days ago. The Driver was dead and the girl was missing.

Jack was a detective. He had to move. He didn't have to wait for the big wheels of justice to start rolling. He was out there alone. Working without a net. He told himself he was going to plan to work some surveillance on 44 Binford Street, with or without the cops. That girl could be there, her time running out. Kelly told his self he would get ready to work the warehouse on Binford St., and if Jesse called, he would deal with her then. She could authorize immediate and around-the-clock surveillance on the warehouse. Freeze the whole scene while she got a search warrant. She could run the Provosts through DMV. She could run a records check. She could check with Probation and Parole. A federal check of agent field notes through the FBI... Kelly wondered why the FBI wasn't there. This was a kidnapping.

Jack realized he no longer had a car since Big Bad Boy Bob Provost decided to roast Mighty Whitey. He called his friend Ed at The Naked i lounge on Washington St. and asked Ed if his friend still owned the used car dealership at Revere Circle. He did. The owner often let Kelly use different cars for surveillance. Jack gave Ed a few ideas and Ed said he'd pick up a vehicle for Jack to borrow for a small fee. Ed said he would leave it in front of Jack's office. Then Kelly called The Musician for a ride.

"Hey, Willie, do you have any other wheels we could use? It would be for some surveillance. You don't have to come, if you're busy."

"I just finished banging out the dents in the rear fenders of the Ford Econoline. The van is all I got, Jack. Can we use that, or is it too recognizable?"

"Well, we been burnt, man, but time is of the essence here. So, wanna pick me up?"

"When?"

"Now."

"How's 45 minutes?" Willie pleaded.

"Make it twenty?"

Jack heard Willie say "Hey Jack. Wanna hear the Joke-of-the-Day?" as he hung up the phone.

Jack grabbed his black backpack with his surveillance equipment and put it by the door. He put on some black cotton pants, black patrol boots, a black turtleneck, decided not to use his so-called bulletproof vest, but put on a shoulder holster, a heavy, dark blue Red Sox windbreaker, black ball-cap, shoved his Colt Combat Commander into its holster and headed toward the door. He picked up his cell phone and shoved it in his pocket. Time was not on his side.

Kelly picked up coffee and the Boston Herald at the Chinatown corner store and walked back to the front of his building. Willie was parked out front. Jack hopped in, handed Willie a cup of coffee, and they crossed the Central Artery into Southie.

"I love the Boston Herald." Willie said. "I love those stories like 'CRACK FOUND IN THE BACK OF MAN'S UNDERWEAR,' by Phil McCracken, Dick Fitzwell, and Haywood Jablowmey."

Jack didn't even glance at Willie.

"So how was Lieutenant Jessica Paris? Are you gonna marry her?"

"I told you. I'm not going to discuss that with you."

"Why? Was she kinky? Did she make you do things? Like…"

"Don't start, Willie."

'Hey, Jack. We're friends. I was there for you when your Mom died, I was there when your fiancée died, I was even there when your dog Raggs died."

"Yes, I see. You're bad luck!"

"You love her, don't you? You want her. You want to possess her."

"Zip it!"

"If you love some one, set them free, brother."

It was late afternoon as they passed South Station, the South Boston postal annex, and crossed over the Fort Point Channel into Southie. Jack thought about what he was going to do when he got to Binford St. It had been a bright and sunny day. Clear and cold. The air was crisp. The plows had cleaned, flattened, and sanded the snow on the roads and the old blue Chevy van cruised smoothly and surely.

They passed the rows of old red brick converted factory buildings and Jack asked The Musician to drive right past the entrance to Binford Street, a short dead end lined with factories with a rail yard at the end.

"Look straight ahead, Willie."

"What do you think this is my first surveillance, Kelly? I'm a seasoned veteran now. I'm the Tonto to your Lone Ranger. I'm the Watson to Sherlock Holmes. I'm the Danny Glover to your Mel Gibson. The Clark Kent to your Superman, the Robin to your Batman. I'm the …"

"You're the Jane to my Tarzan?"

They drove past the entrance to Binford St. and the only car on the street was an abandoned white Lincoln Town Car junk heap with no tires. There wasn't any activity at all.

Jack called the Area A station and asked for Paris. Sgt. Medved was still on the desk and told Jack he had paged the Lt. but she hadn't called in yet. Kelly convinced Medved to page her again and ask her to meet Jack at Binford and A Streets as soon as she could.

Willie parked the van behind the vacant guard shack in the A Street parking lot across from the entrance to Binford Street. Willie turned and said, "So you want to hear the Joke-of-the-Day?" Jack got out of the car, slammed the door and walked toward Binford St.

Jack Kelly walked down the sidewalk towards the last brick factory on the left. The street was empty as Jack walked over the sidewalk where the snow had been trampled flat by footsteps.

"This is the part where the detective wings it." Jack whispered as he approached the building, glancing nonchalantly up at the windows for any signs of life. The entrance was a small alcove with six mailboxes. Kelly scanned the names.

"Well, I'll be. Reno Waste Management, ground floor right rear."

Kelly tried the massive front door and found it to be unlocked. He backed out onto the sidewalk, looked upward, and walked briskly back down the sidewalk towards the A Street lot.

As he jumped back into the warm van, The Musician continued, "So, a businessman boarded a flight and was lucky enough to be seated next to an absolutely gorgeous woman. They exchanged brief hellos and he noticed she is reading a manual about sexual statistics. He asked her about it and she replied, 'This is a very interesting book about sexual statistics. It identifies that American Indians have the longest average penis and Polish men have the thickest average penis. By the way, my name is Jill. What's yours?' He coolly replied in a deep voice, 'Tonto Kawalski, nice to meet you.'"

Jack was about to call Area A again when he saw Jessica Paris's unmarked gold Ford Taurus coming down the street. Willie flashed the headlights on the van and Paris pulled into the lot, parking side-by-side. The window of the Taurus slid down as Jack cranked the van window down.

"Jesse, the Provosts left the mansion in Belmont around the time of death of the Chauffeur. They put a footlocker into the trunk of their Caddy. We followed them to 44 Binford, over there. They most likely pulled the trunk inside. What if Suzanne Stanton was in that trunk?"

Lt. Paris breathed outward and looked over at Binford Street as if it could provide some kind of answer. Then she looked back and said, "Hi, Willie."

"Hi, Jesse."

Kelly interupted the love-fest. "I think you've got enough for a search warrant. I pray she wasn't in that trunk, but... it could happen. It probably did. We can place them at the mansion at about the time of Mr. George's death and before the girl was discovered missing. They left with a trunk. These Provost Brothers are of extremely dubious character…"

Jesse glanced at Jack and said, "You've been a one-man wrecking crew with these Provosts! They're going to sue you for harassment."

"Some of the warehouse space is listed to Reno Waste Management."

"Isn't that the company owned by Thaddeus Reno, the serial killer that tried to throw you off the top of Mass General? The Herald printed your picture with *'Suspected Serial Killer'* under it." Jesse and Willie were now looking at each other grinning from ear-to-ear, thoroughly enjoying the moment.

"Time is critical here, my comedically challenged friends. Do you want to get a warrant or should I go to the FBI directly?" Jack said as Lt. Paris sat bolt upright, Jack having administered a shock to her system. She pulled up her car phone and got on the line to headquarters.

With blistering efficiency Paris had a clerk typing out the warrant as Jack fed her the particulars. The exact location, floor, side, and unit of the structure to be searched, the things to be searched for, and the probable cause to search for them.

"It'll be at least an hour before we can execute." Jesse said to Jack as she put down the phone. The Musician filled the silence.

"Hey Jesse?" Willie said.

"Hey what?"

"This loser couldn't get a date. He goes to a bar and the bartender says, 'Just say you're a lawyer.' So the guy asks a pretty woman to go out with him. After she says no, he says, it's probably a good thing because he has a court case early next morning. She says, 'Oh, you're a lawyer?' He says, 'Well, yes I am.' She likes the idea and they go to his place. When they start making love, he starts to laugh to himself. She says 'What's so funny?' And he says, 'Well, I've been a lawyer for one hour and I'm screwing someone already.'"

Jack fumbled for a jazz or classical station on the radio.

"Jesse. Did I ever tell you about the rooster?"

"I don't think so, Willie," Lieutenant Jessica Paris said. Kelly looked at her and shook his head as if to say, 'Don't encourage him,' as The Musician continued.

"A farmer's chickens were producing less and less so he went down the road to the next farmer and asked him if he had a rooster for sale. The other farmer says, 'Yeah, I've got this great rooster, named Little Red. He'll service every chicken you've got. No problem.'

"Well, Little Red the rooster is a lot of money, but the farmer decides he'd be worth it. So he bought Little Red. The farmer took Little Red home and set him down in the barnyard, giving the rooster a pep talk, 'Little Red, I want you to pace yourself. You've got a lot of chickens to service here and you cost me a lot of money and I'll need you to do a good job. So, take your time and have some fun,' the farmer said with a chuckle. Little Red seemed to understand, so the farmer points him towards the hen house and Little Red took off like a shot ~WHAM~ He nails every hen in the chicken coop three or four times and the farmer is just shocked. Little Red runs out of the hen house and sees a flock of geese down by the lake ~WHAM~ He humps, bumps, and services all the geese. Then Little Reds' up in the pigpen, mounting the pigs. He's in with the cows. Little Red is jumping on every animal the farmer owns.

"The farmer is distraught; worried that his expensive rooster won't even last the day. Sure enough, the farmer goes to bed and wakes up the next day to find Little Red lying under the hot sun, in the middle of the yard.

"Buzzards are circling overhead. The farmer, saddened by the loss of such a colorful animal, shakes his head, bends over the skinny, disheveled rooster and says, 'Oh, Little Red, I told you to pace yourself. I tried to get you to slow down, now look what you've done to yourself.'

"Little Red opened one eye and looked towards the buzzards flying overhead and said, 'Shhh! They're getting closer....'"

After a moment of silence, Jesse picked up her car-phone and checked in with the police department clerk who was typing up the search warrant. It was almost done and she would soon have it sent over to a judge's house to get it signed. She also arranged for a search warrant team and two marked units with two patrolmen in each to stand by at either end of A Street.

"I've got a little more info on Lindon Chase, Jack. I talked to a fraud squad investigator from the Connecticut State Police who went through some old records. He told me Chase worked his way through Yale Law School by working boiler room operations selling bogus oil and gas shares. He ran a phony travel sweepstakes ruse and some credit card fraud before he graduated and passed the bar exam in Massachusetts. His upbringing involved some kind of B.F. Skinner type project whereby his parents attempted to engineer a brilliant child. But," Paris raised an eyebrow, "something went horribly wrong, manifesting itself deep in the psyche of Lindon Chase. And this resulted in a lifetime of therapy for Attorney Chase."

"The monster lives." Jack said.

"No outstanding arrest warrants on the remaining Provost brothers, Jack. But there were six out on Ricardo Provost, the one you called, Bob." Jesse said with a smile.

"Well, we won't ever serve those warrants, will we? I guess he's paid his dept to society, though. I wonder if I'll still get a tenth of Izzy's bail-jumper money."

"Can we get some coffee, Jesse?" Willie asked.

'What do you think she's your waitress? Do you want to order some dinner, too?" Jack said sarcastically. "Why don't you go get it, Willie? I'll have a medium, milk, no sugar. Jesse?"

"Tea. Black. Please."

Willie pulled the van up and Jack hopped out and slid into the passenger seat of the gold Ford Taurus. Jack and Jesse watched the van head into the early sunset of this clear, cold December evening, towards Southie. Jack squirmed a little in his seat.

"About the other night..." Jesse said.

"Oh, no, you're not going to apologize, or tell me you were drunk, are you?" Jack asked, being a sensitive guy.

"No! I wanted to tell you how much I enjoyed... your company, Jack."

"It was good to be with you too, Jess."

"Maybe when, when this is over..."

"Yeah, maybe. That would be good. Jesse, why would they want to keep Suzanne alive? They haven't tried to collect a ransom."

"Well, if this lawyer, Chase, wants to take over the estate and the management of this mega-fortune, the girl would have to be completely incapacitated, or dead, right?"

"I'm with you so far," Jack said.

"So, I don't think they want to keep her alive."

A cold chill ran up Jack Kelly's back as he again thought of the girl. Jack had to hope she was still alive. Lt. Paris continued.

"There would definitely be complications if the girl's death were linked to the lawyer. Maybe they're trying to dispose of Suzanne. Maybe something went wrong."

Jack couldn't believe how matter-of-factly Jesse described the probable outcome. Then he remembered how Jesse had risen through the ranks of the police department to the rank of Lt. Detective. Through hard work, long hours, and consistently good work. He wondered just how streetwise, jaded, and cold she had become. Lieutenant Detective Jessica Paris was a professional.

Willie got back with the coffee but they didn't have time to drink it as an unmarked unit delivered the signed search warrant to the lieutenant. A young plainclothes Detective Tim Watkins told Jesse that nine members of the Boston Police Warrant Service Team were standing by in two vans at A Street and Summer.

"Who's the team O.I.C.?"

"Captain Granfield Nelson is in charge." Timothy Watkins said with an air of pride. Jack knew Granfield. He was a safety first, conservative, deal-from-strength, no nonsense guy. He was a cop's cop.

"What channel is he on?" the Lt. asked.

"Primary, I guess, until you tell him different." Watkins said.

Jesse picked up the squad car mike. "Three-sixteen to Two twenty-two."

"Go ahead Three-sixteen."

"Go to Tac-4."

Jesse switched her car-to-car radio to channel four and asked Captain Nelson, "When would you like to execute?"

"As soon as you want to move on it. We've got a four hour minimum and we're ready to stage, go ahead."

"O.K. Granny, it's a go, lets do it. What do you want from me?"

About a minute went by and Granfield hadn't replied. Jesse hung up her mike and looked over at Jack, and they both shrugged. Jack looked down Binford Street and saw three of the SWAT team personnel come out around the corner of the building at

44 Binford. Kelly looked back at Jesse and saw the head and shoulders of a gray haired sixty-year-old man in the car window. He seemed to be sniffing Jesse's hair, as she looked straight ahead.

"I'll tell you what I want," his voice boomed as Jesse turned in fright, her hand reaching for her revolver.

"Jesus Christ! Don't do that, Granny!" Jesse blew out some air.

"Hi, Jack." Captain Granfield Nelson said.

"Hey, Granny. Patriots made the playoffs this year."

"They did, or Bill Belichik would be gone. We need a guy like Parcells back. Or the Gipper! Goddamnit. Or Ditka. That's who we need. Iron Mike. By the way, sorry to hear about the Schoolteacher, Jack."

"Yeah."

Captain Nelson's radio crackled and a voice said, "One through four ready, One."

"Lets go, Jesse." Granfield said as he spoke into his headset, "Command One to Leader One, let's advance. Make entry and secure the premises. Acknowledge."

"Ten-four, copy make entry and secure," a voice on the radio said.

Willie got out of his van and Jack got out of the unmarked and they fell in behind Capt. Nelson and Jesse. As civilians, they weren't specifically invited, but Jack knew enough to tag along.

Jack could see the officers dressed in all black, with their helmets, body armor, and automatic weapons at every corner of the building. A stack of five officers went through the front door as Kelly and The Musician struggled to catch up and fall in line.

"Let's get up front." Jack whispered to Jesse.

"You got a vest on, Jack?" Jesse asked, knowing the answer.

"I'm bulletproof." Jack lied.

They were through the front doors and shuffling quickly and quietly to the heavy wooden door marked Reno Waste Management under a flight of stairs. As Jack rounded the corner he heard the shuffling ahead of him stop. Then he heard the pounding of a fist on a door.

"Boston Police! We have a search warrant! Open the door! Boston Police! Open the door! Search warrant!"

Crack! Jack jumped as he heard the sound of a battering ram on a metal door. Crack! Again. And then the sound of shuffling feet and the voices of the five members of the Warrant Team, "Boston Police! Boston Police! Search Warrant! Police. Show me your hands!" Then "Open door! I need a cover!" Then, "Rooms clear, 2." And again, "Rooms clear, 3." The voices seemed to have a ring of disappointment.

As Jack Kelly entered the loft the strong beams of the flashlights of the Warrant Team flashed in every direction and then went out as someone flicked on the lights. Jack felt the disappointment too, as he entered the bare loft and began to slowly realize that there was no one and nothing there. No girl. No dirt bags. Not even furniture. Nothing. Just an empty vacant loft space with dirt, papers, and empty food containers strewn about.

"I got three things to say." Jack said. "It ain't right. It ain't fair. And it ain't right."

"It's like we threw a kegga and nobody showed up." The Musician said.

As the Entry Team began to filter back out the door, Captain Granfield Nelson put his hand on Jack Kelly's shoulder and said, "Sorry, Jack. But next time get some solid Intel, OK?"

"Yeah, Granny." Jack said, dejectedly.

Granny added, "What do you think about our execution?"

"I'm all for it." Jack mumbled as the captain and his SWAT team shuffled out the door.

Jack and Lt. Paris began to wander around the empty loft space, their disappointment obvious.

"What the fuck, Jack?" Paris said, more in shock than in blame.

"I never should have taken my eyes off this place." Kelly realized that Suzanne Stanton might have slipped through his fingers. He felt like the losing quarterback in a big game, and said, "Sorry, Jesse," as he kicked some crumpled newspapers into a corner of the loft.

"It was a good shot, Jack. Let's put a BOLO out on the vehicle. What was it a black Caddy?" Lt. Paris suggested.

Kelly hated being the suspicious pessimist, but he looked for signs in the floor, ceiling, and walls for recent renovation. He didn't want to think about the girl being buried in the floor or in the walls. He was bewildered.

"What do you think, Jack?" Paris asked.

Jack didn't respond as he picked up the crumpled newspaper he had kicked into the corner. He spread it out and began to read it. His eyes searched in vain as he saw a want-add in the Sanford News and he read aloud, "Sanford Cement."

"Say again, Jack?" The Lt. asked.

"There's an add here in the paper that reads, 'Sanford Cement of Sanford, Maine, now hiring for pre-cast cement work, Jersey Barriers for Boston's Big Dig, $19.00 an hour.'"

"You're looking for another job already, Kelly?" Willie said.

Jack sat down on the window seat and scratched his head. He held the crumpled newspaper up to the light as if he might see a secret message. Jack was reaching.

Lieutenant Paris began walking towards the door saying something about Jack not calling the next time he had a hot tip. Jack got up a bit too quickly, his heel slipping out from under him, and he landed squarely on his back with a thud. The quarterback was down.

"You alright Kelly?" Jessica said, turning to see Jack flat on his back.

"I'm fine! Those karate lessons taught me how to fall." Jack said trying to hide the pain in his shoulder as he struggled to his feet. Jack felt the gelatinous cold liquid on the right side of his jacket, wiped it with his hand and looked at his hand in the light that filtered through the unwashed loft windows. Jack held his hand under the dim light bulb above the sink.

"What is this gooey shit?" Jack held his hand up and said, "Christ!"

He leaned over the dirty, paint stained sink, ran the water and stuck his hands in, scrubbing them with a half bottle of liquid dishwashing soap. The reddish liquid began to circle and spiraled down the drain.

Jesse was staring at him quizzically, her eyes wide open and her mouth ajar.

"You been parading around like a ballerina on steroids, Jack Kelly. Let's get out of here... Katrina the ballerina." Willie said.

Jack turned and stared at the window-seat and at what he thought was blood oozing out from underneath, as he said, "Why don't you look in that window-seat before you go?"

Jesse scowled, giving Jack that look that women seemed to give him, as if Jack were in third grade and she were the teacher. Then she looked at the window-seat and saw the thick red coagulating fluid that Jack had slipped on. The fluid that drained from a body gravely injured and stuffed into a small space, housing old hot water pipes.

Lt. Jessica Paris didn't move. Her lips got very dry. Her breathing quickened but she couldn't quite get enough oxygen to her brain. Should she draw her gun? Had something… someone been in there? She finally looked back at Jack and said, "Are you gonna look, Jack?"

"Since I don't see any one else rushing forward," Jack moved toward the window-seat, walking slowly and glancing around the room several times. He hoped it would take longer but after a few short steps Jack was leaning over the window seat and feeling underneath the lid for a handle. He took a few deep breaths and lifted the cover a few inches… and then raised it all the way. He stood there staring down.

The Lt. took several steps forward and pleaded desperately, "Is it her, Jack? Is it her?"

Jack held his breath, refraining from taking any of the odors in through his nose, as he reached down into the window-seat and tried to turn the head so he could see the face. Jack could see the blonde hair, but Rigor Mortis had set in and Kelly had to use both hands to turn the face up into the dim light enough to see.

"It's Justin J. Buxton-Smythe." Jack said flatly.

Chapter 20

Body In the Box

Upon his arrival, Sergeant Donavan told Jack that in all his years with the Boston Police Department he had not seen such a steady stream of bodies associated with one man. At least not since enforcer and hit man for the mob, former New Bedford resident Joseph "The Animal" Barboza, roamed these parts, leaving behind a trail of dead.

Lt. Paris made a few calls and told Jack and Sgt. Donavan that Buxton-Smythe had been bailed out of the Charles Street Jail by his cousin, Gino Provost, brother of "Bob" Provost.

"I had nothing to do with this one, Sarge." Jack pleaded.

"I believe you probably didn't kill 'em directly, Jack, but it still remains to be seen if you had nottin' to do wid it at all. We hauled this Buxton out of your ahffice after he tried to kill ya, just far days ago. And it was just tree days ago that you administered poison to his cousin."

"Poison, Sarge?"

"Lead poison. Administered directly into his farhead." Sergeant Donavan countered, poking his forehead with a finger.

Sure. It was all fun and games for Donavan. He wasn't in it up to his neck, or over his head, like Kelly was. Donavan would go home at the end of his shift, crack a beer, sit down to his evening meal, and tell the old lady about the fine kettle of fish that poor private eye Kelly had gotten himself into.

The forensic boys and the lab techs from the Medical Examiner's Office, with their rubber gloves and dark blue cotton jumpsuits, were combing over the crime scene. Lights flashed as photographers snapped pictures and the M.E. himself was laying out a white plastic sheet on the floor on which to examine the body. He gave the order to remove the body from the window seat and to put it down on the plastic sheet.

Three technicians jockeyed for position over the window seat and struggled to get around and under the body. They soon lifted it up, out, and over onto the white plastic sheet. As flashbulbs popped they backed away, some of their gloves dripping with semi-coagulated blood, to reveal a grown man, Justin Provost Buxton-Smythe, lying dead, springing slowly back into a curled up fetal position.

He had short blond hair and was dressed in a navy blue blazer, black slacks, and black cowboy boots. He had long stopped bleeding, but the left side of his head was covered with thick, coagulated blood. His fists were still clenched. His lips were drawn back exposing his teeth and freezing his face in a grimace.

Jack thought that maybe Sgt. Donavan was right. Kelly had been involved with the death of two Provosts in three days. If it wasn't for bad luck he wouldn't have no luck at all. Jack was deep in thought, leaning on a windowsill, looking intently out at the rail yard when The Musician put his hand on Kelly's shoulder.

"What's on your mind, Jack?"

"I was just thinking about the Provost Brothers, and how I first ran across them…. They had ransacked my office, slapped me around, thrown my accountant out a third floor window, shot him, then ran him over with a car. All while they worked for the Fat Man. I can still feel his damnable presence."

"Yeah, that Reno," The Musician said, "When the Fat Man entered a room, he was so evil, so sinister, I could almost hear the brooding cellos playing a dark and suspicious refrain."

"Cellos?" Jack said.

"There's always room for cellos."

After a long pause, Jack looked at Willie and quoted from Mary Shelly's *Frankenstein,* "'I beheld the wretch- the miserable monster I had created.'"

"You talking about me? Yeah, you are. I know. Hey, you wanna hear the Joke- of-the-Day?"

Jack was thinking he had already been subjected to The Joke-of-the-Day when Willie took Kelly's non-responsiveness to be a yes, glanced over at the body lying on the white plastic sheet in the middle of the floor, shrugged, and forged ahead.

"A very young and new nun goes to her first confession. She tells the priest that she has a terrible secret. The priest then tells her that her secret is safe in the sanctity of the confessional.

"She says, 'Father, I never wear panties under my habit.'

"The priest chuckles and says, 'That's not so serious, Sister Bernadette. Say five Hail Marys and five Our Fathers.'

"'Thank you, father.' The new nun said, and then the Father added, 'And do five cart-wheels on your way to the altar.'"

Chapter 21

Case In Point

Jack got back to his office late again, dropped his keys, found the jazz station, and took a long hot shower. He scrubbed every part of his body, trying to wash away the scent of death. He washed his hair twice and yelled out in the shower, "What's next?" He was too tired to eat and just lay down on his bed for what seemed like too short a time.

Jack Kelly had planned to sleep late, but the phone rang at 8:05 AM.

"Jack? It's Jesse. We've got a meeting at 9:30 with the lawyer, Lindon Chase. He's gotten a ransom note for Suzanne. Can you sit in?"

Jack exhaled slowly and loudly and then answered, "Yeah. You gonna have coffee?"

"Yes, Jack we'll have coffee for you. Want some sticky buns?"

"Maybe later, Jess." Jack said and hung up.

Jack arrived on time and met Lt. Paris at the front desk at the Area A station.

Sleep When I'm Dead

As they walked into the Criminal Investigations Division Paris didn't say a word and Jack didn't ask a question. They entered a conference room next to Lt. Paris's office and Jessica picked up one of six Green Mountain coffee cups and handed it to Kelly.

"How do you like it?" she said.

"How come everything you say has sexual connotations?" Jack asked.

"How do you take it?" Paris re-phrased the question.

"Isn't that rather personal, detective?"

"OK, Jack." The Lt. said getting annoyed with first having to serve Kelly coffee, then having to endure his comedic probe.

A lab tech came into the room and handed Jesse a document incased in plastic. Paris dropped the document on the conference table in front of Jack and asked him to look at it.

It was the original ransom note. Jack read it. It was on white legal paper and read, "To Mr. Chase. We have Suzanne Stanton and you will give us $250,000 in unmarked bills at a location and time of our bidding. Don't contact the police or the girl will die. We will call you and only you at the girl's house."

"What do you think, Jack?" Paris asked.

"Short and sweet. No frills. Amateurish. 'Time of our bidding?' Give me a break. I'd say we have a drama student from Harvard, BU., or Emerson College. White. Male. Between the ages of seventeen and thirty-five, balding, married, two point-two kids, left-handed, a chain-smoker, Irish-Catholic, a republican, uses more pepper than salt, probably a lay-clergy or coach, or a custodian, and sexually stifled. A closet sadomasochist."

"You can tell all that from the note?" Jesse asked.

"No. It's the swirl of his K in Kidnapper. Look I don't have a clue here. I made that stuff up. And you bought it, Paris?"

"Are you serious, Jack? I gotta check everything you say, twice."

"Not everything, Jesse."

Jack thought he saw a quiver in Lieutenant Jessica Paris's lower lip and one of her eyes seemed to glass-over with emotion. Maybe Jack made more of an impression on her than he had thought. Maybe she still remembered the first time around.

The only other person in the room sat at the far end of the conference table, looking through a case file. He was stocky young black man, about 28 or 30 years old, light brown hair, clean-cut and dressed in an impeccable suit, white shirt and tie. Kelly guessed correctly as Jessica introduced him to young FBI agent Arthur Laprise. Jack knew the Feds would show up for a kidnapping case. They loved the high profile stuff.

"Agent Laprise is up to speed and has no problem with you assisting us on this, Jack."

Laprise stood up and offered Jack his hand saying, "Believe it or not I did some work one summer as a P.I. Before joining the Bureau. Workers Comp surveillance."

"Agent Laprise, is it true that the FBI says there are at least thirty-five serial killers active in the U.S at any given time?" Jack asked innocently.

"Fifty to seventy-five, I believe. Minimum."

Jack wasn't impressed and didn't like him already. Obviously Laprise had not been filled in on Jack's many years of service, culminating in a high number of felony arrests and a solid conviction rate. Kelly would not allow himself to be intimidated by the young troubleshooter the Bureau had sent in. Maybe the state and local police bent over for the Feds, but Jack was a citizen, and wouldn't be chewed out by a supervisor if he said something a little too direct, said something out-of-line, or didn't follow protocol.

"This coffee's cold. Could we microwave it, Lieutenant?" Jack said, half- expecting Paris to swing at him. Jack hated the way she was so sensitive, such a feminist at times.

Kelly braced himself as Jessica tensed and was about to say something when Sgt. Donavan walked into the room with a state police detective Jack knew. Sgt. John Abbott was a tall, thin cop with a short black jarhead haircut and a square jaw. With Abbott was another gentleman who held his hands up by his stomach and seemed to tiptoe into the room. He was about sixty-five, with thinning gray hair stretched across his scalp, small eyes, and a long pointy nose. Jack recognized him as the lawyer he had tailed to the girl's house in Belmont. Donavan introduced attorney Lindon Chase to Paris, and as Donavan left the room she in turn introduced Chase to Jack, telling the lawyer that Jack was just 'sitting in.' And she introduced Chase to FBI agent Laprise.

Chase was dressed in some kind of casual attire, like a green velour jumpsuit, he looked like some kind of comb-over velvet Elvis. Chase's eyes seemed to widen slightly and he swallowed as he smiled at the FBI agent. Another groupie, Jack guessed. Then Chase looked at Jack.

"Haven't I seen you somewhere?" The Lawyer asked with a thick lisp.

"No. I've never been there," was Jack's reply as everyone sat down at the table. Paris directed her narrative mainly to Laprise and glanced occasionally at the others as she gave everyone a quick and general rundown of the case. When she finished, Laprise, Chase, The Statie, and Paris all looked at Jack.

"Well, Mr. Kelly, you seem to have a penchant for being in the wrong place at the right time. Or is that the right place at the wrong time?" Agent Laprise said.

Kelly just looked back at Laprise wondering if he was developing Jack as a suspect.

Paris got everybody back on track by passing the ransom note around and saying, "We've got the note and I'll read you the forensics report on it, 'No fingerprints, common stock paper, run off of a Cannon BJC 4100 color ink jet printer, very common. No human traces, no follicle or secreter's trace oils, no microscopic skin cells, blah, blah, blah… No nothing.'"

"So where do we go from here?" Chase asked FBI Agent Laprise, obviously taken with him. Agent Laprise in turn looked at Jesse as she answered, "We're going to ask you to do as the note instructed, Mr. Chase. You don't have to sleep there, but could you wait at the girl's Belmont residence to receive a call from the kidnappers with further instructions. If you wouldn't mind?"

"Of course, Lieutenant. I'll do anything I can to help… get Suzanne back."

Kelly had to exercise strong self-control not to show his disgust with the filthy lying bastard. Jack wanted to grab the attorney by his scraggy neck and shake him until he confessed and told them where the girl was.

"Well, we ought to get you right over there, counselor, with a couple of our plainclothes guys." Paris suggested and they all stood up.

As Chase was leaving with Sgt. Donavan he turned and asked Agent Laprise if the phone at the Stanton Mansion would be tapped.

"Already done, sir." The State's detective, John Abbott replied loudly, adding more softly, "And your home phone and office, Slimeball," as Chase walked out of earshot.

"I'd like to take him out at the knees," Paris said.

"Finally, a plan that might work." Kelly added.

"It would make me feel a lot better." Abbott chimed in.

Jesse said, "I've got two of my best homicide investigators who will be watching him more than they'll be watching *out* for him. Burns and Flood."

"Film at Eleven," Jack said.

"Huh?"

"Burns and Flood. Sounds like a disaster on the Eleven O'clock News." Jack couldn't resist.

"This meeting is officially over." Paris announced.

"Want me all to yourself, don't you?" Jack suggested wryly to Lt. Paris as the others left the room. The Lt. turned and glared at Jack.

"Jack Kelly, there is an eight-year-old girl out there in the company of some sick and murderous deviants. Come up with something, Jack!"

"Hey! I'm on standby. I'm prepared to launch into action at any moment, when the situation calls for it. I'm quiet right now, but if need be, I'll take a stand for what I believe in at any given moment. I am a soldier for truth and beauty, the good and the just. I'm just on standby. When needed I'll step-up. And there are a lot of us, silently toiling away, our heads down. But when we're needed our hearts will sing and we will rise up and lay down our lives for our beliefs."

"Shhh. I thought I heard the Star Spangled Banner playing in the background, Jack." Paris said, "Look, I don't mean to get on you but these wiretaps might not be enough to do it." Her face was stressed and lined. Jack had no way of knowing that Jessica had been molested repeatedly by a friend of her father's when she was eleven. It was a dark little secret buried so deeply she had never confronted it, and it was still unresolved. She still felt the pain. Something about the little Stanton girl had really hit home with her.

The Lawyer and the two homicide detectives arrived at the Stanton Mansion and settled in. Chase gave the detectives a tour of the house pointing out the locations of the four telephone outlets. The Lawyer offered Burns the Chauffeur's room, but Burns declined, instead opting for the couch in a small library off of the dining room. Flood took a bedroom upstairs and down the hall from Chase in order to keep a closer watch on him.

Late that afternoon a technician arrived from BPD technical support. He showed Burns and Flood which buttons to press to record conversations on a small rack of recording equipment with its own phone extension set up on a table by the mansion's main telephone.

Shortly after the technician left, the phone rang sending Burns, Flood, and Chase into a mad scramble to set up by their respective phones. Chase had run down the stairs and was finally ready to answer the phone after the sixth ring. But the phone did not ring a seventh time. After a long and tense pause, Burns finally picked up the receiver and yelled, "Wait!"

Of course there was no one on the line. Flood scowled at Burns and the three began to turn away to head back to what they had been doing before the phone rang. The phone rang again, this time the three were set when Chase picked up the phone at the beginning of the third ring.

"Hello?"

"Chase? This is Lt. Paris. Please put the nearest detective on the phone."

"They're both here. Which do you want, Lieutenant?"

"Flood." Paris said, selecting the more senior sleuth.

Detective Flood, listening on the other phone winced and then said, "Hi, Lieutenant."

"You're going to have to get set up to answer that phone a lot quicker, Flood. It rang six or seven times before I hung up. We don't want to miss the call do we?"

"Yes, sir. I mean no, Ma'am." Flood stammered.

Paris, sensing Flood's floundering, was tempted to push him further with a 'Don't jeopardize this mission or that little girl's life, mister!' speech, but let the young detective off the hook. "Have the techs come and gone?"

"Yes."

"Are you alone? Is the Lawyer in the room with you?"

"Yes." There was a long pause.

"Never mind. Listen. If Chase so much as shows a strange look, or does anything out of the ordinary, document it in your notes."

"OK, Boss."

"You've got my pager and cell-phone numbers?"

"Yes, Boss."

"If you get a call, from the bad guys, you do not move, other than to call me! Is that understood?"

"I got it."

"If I don't hear from you tonight I'll call you in the morning, OK?"

"OK."

"Be careful out there, detective."

"Don't worry, Boss. I helped pull the body of the Chauffeur out from the little duck pond out back. This place gives me the creeps."

Chapter 22

Diamonds In the Night

There were two detectives with Attorney Chase at the Stanton Mansion but as evening fell Kelly and Paris drove out to the neighborhood in Belmont where the little girl lived, anyway. They didn't have any major objectives, just some case discussion and some light surveillance.

Paris and Kelly drove right out of the city. Out Storrow Drive to Fresh Pond Circle. They drove up the big hills on Route 2 and on up to Belmont. Paris pulled off at the top of the hill, swung to the left then once to the right. They drove down the little girl's street until they were a few houses down from, and diagonally across from the Stanton Mansion. They pulled up to a little park with a tiny ball field and a bench overlooking the city. They got out and walked past first base and sat down on the bench where someone had brushed off the snow. It was cold out but they didn't feel it. There was a spectacular view of Cambridge and Boston below. The lights from Christmas decorations were shining from almost every house. Christmas lights seemed to be everywhere. Red and white car lights as well as building, house, and store lights twinkled and merged with the planes taking off and landing at Logan in a backdrop of stars.

Jack sighed deeply as if he could expel all the recent events from his soul.

They were quiet for a long while as they looked out over the Hub, perhaps putting things in perspective. She spoke first.

"It all seems so simple. Everything down there appears to be so orderly."

"If you really want to see simplicity and order, set your sights a little higher. Look up at those stars."

"See that dense little group of stars?" Jack pointed. "It's the Pleidaes. A compact group of glowing suns approximately the same size as our sun. Each has a good shot at having planets revolving around them, and moons around the planets. And, there are Amino acids; the building blocks of life, in the interstellar dust scattered throughout the universe. And for life to 'happen,' all you need is a few base elements, air and water, and the planet should be at a distance from a sun that is not too hot or too cold."

"What if there were three or four suns in the sky?" Jack asked and then answered, "There are probably places like that in our local galaxy alone. Imagine multiple shining orbs in the sky. Multiple moons. Glowing all night." Jack and Jesse looked up at the stars. The wind was blowing through the trees. There was no moon. The stars stood out. Planets, constellations, and faint galaxies lit the blackness. A shooting star, a meteorite, streaked straight across the heavens. Jack wondered why people hardly ever looked up at this fantastic, glorious, really big show.

"On a night like this I can't imagine not having this beautiful breathing darkness. I love the freedom from the light. I love the exquisite night, where city lights illuminate the horizon and a star-studded canopy is overhead. They say it all started with The

Big Bang." Jack was getting tired of listening to his voice drone on and realized that she must be tired of it too.

"Is that when the Nova crashed? Crashed into a Pinto, didn't it?" Jessica asked rhetorically, and added, "Well, what was before that? Something must have happened before The Big Bang?" asked Jessica.

"Before the Big Bang? Dinner and a movie."

She punched his arm.

"Simple, huh?" Jack said.

"Well, uh… yes. Yes, you are. I see it all now." She said looking at Jack with a wry smile and moved closer to him. She kissed him slowly and passionately and then asked Jack, "Do you think about these things much?"

"Yes, when I can. Unfortunately I'm continuously interrupted by petty needs. Like work, water, food, shelter, basic transportation, some clean clothes, and I shower when I can."

"I hope this was one of those days that you did," she smiled as she leaned closer in the cold night and kissed his lips softly.

Kelly had needed the touch of a beautiful woman and kissed Jessica back hungrily. Jack slid his hand through the opening between the Velcro fastenings of her ski parka and slid it along her midsection grabbing her gently. The heat from her body felt good as he held her tight to him. Her breasts stood hard against his chest and she let her left hand drop down to below his waist. He kissed her deeply. But the deep soul kiss was interrupted when the beeper in her coat pocket activated, emitting a cascade of descending scales.

"What's that? An alarm sounding the invasion in the private regions of the Paris Temple by the Roman hands and Russian fingers of Jack Kelly?"

"Let's get to the car, Jack. I left the cell-phone there." As Paris stood up and looked at the number on the pager, she looked at Jack, and then to the Stanton Mansion diagonally across the street and said, "It's coming from the house."

Jack and Jessica got back in the car and Jessica started the engine and got the heat cranking. She picked up the phone and dialed the call back number on the beeper. It rang three times and Paris was just ready to leap from the car when Detective Burns answered.

"It's Paris, what's going on?" Jessica inquired with some urgency.

"Sorry, Boss. We had to set up the recording equipment before we answered. We're jumping around here like raped apes, Lieutenant. We got a call from the kidnappers five minutes ago." Burns added, "You better drive out and listen to this."

"Kelly and I are across the street. We'll be right in."

Kelly and Paris pulled the unmarked cruiser down the driveway to the archway by the kitchen door. Paris knocked lightly on the door as they walked into the huge kitchen. A young girl's blood curdling scream greeted them loudly, startling Paris and Kelly. Lt. Paris fumbled under her parka for the .38 caliber revolver she carried. Jack reached under his coat and pulled out the .45 caliber automatic from under his left armpit but the gun slid from his cold hands and clanked loudly across the kitchen floor.

Jack flinched instinctively when his gun hit the floor and now the fight or flight response was controlling him as he looked for cover or a direction to run. He and Paris almost knocked heads as he moved left towards his fallen gun and she moved right, towards the doorway of the living room where the scream had come from.

Paris peered around the edge of the doorway to see detectives Burns and Flood standing over the tape recorder.

"Turn that fucking thing down, Flood," Burns was yelling as they both turned in surprise to see Paris and Kelly, with their guns pointing at them, peering around the corners of the doorway.

"Jesus Christ, guys!" Paris said. "Who is fucking screaming?"

Paris and Kelly holstered their guns and walked to the table where the recording equipment was set up. Burns and Flood did not say a word. They just stared at Paris and Kelly as Flood hit the play button on the recorder, this time the volume at a slightly lower level.

The sound of the ringing phone was recorded clearly. It rang four times and on the fifth, the receiver was picked up and the Lawyer's voice was heard to say, "Hello, Stanton residence."

The next voice was that of a male with a deep and raspy voice doing a poor job of imitating a Jamaican, saying, "We have the little bitch. We want $250,000 in unmarked bills, mon. Put the cash into one of those aluminum suitcases. You have twenty-four hours to get the money together, mon, and then we'll tell you what to do next. If you want to see the girl alive do exactly as we say."

"Who is this?" The Lawyer seemed to stammer. "Where's Suzanne Stanton?"

"We don't want to hurt her but we will, mon. Please cooperate and we won't. But if you defy us..." The sound of a hard slap and the unnerving loud scream of a young girl could be heard. Then the phone line went dead. The hair on the back of Jack's neck stood on end. The four detectives stood motionless and in silence as the gravity and reality of the phone call took hold of each of them.

"The good news is that Suzanne Stanton is still alive. The bad news is those fucking creeps are abusing her. If I get my way, I'd like to see them executed." Lt. Paris said.

"I could follow those orders, Lieutenant." Flood remarked with a great deal of sincerity.

"Come on, now." Jack pleaded. "Let's not talk about violating anyone's rights. Least not in front each other. It's innocent 'til proven guilty. There's good and bad in everyone. I certainly bear the Provost Brothers no animosity," Jack said as his voice got louder and louder until he was practically shouting. "I have no personal dislike against those two-timing, back-stabbing, lying, kidnapping, child abusing, mother-fucking, Mongoloid, Cro-Magnon murdering assholes."

"Jesus, Kelly," Flood said, not knowing Jack too well.

"OK. I made up the 'back-stabbing' part."

"Where do we go from here, Lieutenant?" Burns asked.

"We make a tape copy for ourselves and then get that original tape immediately to the lab so the technicians can break it down. They'll bring out the background noise, identify every sound, stress analyze the voices, see if they can pinpoint the brand of tape and where it might be sold. Then I call the Captain, he calls the Shift Commander, who calls the Bureau Commander, who calls the Chief, who calls the Mayor."

"Neck-bone connected to the head-bone," Jack interrupted.

"Yes, we'll also be calling the Neck Bone and Head Bone." Paris added, "Detective Sgt. John Abbott of the Mass. State Police and young agent Arthur Laprise of the FB fuckin' I."

Jack amused himself briefly with the realization that he wasn't on the clock and could go home anytime. But Jack was simultaneously deep in thought. A feeling of helplessness was creeping into his blood. It was the echo. He could not get the sound of Suzanne Stanton's scream to stop ringing in his ears. It bounced around inside his head but couldn't find its way out. The scream mocked Jack Kelly. It laughed at him. The screaming echo was there and would not fade away.

"Flood, how do you think the Lawyer reacted to the voice of the kidnapper?" Jack asked leaning across the table and lowering his voice to nearly a whisper.

"It was like, he knew the script and was trying to stick to it. At one point the Jamaican, if that was, in-fact, a Jamaican, sounded like he was reading and skipped a line and Mr. Chase seemed to hesitate to let the other guy finish... I don't know."

"Yeah, I got that too. How about his facial expressions?"

"I've been thinking about this long and hard. Well, not that long. But hard. Well, not that hard...." Flood sat down at the table.

"Go on, detective," Paris urged.

"I wouldn't even write this into a report, but, it's just that, Chase's eyes rolled up, he kinda... looked up into the memory corner of his brain and was reading a short script, and wanted to stick to it. And he didn't seem to be really... like, shocked about the whole phone call. Like he knew what to expect." The rookie detective spoke with conviction. Kelly agreed with him and was impressed.

"Excellent observations, detective. Paris, I recommend this young man move right up the ladder. Perhaps, even into your shoes. You'd look nice in those navy-blue pumps, Flood.'

"If your opinion meant anything, Kelly," the young detective was right again.

It was 12:30 AM on a Tuesday night. Jessica had other cases to work the next morning and she suggested she drop Kelly off and try to get a night's sleep. As Lt. Paris was giving Jack a ride home she spoke in a hushed quiet tone.

"I feel so ineffective and powerless." Paris said.

"I hear you."

"I'll brief the others and we'll formulate some kind of game plan. Maybe the lab guys will come up with something. Patrol is going to start driving by the Provost family home in East Boston every hour, running every plate on every car that stops there. There's nothing I can think of doing tonight? Maybe we can get some sleep."

"You want to stay at the office, Jesse?"

"I don't think we'd get that much sleep."

"I'll sleep when I'm dead. But I know we'd get some. Or you'd get some. And I'd get some, too. Sleep, that is. I know we'd get some, sleep, I mean." Jack said, not knowing what he meant at this point. Oh, the pull of the beast was so strong.

In a very old factory-warehouse in Southie, on the Binford Street dead end, near the piers on Atlantic Ave., Suzanne Stanton was screaming and crying as her thin frame was dragged across the old wooden floor. Pulled by her once clean and cared for blonde curls, she cried out and struggled but her captor was so much stronger. Her clothes were filthy and she was covered by dirt. She had not washed or bathed for three days. Abrasions, bruises, and dried blood covered her arms. She was being dragged down the basement stairs, pushed and pulled along the dirty cement floor and shoved forcefully back down into a six-by-four foot cast-iron coal bin cut in the back wall behind a furnace. She cried out as she was pushed into what used to be a wood and coal storage area.

"Look! Shut up! We been treatin' you good! You ate some beans. Shit! You ate more fuckin' beans than I did. We gave you a chance to use the bathroom. You should have taken the opportunity when you could. So what if my brother likes to watch? We let you scream your 'hellos' over the phone to that nice Mr. Chase."

Suzanne Stanton screamed at him. "He's trying to poison me! And I heard you talking to him on the phone. He wants to put me away in a hospital."

"And we know your friends from the police department were there. Now shut the fuck up!" the thin Provost screamed at Suzanne as she cried quietly in the dark and dirty box. The huge black cast-iron door slammed shut.

Chapter 23

Dead Stop

Jack dreamed of Johnny's Jazz and Blues Club, the hole-in-the-wall nightclub he would own someday. He dreamed he was sitting at his usual spot at the end of the bar. The club was up and operating this night and all Jack had to do was sign a few things, adjust the lighting, and make sure tonight's jazz band went onstage on time. He ordered some small Italian appetizers, some manicotti and eggplant, and a good upstate New York red table wine. A second later the food had been delivered, eaten, and a pretty new waitress removed the dishes from the bar as Jack rubbed his full belly and tasted the remnants of the pasta in the spaces between his teeth. Jack leaned back in satisfaction and lit a $14.00 Cuban cigar. Jack had never smoked a cigar that cost $14.00 and was taking stock of the expensive smoke when the waitress returned. Jack smiled and noticed the shimmer in her curly blond hair and the gleam in her bright blue eyes. She smiled back at Jack, shook her head slowly from side to side and asked him, "Aren't you going to find me?"

The smile faded from Jack Kelly's face and was replaced by a blank stare as he replied, "What?"

He was dumbfounded as she continued to look into his face. The lights and sound of the room began to fade as the young girl's face consumed Jack's attention. It was all he could see. Her face began to change slightly and started to resemble more closely the photograph he had seen of the poor little rich girl, Suzanne Stanton. Kelly wanted to remain in the dream world but he knew he was slipping out from his dreamy visit to Johnny's. She said it again, as Jack realized, from within his dream, the horror of reality.

"Aren't you going to find me?" she said, as Jack looked into the blue-eyed face of the missing child.

Jack sat bolt upright in bed, sweat beading on his forehead and trickling down the back of his neck. He walked over to the window and opened it, taking a deep breath of the cold air. He felt guilty about lazily dreaming of his nightclub while the girl suffered, perhaps, unspeakable abuse. Jack had gotten the message sent by his unconscious mind.

In his frustration, Jack did the usually unthinkable. In a major personal statement of commitment he picked up the TV's beloved remote control and threw it against the wall, plastic and batteries scattering on the floor behind the TV.

Jack was near desperate as he strained his brain trying to think of where the Provosts and the girl had gone. Why was the Provost cousin, Buxton-Smythe, killed? Did they really want the ransom money? Will they kill her, one way or the other, anyway?

At 9:45AM Jack left a message at the PD for Lt. Paris to call him and then got ready for a day of action. Soon it was late morning and Jack could no longer sit around. He would have to get out and do something. Anything, he thought. He had to shake off the feelings of inadequacy and the overwhelming feelings of helplessness that were shaking him, more and more.

Sleep When I'm Dead

Jessica Paris called and told Kelly that the forensics lab people had found several long blond hairs under the body of Buxton-Smythe Provost found at the warehouse in Southie, and they had matched them to the Stanton girl. And she told him Reno Waste Management owned the whole warehouse.

"So she was probably there and gone now. Was Bucky's next of kin notified, and if so, who might that be?" Jack asked.

"I don't know, I'll check. I know we have not released the body, yet."

"The kidnappers called at around 5:30 yesterday. Can we go out to Stantons' to see if they call again today? I can't stand the waiting! I have got to do something!"

"OK. Yes. Pick you up at 4:30." Paris promised, and she did.

Flood, Burns, Paris, and Jack were in the small living room of the Stanton Mansion awaiting a call from the kidnappers. The Lawyer, Lindon Chase, walked through several times and Jack and Paris did their best to make him feel that they did not suspect him of anything.

All four detectives jumped when the phone rang at six o'clock.

"'Anonymous,'" said Flood, reading the caller identification display and pushing the record buttons on the tape recorder.

Kelly heard the footsteps of the Lawyer scurrying from another section of the big house. Kelly involuntarily held his breath.

On the fourth ring, as Flood and Burns nodded their consent, the Lawyer and Flood both picked up receivers, the Lawyer saying, "Hello?"

"Do you have the money, mon?" the gruff voice demanded.

Chase looked a little pale as he stammered. "I... I..."

"Do you have the money, mon?" insisted the voice of an adult male, with perhaps a slight Jamaican accent.

"I can get it right away."

"I told you to get $250,000 yesterday. What the fuck do you think, I'm calling you for, man? Do you want me to send one of her fucking fingers over?" The pretence of a Jamaican accent was almost completely gone now and a Boston accent was creeping in to the caller's voice.

Chase looked puzzled. Paris whispered, a little too loudly. "How's Suzanne?"

"The girl is fine!" the kidnapper shouted, and then added, "Who the fuck is that?" Paris wasn't standing near Chase but she was next to Flood and the receiver had picked up her voice.

"That's the maid." Chase said, looking at Paris and shrugging his shoulders.

"OK. Yeah. You fuckin' 'bus chaser.'"

"That's 'ambulance chaser,'" the Lawyer corrected.

"Do you think I'm fucking stupid, you cheap mouthpiece? You prick lawyer!" The kidnapper said with quiet resignation in his voice, and then screamed, "I'll start sending body parts over by Federal Express!"

"No. No. We'll do whatever, anything we can..."

"Shut up and listen, I got 15 seconds left. We are now going to bury the girl up to her neck. Don't fuck up again, mon." The phony accent had returned.

"Don't leave her there, in the heat, too long! Please!" the Lawyer shouted into the phone, looking up to Paris for approval.

"Time's up, counselor. Have that money ready to travel by tomorrow evening or she dies. Got it, shyster?"

"Yes." Chase said with a look of bewildered puzzlement as both parties hung up.

"Did we get the trace Burns?" Paris asked the young detective.

"Disconnected at fifty-two seconds. Nope, no trace."

Chase excused himself saying he had to go and lie down. He held his hands to his chest and pranced out of the room.

"Did you see the look on his face when the kidnapper jumped on him. I don't think he expected his employees to disrespect him." Burns whispered.

"That phony Jamaican kidnapper seemed to be enjoying that a little too much. I think something wrong is going on. The script is changing. What if the Provosts decided on their own that instead of just pretending to, they were really going to ransom Sarah?"

"Suzanne!" Paris corrected Jack.

"Really ransom *Suzanne*, for the $250,000, and then take off?" Jack Kelly asked.

"Chase would never pay them that kind of money. Or they can try and get the ransom money, and then kill her anyway." Paris added.

"Did you hear the Lawyer's phrase, 'Don't leave her in the heat, too long?'" Jack asked the group quietly. "Doesn't that indicate some knowledge of where she is being held? I mean, it's freezing outside."

It was jet black outside and late as Jack left the Stanton Mansion in Belmont. Lt. Paris dropped him off at his office. Kelly needed to locate the girl before she was hurt further or killed. He picked up the old set of license plates that had been taken off of the burnt shell of Mighty Whitey from the top of his file cabinet and wiped off the soot with a paper towel. He called Ed at The Naked i in the Combat Zone. Ed got on the line and over the phone Jack could hear Ed yelling to the club patrons. It was late and he was trying to shut down the bar. "Let's go! You don't have to go home but you can't stay here… And for you honey, you can help me clean up. Sorry, Jack. There is a black Jeep Cherokee already parked down on the street for you, brother. Willie dropped it off. Keys are on the gas cap. It's in the front of the lot right across from your office."

"I love working with professionals." Jack said and headed for the door.

Kelly took the license plates down to the parking lot across Kingston Street and attached them to the beat up old 1994 black Jeep Cherokee with tinted windows. The Jeep ran well and Jack put the transferred registration into the glove box. He picked up a switchblade comb from the center console and flicked it open. "Maybe I'll buy this Jeep." Jack said, laying the comb back down and heading for the warehouse on Binford St. in Southie. The packies were closed but on Broadway he beat last-call at the mobbed-up bar the Triple O' Lounge and Jack downed a shot of Jose Cuervo Especial Gold Tequila and bought three one-pint cans of Fosters Australian beer to go. He asked the bartender if they still made Shlitz Tall Boys. The bartender, a clean-shaven twenty-five year old, had black hair, wore a Kiss-Me-I'm-Irish button on his shirt, had a strong Irish accent, and didn't know, but recommended heartily, a stout Guinness.

Kelly left with the three pints of Fosters and drove his black Jeep Cherokee to the Binford Street warehouse. He didn't know what else to do so he had returned to the last place that he knew Suzanne and her captors had been. He parked the Jeep just out of sight around the back of the building. He tried the building's front doors but they were locked. He stood out front, looking up, but there was not a light on in the building. There was a doorbell for the mammoth graveyard of books, Beverly's Book Repository, but no one answered. Jack knew this place was chosen because Reno Waste Management owned the whole building. Did Reno own any other buildings in the area? Jack didn't think that anyone still lived in the building. There were no cars parked on the street and not a sign of life. Jack pulled the flashlight out from his waistband and slipped around the corner. On the ride over, Jack had finished off a can of Fosters and thought that the dark side of the building next to the freight train yard might be a good place to take a leak.

Jack was halfway through drawing a large, yellow, mystical eyeball in the moonlit snow when he looked up and noticed the black Cadillac down in the alley next to the building under the Summer St. Bridge. The trunk was open. The Caddy looked a lot like the Provost's ride. As Jack zipped up and began to walk slowly in that direction he noticed the multiple tire tracks in the snow, running from the warehouse on Binford Street to the dirt, then the tar. The crunch of snow beneath his feet was deafening. "Jesus Christ," Jack exhorted under his breath. The dead-end street was ordinarily covered with ground down crushed glass and tiny metal fragments from the freight car shipments of junk. But tonight the snow covered everything and turned tunnels, trestles, train tracks, trains, from locomotive to caboose, a soft, clean white. The bridges, cars, trucks, and scrap heaps were now God's snowy sculptures.

As he approached the Caddy he didn't see anyone. Jack pulled his gun and shined his light into the interior of the car. The Cadillac was definitely the Provost's car. It looked abandoned. The keys were in the ignition. Maybe they were hoping someone would drive away with it. Or maybe they would report it stolen.

Jack put his .45 back in its holster. He got into the driver's seat and turned the key. The car started right up. Kelly shut the engine off and stepped out from the vehicle.

There appeared to be somewhat of a path from the trunk of the Caddy to the closest building, the same warehouse at 44 Binford, but a back door about 50 yards away. Kelly instinctively began following the trail. As he walked between two abandoned washing machines he heard a noise and looked to the left.

It was then that he felt the somewhat familiar and unmistakable thud of a blunt object on the right side of his thick skull.

Chapter 24

Fade To Black

Kelly was unceremoniously dragged by his hair and one wrist down the dirty gravel path, through the cellar doors in the back of the warehouse, down a few stairs, and into the cellar of the six-story red brick abandoned building. He was dropkicked onto the cement floor and still hadn't regained consciousness. The metal pipe had left quite a goose egg on the right side of Kelly's head.

"I got a present for you, Billy." Gino Provost yelled from under his backward worn black WWF baseball cap and through his biker beard as he leaned back and admired his catch.

Billy Provost charged into the room. He wore black denim coveralls and a black dress shirt over his skinny body and his arms and neck were covered with jailhouse tattoos. The thin Provost Brother had his ever-present chauffeur hat over his long black hair.

"I don't believe it! That fuckin' dick that has been a motherfucking plague on this family." Billy kicked Kelly square in the stomach. Then he knelt down by Jack and grabbed him by the front of his shirt pulling him up with his left hand and punched him in the face four times.

"Wake up, you fuck!"

Billy threw Kelly back down on the floor in disgust. Blood began to pool under Jack's face from cuts that ran from his lips, nose and right eyelid.

"Did you check for his gun or a knife?" Billy asked Gino.

"Yeah… " Gino said rather unconvincingly, handing over to Billy, Jack Kelly's .45 automatic.

At that moment the brothers heard the ringing of a cell phone coming from Jack's pant's pocket. As the phone rang, Billy looked over at Gino and said, "I guess you checked him real good, huh, Gino? So good, you didn't find the fucking cell phone in his pants pocket? So fucking good, you checked him, that he probably has a fucking couple of knives, so I can get my fucking guts sliced out on to the cellar floor, here Gino? Is that how fucking good you checked this motherfucker, Gino?"

"Just a pat down." Gino said, sheepishly.

"'Just a pat down.' Oh? Now you're a fuckin' cop, Gino? Did you violate his rights? Did you advise him of his right to hurt our family, Gino? How 'bout his right to fuckin' die for shooting your brother, you porky fuck."

"Don't call me Porky." Gino said as they both looked down at the unconscious Kelly.

The cell phone was still ringing and Billy picked it out of Jack's pocket and placed it on the ground. "You have the right to shut the fuck up," he said and stomped the phone into pieces.

Gino, in an effort to redeem himself, checked all Kelly's pockets, finding the black mini-mag flashlight with "Kelly" written on the side and scooping the $65 from Jack's pocket into his own.

"You sure nobody else was with him?" Billy asked Gino.

"Check it out and I'll put that cheap dick in the coal bin next to the girl. Later on, we'll have a little kangaroo court for Mr.

Kelly. He's got some payback comin' for taking out Rick." Gino said with a sickly evil smile.

Billy grabbed a two-foot long metal pipe and a baseball bat and shuffled out the door.

The portly Gino took hold of Kelly's ankles, put them under his arms and began pulling him along the cement floor, across the room, and toward the furnace.

"Holy shit," Gino said and took a minute to catch his breath, dropping one of Kelly's legs and throwing his baseball hat into the corner.

He dropped Jack's other leg and opened the cast-iron door to one of two dark and dirty bins in the wall where coal was once stored. An unconscious Jack Kelly was dragged and pushed over the several boards at the bottom of the coal bin's doorframe, feet first. Gino closed the large black cast-iron door on the top of Jack's bloody and swollen face, knocking him back into the old coal bin.

Chapter 25

Voice In the Night

"Now I lay me down to sleep, I bless the Lord my soul to keep. And if I die before I wake, I give The Lord my soul to take. Now I lay me down to sleep…"

The girl's chanted words echoed into Jack's ears and rolled around, circling slowly, closer and closer to his inner ear and the transceivers that make syntax coherent. But Jack Kelly did not hear them.

Jack knew he was dreaming and he purposefully walked into his nightclub, Johnny's Blues and Jazz Club. There were only about twenty-five customers scattered around the small club but Jack knew that the power-suited workforce employed in this corner of downtown Boston would soon be hearing that ending day bell and heading toward the more popular watering holes in the area. Jack sat at the end of the bar and his favorite bartender, Jimmy, got him a large Dewar's scotch on the rocks with a twist of lemon. Jack breathed the air in through his nose, taking in the smells of the club. His eyes roamed the small club looking for anything out of place as he began to plan the operations for the upcoming night. He listened intently to the classic jazz tape-loops that he had personally recorded for use at the club. But the Miles, Mingus, and Monk seemed to fade as Kelly heard a voice in the background coming out of the speakers. It was a cadence. Like poetry. It was a young girl's voice...

"Now I lay me down to sleep..."

Jack sipped the scotch and the jazz was again dominant. He idly watched a pretty dark haired waitress move across the room in front of the stage as the cadence began again to emerge from behind the piped-in jazz.

"Now I lay me down to sleep..."

Jack shook his head and looked down at the scotch and then took a sip. He tasted it slowly, sucking his tongue against the roof of his mouth. But it was like he had a cold and his tastebuds were not working. Was that dirt in his mouth? What was going on here? He thought that since he was dreaming, he just needed to concentrate more on imagining the taste of the scotch, remembering it. But his senses were fading in and out. The jazz was being drowned out by the young girl's voice reverberating inside Jack's head.

"Now I lay me down to sleep, I bless the Lord my soul to keep. And if I die before I wake, I give the Lord my soul to take. Now I lay me..."

It was jet black. Jack shuddered and his left eye popped open. The right eye was swollen shut. He did not know where he was. He was sweating, sore all over, and had a pounding headache the size of the old Boston Garden. He could taste the blood in his mouth as he tried to swallow. He tried to move his legs and arms, one at a time. They seemed stiff and sore but not broken. He reached up and felt the bump on the side of his head as some memory began to return to his addled brain. He stopped his systematic damage check and his shuffling. In the enclosed coal-bin he heard Suzanne's muffled voice echoing from somewhere nearby him.

"And if I die before I wake, I give the Lord my soul to take…"

Jack spit blood and coal dust out of his mouth and ran his tongue around the roof of his mouth. It was so dark. Kelly bit off tiny pieces of skin off the inside of his top lip and spit them out as he struggled to move his aching limbs. He lay back on the chunks of coal and stretched up his arms. He slid his hands along, feeling the black coal-dust clinging to the arched roof of the coal bin. Was this some kind of furnace? It was so black. Jack saw a thin crack of light, above his head, at the top of the cast-iron door.

Approaching footsteps echoed louder and louder. The heavy metal door creaked loudly as it swung open, letting in what seemed to be a flood of light, blinding Jack. He heard muffled voices and squinted into the light, trying to shield his eyes. A strong hand grabbed his wrist and pulled him across the bed of coals and out the door. Jack covered his head with his arms reflexively, wondering if he was about to be kicked, punched, or hit with an object.

"Drag him out so I can get his fucking feet, Gino!" the gruff voice, yelled.

Jack was a wounded animal. He was too hurt to struggle as he was dragged from the hole, but would save his energy for a last ditch effort if needed. His eyes began to adjust to the naked light bulb hanging from the ceiling. He was glad to be out of the hole and did not want to go back. Jack was not compliant, but was overpowered by the two Provost Brothers, one pulling his feet and the other holding his arms. Then Jack felt the zap of a stun gun in his ribs. He didn't pass out, but the voltage took its toll and Jack stopped resisting, staring straight ahead, somewhat out of focus. Jack thought of how, in the old days, a cow would be taken to the slaughterhouse. He pictured the beast being hit in the head with a sledgehammer, dazed and confused, its legs beginning to crumble.

The Provost Brothers dragged Jack across the floor, up some stairs, and into a larger room with a wooden floor in the brick factory building. The kitchen was bare accept for a table and several rickety wooden chairs, a huge meat freezer, a refrigerator, and a sink. Jack was coming around but maintained the distant look in his eyes while he took stock of his surroundings. As he lay crumpled in the middle of the floor the brother Jack knew as Skinny rolled him onto his side and crooked his legs.

"I'm really not that bad a guy, Detective Kelly." Skinny whispered in Jack's ear.

Jack mumbled back, semi-coherently, "I'm sure you were one of the nicest guys on your cellblock. And now that you're out of jail I bet you feel like a new woman. But you run with the dogs, you get fleas."

"Oh come on, Mr. Kelly," the thin Billie Provost pleaded.

"You hang around garbage long enough you start to stink. I know its' your brother whose been pushing you to do these things. He's the fly in the ointment. The monkey wrench thrown into the gears. The saboteur. The bad apple that spoils the barrel. The lump in the gravy. The hair in the pie."

Skinny stood up shaking his head from side-to-side and looked down on Jack as Gino stood next to him. Jack coughed and looked out through the small kitchen window to see beads of rain water collecting.

A wet snow had crossed over to light drizzle and then the rain became steadier outside and had finally exploded. Soon the torrential pounding on the tin cars outside drowned out any other sound. The lightning was flashing and flickering like a bad neon light bulb in an all night Laundromat.

The other brother, Gino, stuck a wooden kitchen chair under Jack's ass and they both lifted him up to a sitting position. Skinny ripped a two-foot strip of duct tape off the roll, strapping Jack's left wrist to the chair arm. Jack tried to jump up when he heard the tape ripping off the roll but the overweight Gino pushed him down. Skinny quickly taped the right and left wrists down and then his feet to the chair's legs.

"You think you're fuckin' smart, don't you wise ass?" Skinny screamed into Jack's face. His hot breath stank of the garlic-laced pizza big Gino had picked up at the North End Regina's. Skinny slapped Jack across the top of his head.

"What are we gonna do with this fuck, Gino?" Billy said.

"Don't say my fuckin' name, Billy!"

"Oh shit, man. I think he knows who we are, for Christ's sake!"

"We're gonna have ta…" And then Skinny's voice trailed off, he looked away from Jack and he said to his fat brother Gino in a muffled voice, "Kill 'em." He made the gesture of a knife sliding across his neck.

The room was lit by two light bulbs hanging on black wire. Billy walked across the room and got a Bud Light from the dusty refrigerator, tossing it to his brother and getting another for himself. Billy cracked open the can, took a long drink, and belched.

"I'll take a frosty brewski, man, if you can spare it." Jack's hoarse voice rang out as the two Provost Brothers stared at him in disbelief.

"You know what? You lack respect, Bitch." The heavyweight Gino said, struggling to pull Jack's .45 from his own waistband. Jack recognized his voice from the call to the Belmont Mansion.

He walked toward Jack in a menacing and agitated manner. Jack didn't have much going for him but he clung to the only thing he knew. That wise-ass wit of his.

"Hey? Where's that half-ass phony Jamaican accent you've been sporting, mon. Have you guys been shell-shocked, mon, by too many planes flying over East Boston on their landing approach to Logan? And who you callin' Bitch? Do you want this dance, Porky? Cut my hands loose, Fat Boy. I'll show you the Southie Shuffle. Drop you like you was a bad habit. And I'll save the last dance for your Skinny rat brother."

The two Provosts moved toward Kelly. Jack yelled, "I've got a gun!"

The brothers stopped, looked at Jack, looked at Jack's gun in Gino's hand, back at each other, and then at Jack again.

"Its' another gun!" Jack said a little less convincingly.

"Its not here. It's at home. But I've got another gun." Jack added mildly.

"Let's boil some water, Billy!" Gino said, with an evil grin. "See how he likes that. You like hot water, you fuck? That butler at the girl's house went for a little swim in the cold water of the duck pond. You can drown in a pan of water, you know, cop-fuck. We got a spaghetti pot, Billy?"

"That takes too fuckin' long, Gino!"

"Yeah, but we got some spaghetti and we can cook it up first."

"Shut up, Fat Boy!"

"But I'm hungry, Billy! And don't call me Fat Boy!"

"I know," said Kelly, "That is so insensitive. You skinny bastard."

Gino lit a Marlboro and the smoke curled up towards a light bulb. He passed it to Skinny and said, "Let's teach him some respect." And he began to slowly wave the flame of the lighter in front of Kelly's face.

Gino hesitated and Billy added, "For Rick," regarding the brother that Jack had shot square in his large white forehead while at the Charles Circle gas station.

Jack's eyes grew larger as Gino moved in. Billy passed the cigarette to Gino and got behind Jack holding him tightly as he struggled and rocked the wooden chair. Gino stuck the hot end of his cigarette down onto Kelly's forearm, grinding it into the flesh. Jack could hear the sizzle and smell the burning flesh as he struggled. He shook and pushed with his legs but could not shake the hot coal of the cigarette butt.

"AAAAHHHHGGGGG!" Jack Kelly screamed into the cavernous factory building with all his might. The pounding rains and the rumble and screech of the locomotive engines hooking up with long lines of freight cars in the rail yard drowned out his repeated cries.

"Shut up, Bitch!" Billy screamed and zapped Kelly three quick times in the ribs with the stun gun. Gino hit Kelly on the legs several times with a broken pool cue. Jack's screams echoed throughout the building. Gino ripped off a foot of duct tape and stretched it across Jack Kelly's mouth.

"What happens if I stun his head?" Billy asked.

"I don't know, Bill," Gino answered, smiling.

Billy stuck the two prongs of the stun gun into the back of Jack's skull and pushed the button. Jack's head shot forward involuntarily as he saw the electricity spark across his eyes from his upper eyelids to his lower. Kelly was numb with pain and felt punch-drunk. His shoulders twitched slightly.

Jack was taking another beating and resembled the monster that Dr. Frankenstein had assembled. His clothes were dirty and ripped. His hair and skin were covered by soot. Blood from his scalp had trickled down his swelling forehead and ran down the side of his neck where it had dried. Under the silver duct tape his lips where split and swollen to Ubangi proportions.

But Jack managed to look up sweetly, with what would have been a soft smile, and in a singsong voice he mumbled something under the duct tape. The Provost Brothers looked quizzically at each other and skinny Billy said, "What?" And again Jack smiled and mumbled louder.

"I think you've blown his fuse, Billy," Gino said as he ripped the tape off Jack's mouth. "Now, what did you say, cop-fuck?"

"I said, thank you, boys. My headache is completely gone." Jack said with slurred speech, unable to hold his head up.

Fat Gino half-heartedly attempted to shove the pool cue into Jack's mouth. But Kelly wasn't taking it. Jack smiled, looked up, and said, "You pussy-boys like a little foreplay don't you? Why don't you just come out of the closet? Maybe you'd feel better if you slapped the little girl around for a while. By the way, are you girly-men doing each other? You're gay guys, right? Butt blasters. Well, different strokes, if you know what I mean. You ride the baloney pony, huh? At least your brother took it like a man when I put a bullet in his forehead."

Gino swung the pool cue hard, breaking off the fat end as it hit Jack across the top of his head. The chair, with Jack still in it, landed back on the dirty warehouse floor. Jack Kelly was out cold.

Chapter 26

The Soul Brothers

    The Musician had not heard from Jack for three days. He had left messages for Kelly on his office answering machine and cell phone voice mail with no return call. But Kelly had been known to take off for days at a time and didn't report in to anybody. He would take off for the islands on a boat. Sometimes he'd drive up the Maine coast or down to the Cape and walk the beaches for a couple of days. He had been doing this more often since his schoolteacher fiancée died.
    The Musician began to sniff around. He called Area A. Lt. Paris hadn't heard a word. The only movement on the case of the missing eight-year-old girl had been to contact every agency that could help, distributed flyers at Logan, the train and subway stations, and bus depot. The TV and newspapers were running pictures. The usual teletypes had gone out on regional and nationwide law enforcement networks. And the FBI had scheduled another task force meeting at Area A for tomorrow afternoon. And they expected Jack Kelly to be there.
    The Musician called Cooper, Kelly's long time photographer and blues guitar playing friend. Nowadays Cooper was a bit

older and had to play live music with the band a lot less and be the professional photographer more. Cooper is a bright guy, heading towards fifty, with short well-groomed hair and round penetrating eyes. He critically analyzed everything through his big corrective transition glasses. He was well read and knowledgeable on a wide variety of subjects. Just like any of the typical know-it-alls almost everyone knew. Cooper and Kelly had bet on every NFL game played for the last fifteen years and they kept in touch regularly.

"Hello."

"Cooper?"

"Yes. I know that golden-toned voice. That Basso Profundo. It's the Big M, isn't it? The Musical Man From Southie. Who lives in a shoe and has so many kids he doesn't know what to do."

"Hey, Coop. How's it goin'?"

"Well, I couldn't perform last night. Couldn't get it up last night."

"You mean, sexually?" Willie asked.

"No! I couldn't get it up to perform as Hamlet at the Wilbur Theatre for the Queen of England. Yes, sexually." Coop confessed. "Poker game next Monday night. You in?"

"Yeah. How's 'bout Jack? He gonna play?" The Musician asked.

"Sure. Ed, Andy, Brownie, me, you, and Jack if he's around."

"You heard from the boy?"

"Jack? No. Not for about three or four days. He's hot on the trail, you know. Well, you been workin' with him, right? The little girl from Belmont, that's in all the papers and on the TV, right?"

"Yes, but I haven't heard from him in three days, either. I don't like it. Was he going away, or anything? That pretty blonde up in Maine, maybe?"

"He didn't tell me about it." Cooper said.

"No. If he's working a case I doubt if he took off. He would have said something. I left a few messages on his machine, but no word. I called his cell phone day before yesterday, I thought someone picked up, I heard loud noise for a second and the phone went dead. Now it says, 'Out of service.'"

"That's a bit odd, no?" said Cooper, who is usually much more involved in the misadventures of Jack Kelly and added, "So, where's the young heiress and who killed the servant guy, ah, the chauffeur up in Belmont? I heard, well I read it in the Boston Globe, his neck was crushed in by the limo's power windows and then he was dragged out to the pond in the backyard and drowned."

"I don't know."

"Hey, Willie? You gonna tell me the Joke-of-the-Day?"

"Nah..."

Cooper was astonished, and said, "You ran out of jokes? Are you kidding me?"

"Yeah, I am for sure. Here you go. A young man walked into a barroom and sat down at the bar... 'What can I get you?' says the bartender.

'I want 6 shots of Rum,' responded the young man.

So the bartender lines up six shots and the young man starts drinking one after the next. So the bartender says, 'Six shots? Are you celebrating something?'

'Yeah, my first blow job,' the young man answered.

'Well, in that case, let me give you a 7th on the house.' The bartender offered.

'No offense, sir,' the young man said, 'but if 6 shots won't get rid of the taste, nothing will.'"

Cooper raised up his large frame and laughed saying, "You are one kooky, crazy, gone cat, man. Too hip to trip, Willie."

"I gotta find Jack. I know he wanted me to chase down some leads. Something's not right. You have him call me as soon as you hear from him, OK?"

The Musician decided to head out in search of Jack. He wasn't quite sure where he would begin. Willie's wife asked him to stay home tonight but he grabbed his van's keys and left her standing by the door of their second floor walk up on M Street. He left his nine children, six of who were home and monopolizing the TV and one-and-a-half bathrooms. He quietly made his escape.

He drove the few miles from Southie to Jack Kelly's office in Chinatown. He noticed Jack hadn't scooped his mail from the downstairs mailbox and climbed the four flights to the office. The outer doors were open but the inner doors were locked and nothing seemed to be out of place. Willie knocked loudly. If Jack were in his office or in his tiny kitchen and bedroom in the back, a TV would be on. It was the soundtrack of Kelly's life. Jack might not be watching it. But it would be on. As well as some music. Loud music. Jazz, blues, rock, classical. Even while he was working. Willie Ellis Crawford knew Jack always had music playing.

The Musician drove down A Street to 44 Binford Street, toward the old factory warehouse. There were a small group of five young blacks hanging around the loading dock by a makeshift basketball hoop at 42 Binford. They had shoveled away the wet snow and cleared off a court. The young men wore similar red and gold jackets with lettering on the back. Several even wore their hair in the old afro-style. They had the requisite boom-box radio blasting out the hip-hop voice of FM radio. "This is

JAMN 94.5 Boston with a shout out to Mouse in New Bedford. Listen while I'm dropping Dr. Dre with Eminem asking, did you 'Forget About Dre?'" This intro was followed by a thumping bass and backed by a synthesized drum machine and the staccato poetry of the young rappers.

The musician got out of his van mumbling to his self, "Just sit back and watch the magic." He stepped into the snow, his long brown hair blowing in the strong wind coming out of the rail yard. Willie wore no winter jacket, just his white sneakers, jeans, and a brightly colored Jimi Hendrix T-shirt.

The young thin black man stopped bouncing the basketball and coughed into his hand the word "Honky," and the others giggled. One said, "Shit," and they began to posture and pose. The smallest kid stood out in front of the pack, crossed his arms, tilted his head back and looked down his nose at Willie.

The Musician took a few steps in their direction and the biggest kid stood up, intently staring straight back at Willie, placing one hand in the small of his back. A sign the Musician understood.

"Easy, brothers," Willie said getting to within 10 feet and stopping.

"What makes you think we're brothers?" the smaller said.

"Hey. We are all brothers. I got seven blood at home and five sisters." Willie said, affecting a street rap. "Shit, the only birth control my family practiced was when my old man got so drunk he passed out."

One kid started chuckling loudly and then stopped abruptly when he saw nobody else was laughing.

"He's the White Devil." One kid said, trying to incite the group.

"Yeah, so I'm white."

"White? Your ass could provide light in a cave, Whitey," the kid said.

"Hey," The Musician said holding up one hand. "And I ain't the Devil. But I ain't afraid of the Devil. I been married to his sister for 17 years."

"You got any money, Whitey?" the smallest said.

"Hey! My father was black," Willie lied, "and my mother was a white missionary. Well, she was in the missionary position, anyway. I grew up on the streets of the Berry. That's right. Roxbury. Tremont, Columbus, and Mass. Ave. Now you got to give me my props or I'll turn you upside down and check your pockets. I will school you 'cuz you ain't representin' you shaming. That's right. See what I'm sayin'?" The Musician was walking back and forth and waving his arms but the boys were not in the least bit intimidated.

"Crazy cracker. Must be slammin' crack," the little leader said.

"Gimme the rock." The musician motioned for the basketball.

"What the fuck kinda game you got?" The kid with the ball said adding, "Cracker time?"

With that they all laughed.

"Life is like basketball," Willie began. "Or basketball is like life... a series of victories and defeats. But what is it really all about? It's how you handle those victories and defeats. If you can take something positive from each defeat and each victory, then you on the..." and he shouts, "road to freedom!"

"OK, Coach. What are you? Martin Luther Queen?" the smallest said, getting hi-fives all around.

"OK. But you got to give me my props." The Musician insisted.

"Why we gotta give you anything?"

"Hey man, before the drugs, the booze, and the hookers, I used to be somebody. Yeah. I was an actor. That's right. You ever see 'The Warriors?' And I did the death scene in 'Raging Bull,' with Bobby DeNiro. Yeah. They paid me to die… Just like the Red Sox."

Nothing. Tough crowd. But the thin brother shot over the basketball with a quick bounce pass. Willie scooped it up and got the ball spinning on the end of his thumb.

"I am representin'. On the local b-ball courts, they call me 'White Chocolate.'" Willie said, bouncing the ball through his legs, around his back, down one arm and up the other. He had reduced the situation to a stand-up comedy battle showdown and started to draw on his banked reserves of vaulted shtick.

"You are one fuckin' crazy motherfucker… White Chocolate," the smaller guy said in disgust and disbelief as Willie stood before them with the basketball spinning flawlessly on top of his thumb.

"Crazy enough to know, we got to get along. We *got* to get along. And learn to speak Spanish, if you know what I mean." The Musician delivered the last words with a wink and a nod, still spinning the ball.

"Hey! I'm half Spanish," the big guy on the stairs and in the back said as he started to step forward, pointing at Willie. The Musician began to back up saying, "Let me esplain… my muchos macho hombre brother, so you never has to ax me again."

Willie's eyes darted from left to right, looking for any possible avenue of escape as the larger brother said, "You' in that band with Reggie's brother Shawn. That Southie band there… Uh… uh," the big guy said.

"The Back Bay Beats," Willie offered as the air went out of his sails. Oh, the crossover abilities of the talented operative. He had enjoyed the confrontational rapport and repartee of the street delinquents.

"These guys are Phat!" the large brother yelled enthusiastically to the others, pointing, walking closer to Willie and putting his arm around his shoulders. The Musician glowed in the moment, until the young man added, "They double-billed with RUN-DMC back in the day. That's how old school. They are beyond Old School. They are ancient." The Brother continued as Willie shrank. "They are older than dirt. They are…"

"OK, OK. Thanks…" The Musician said humbly.

"We are The Soul Brothers," the little leader said turning to show Willie the words embroidered on the back of his jacket. "Cool, huh? Its retro."

"Yes. Maximum cool."

Then Willie gave them The Joke-of-the-Day.

"Hey listen Brothers. There's this old, like 88 year old, rich, white dude, lives in a mansion by the ocean, right. Well, everyone in town is amazed when he gets his young wife pregnant. She goes to the hospital and has a baby and the nurse says to the old dude, 'How do you do it?'

'Gotta keep the motor running,' the old man says.

"Next year the young wife goes to the hospital and has another baby. The nurse says to the old man, 'Again? How do you do it?'

'You gotta keep the motor running,' says the old man.

"Next year he comes into the hospital with his young wife, and she has a baby boy.

The nurse, holding the baby, says to the old man, 'How did you do this?'

'Gotta keep the motor running,' the old man says.

And the nurse says, holding up the baby, 'Well, you better change your oil, 'cuz this ones black.'"

The young black men were falling on the stairs and holding their sides.

"I can see my job here is done," The Musician said turning back toward his van.

"Look, guys, really though, have you seen a white dude, 'Honky' if you will, by the way I haven't heard that one since 1972, he's about 5'11" reddish brown hair, medium build... no facial hair...drives a black Jeep...tinted windows.... No hat...?"

By the look on the dark skinned Soul Brother's faces, he knew the answer. "How 'bout a thin, skinny-skinny, white guy, pale, six-foot, chauffeur's hat...in a black Cadillac?"

"Well, that's life in the big city." Willie said and got back in the van.

He had driven right down to the front of 44 Binford Street where Bucky's bloody body and strands of Suzanne's hair had been found and where the trail went cold. But Willie didn't see Jack's black Jeep Cherokee with tinted windows that sat 200 yards away, right where Jack had left it parked behind the building. And Willie didn't know that Jack Kelly and Suzanne Stanton lay half-dead in two coal bins about four hundred yards away. So close, yet so far.

Chapter 27

The Long and The Short

The Musician waved, bidding his newfound brothers ado and decided to cruise by the Lawyer's office. Maybe Jack was doing some surveillance in that neighborhood. Jack would probably see Willie before Willie saw him. The Musician knew Jack's white Crown Vic had burned to a crisp at the Charles Circle gas station and Willie had delivered Jack's rented black 1994 Jeep Cherokee, with 196,000 miles on it and knew what it looked like.

Willie drove out Comm. Ave through Kenmore Square and to the building at Harvard Ave. in the Brighton section of Boston. He parked, bought a paper, and walked in and out of the lobby at the Lawyer's building. No Jack. He surreptitiously walked past the Lawyer's office up the stairs and it looked closed. He called Jack's cell phone again from a payphone but there was still no answer. A robotic voice said "out of service."

Willie mumbled and wondered aloud if he was wasting time at this location as he watched two knee-soxed and uniformed schoolgirls walk past giggling to themselves.

"Hoodsies are my favorite treat. Short and sweet and good to eat."

It was now 7:45pm and The Musician was shooting in the dark, but he took a ride by the girl's mansion in Belmont. He saw no activity there and Willie didn't think anybody was there until he saw a light in the back kitchen go on. He parked his blue Econoline van by the little park overlooking the twinkling lights of Cambridge and Boston. The Musician was a fairly talented operative, for a part-time professional. He could talk his way out of a dead end. If the truth be known, he developed the talent walking through Southie's toughest neighborhoods carrying a violin case, from the ages of 6 to 11.

He slipped out of the van and made his way down the driveway. He looked into the garage and saw Attorney Chase's cream-colored Mercedes parked alongside a cranberry Mercedes limo then walked on to the mansion. He walked past the kitchen doors to the window and saw the Lawyer using the wall phone. He was talking to Skinny. All Willie heard was "What the fuck is he doing there? You fuckin' guys brought him in. His connection is to you! You will have to take care of him. No! I don't want to know. And clean her up and take care of her, no damaged goods; this has gone far enough. I am going to cash this thing in…" and "OK. Like you say, keep him secure and we'll dump the body later."

The Musician was intrigued, to say the least. He knew right then and there he would have to keep a tail on the Lawyer. He wished he had some way to tell somebody, Cooper or Lt. Paris, what he had heard. He thought Kelly should have provided him with a two-way portable, or a cell-phone, or something. The Musician thought about going on strike, or asking Kelly for more money, but he knew he would help out Jack anytime he needed it. Willie wasn't a professional operative, he was just a guy Jack used from time to time.

The Lawyer hung up the phone and Willie moved back from the kitchen and walked out of the driveway. He got back in the van and pulled it up a little closer and began his surveillance. The Musician was just starting to doze when the Lawyer pulled out of the garage with the cream colored Mercedes. He followed the car out of the neighborhood, down Route 2, Memorial Drive, and across the BU Bridge. A couple of lefts and rights and the Lawyer parked behind his condo on Green Street in Brookline. Willie watched as Chase did his funny little light-in-the-loafers walk and swished into the building.

The Musician settled into the surveillance until the Lawyers third floor condo lights went out, about an hour and a half later, at 11:45. Willie knew that if he stayed vigilant all night he would not be in any shape to continue in the morning. The Lawyer was going to sleep and since he had no food or drink, Willie decided to do the same. He headed home to catch five hours, stock-up on food, and grab some surveillance equipment. He would need a camera, clothes for different situations, his wife's cell phone, and since he didn't have a Mass. License-To-Carry a Firearm he would bring a baseball bat. It was his weapon of choice.

He didn't have Kelly's authorization to work for these hours. That would be one more item to write down onto his list of demands when he went on strike. This time Jack had gone too far. "Son-of-a-bitch doesn't tell anybody what he's doing… where he's going… Working without a fuckin' net," the Musician mumbled as he pushed his wife over onto her side of the bed and pulled the covers over his head.

Jack Kelly was still asleep, waking slowly this morning from his dream world. Although still half-dreaming, he was trying to remember a poem he had to memorize when he was in grade school. His lips moved as he mumbled, "Out from the night that covers me, black as a pit from pole to pole, I thank whatever gods may be for my unconquerable soul." He felt the distant pain, but struggled to remember, "Out of the felt circumstance… bloodied but unbowed… Out to the bludgeoning of chance, my head is bloodied but unbowed."

No! It was all wrong. He couldn't focus. And why was he so uncomfortable? He tried again to remember the William Ernest Henley poem Invictus he had learned as a schoolboy.

"Out from the night that covered me, black as a pit, from pole to pole. I thank whatever gods may be, for my unconquerable soul… Under the blud… Under the bludge… of chance I have not winced or cried aloud…" Jack was waking.

He wondered how long he had been unconscious. Was it a couple hours or a couple of days? He knew he was hungry, tired, hurt, and filthy.

He felt the dryness in his mouth and his swollen upper lip. His right eye was still swollen shut. In the darkness he shuddered, even though it was not cold. His mind was addled and tired. He thought of sitting in a chair in the sun. He imagined breathing in fresh air and maybe sipping a drink. A Cape Codder with Grey Goose vodka, Ocean Spray cranberry juice, and a wedge of fresh lime. And some shrimp cocktail with fresh squeezed lemon. And maybe some lobster meat and melted butter to dip it in. And fresh bread. Baked Pesto encrusted Salmon, smoked Bluefish with a dill sauce. Or just some crackers with a light cheddar cheese. Jack was easy to please. He didn't want much. He didn't need much. Just the good things in life. The things that mattered. What was everybody running around worrying about anyway? Life could be OK. Life could be good. As long as you had some money in the bank. A good job. A good supportive family structure. Medical insurance. Good health. Great looks. A future.

It's hopeless.

"Beyond this place… of wrath and tears, looms but the horror… of the shade yet he still… or they still… will find me unafraid?' Who? 'The… the… menace of the years, finds and shall find, me unafraid…" Jack's voice grew stronger as he struggled to remember the last few lines. "I am the captain of my ship… the master of my soul."

Then Kelly heard the young girl's voice singing back, a child's nursery rhyme.

"Two little monkeys jumping on the bed. One fell off and bumped his head. Mama called the doctor and the doctor said. 'No more monkeys jumping on the bed.'"

"Hello?" Jack heard the small voice and was startled.

"Hello?" the girl's voice sounded weak and afraid.

"Hi. Are you Suzanne Stanton?" Kelly asked.

Chapter 28

Who's Your Daddy?

Although his wife did not stir, the Musician awoke in the morning when his five-year-old jumped across the bed at 6AM with the German Shepherd chasing him. It seems that the boy, this one The Musician named John Lee after John Lee Hooker, stole the dog's favorite tennis ball and had been taunting the hapless canine for half an hour. The musician looked at the clock.

"John Lee, what's going on, here? Jesus H. Christ! It's 6 O'clock."

"Mommy says that you shouldn't take the Lord's name's veins," his boy said.

The Musician washed, put on the clothes he had laid out the night before, picked up the duffel bag he had packed, ate a handful of vitamins, drank a carbonated water, kissed the boy, told him to go wake up Mommy and headed out the door.

He pulled up to the Lawyer's neighborhood condo at 6:48. He had planned to be there early enough so that he could have seen the lights in the Lawyer's apartment come on. But the cream colored Mercedes was still parked in the rear of the building. He hit the local convenience store for coffee and a bagel. Then he set up for the surveillance by jockeying for a parking space that allowed him to see the front doors of the building and the Mercedes. He took one sip of coffee and used his wife's cell phone to call Sgt. Paris at the Area A station but she wasn't in. He checked Jack Kelly's office phone and left another message. He dialed Kelly's cell phone, but it was still "Out of service."

"Who are you?" Suzanne asked.

"Jack Kelly. I'm a private investigator. I was asked by Ric George, your chauffeur, to help the police find you."

"Oh, I knew Daddy would find me," the girl said, confusing Jack.

"No honey… your chauffeur, Ric…" Jack shouted into the corners of the coal bin.

"Ric *is* my Daddy, Mr…"

"Kelly." Jack said inaudibly as he stared ahead, into the darkness. Jack hadn't realized that Suzanne Stanton knew Ric George was her natural father. Then he spoke up, louder this time, "Kelly. Jack Kelly."

"Mr. Kelly, Daddy Ric said we had to keep it quiet a little longer. He told me that after Mother and Daddy Stanton sank in the boat, that Mother's last will and testament told that Mother and Ric had an affair and I was born and Daddy Ric would get a lot of money.

"Daddy Stanton didn't mind so much. He had his own friend. He was a homosexual, Mr. Kelly. I know what that is. It means he likes the same kind. And he and his friend, who was Mr. Chase, would bring young men over the house. I would see them. And listen to them after Mother or Daddy Ric would make me go to bed, Mr. Kelly. I'd sneak down and sit on the staircase."

Jack's head was swimming. Suzanne sounded a lot older and more sophisticated than Jack imagined she would be.

"Call me Jack. How old are you?"

"I'll be nine next month, January. Daddy Stanton has been good to us, Momma said, and he was upset about Ric being my real Daddy and all, but he said Ric was willing to do right by me and it was 'Best for the child,' so…. Anyways, Momma basically was the boss, anyway."

"A familiar refrain," Jack said to no one in particular.

"What?" Suzanne yelled through the wall.

"I'm sure they all loved you, Suzy," Jack yelled back.

"I heard them hitting and hurting you." The young girl's kind words brought a swell of emotion up in Jack's chest and throat.

"We'll get out of here Suzanne, you'll see." Jack said as he began to feel, push, lift, and explore the door with his hands. It was so very dark and the coal under his back shifted with his movements. After a minute, Jack said, "These coal bins were built in 1924 for US Glass Incorporated."

"How did you know that, Jack? Is that destructive reasoning, your training, or some special skill you learned at the police school or something?"

"Yes. Destructive reasoning, for sure. It's the result of prolonged exhaustive and detailed investigation. And it's written on the door. I've been feeling the letters with my fingers."

In some ways Jack had been renewed. He had done what seemed to be impossible a few days back. He had done what he gets paid for. He had found the girl. Suzanne Stanton. And she was still alive. If only he could call in the Cavalry. If only someone knew where he was.

Kelly and Suzanne Stanton spent much of that day and night talking and many hours the next day conversing through the wall of the coal bins. She told him of her plans to be a fashion writer for a big New York magazine and her thoughts on fashion, clothing design, and the sophisticated lifestyles of the rich and famous. Jack was enchanted. They were locked away in a dungeon, without food or water, and they were discussing fashion trends. She was so innocent, and yet seemingly knowledgeable of many of the inner workings of relationships and even some of the dynamics of pursuing a career.

She seemed to take a quick liking to Kelly but Jack shrugged off her admiration. He wrote it off as some warped transference or misguided Stockholm syndrome. She was just a kid. But she was becoming something special to Jack.

Kelly held all women in awe. He couldn't understand them but he knew he loved them. Jack was very susceptible.

And Jack was starving. It had been three days without food, a shower, or any other of the amenities of life. He was too dehydrated to shed a tear. The feelings of helplessness and frustration were overwhelming.

Where was Lt. Jessica Paris? She started this thing. Was she using some vacation time to go away with some guy on a 'Cruise to Nowhere?' Or was it a cruise to her underwear? Jack pictured them clinking their Champagne glasses by a window table on a cruise ship, a waiter bringing Chicken Parmesan, lobster, and Fettuccini Alfredo. They'd be playing tickle-foot under the table. Paris would laugh and say, "That poor slob of a Private Detective should either have that case wrapped up or be dead by the time we get back. Ha ha-ha! That schlep, that schmuck! Ha ha-ha."

Was Jack to die in the dirty coal bin? Along with the child he had been asked to find and protect. Tune in next week.

She would most likely be killed at some point. This was not the way Jack Kelly wanted things to go. And then, like a bubble in a bottle of cheap Champagne, an idea began to rise into his consciousness.

The Lawyer drove out of the apartment complex's parking lot and onto the street. The musician stirred from his sedentary position and swallowed. He slid back into the driver's seat from the backseat. He had shut the van's engine off about a half-hour earlier and it was stone cold inside the van. The cream colored Mercedes drove past him and he started up the engine while praying the Lawyer didn't look in his rear view mirror and notice The Musician following. He slapped the fan switch on to its maximum position, full blast, but the windows were three-quarters covered with frost. When the Lawyer turned a corner on the street Willie turned the old blue van around and stomped on the gas trying to catch up to the Mercedes.

As he rounded the corner he didn't see the Lawyer ahead of him. He gunned the engine and the van slowly responded. The windows were clearing as his eyes searched the traffic for the Mercedes.

"Oh no! If I sat there so early in the morning and lost him in the first thirty seconds of this moving surveillance I'll freak!" The Musician had a fifty-fifty shot. He looked over the BU Bridge and down the hill into Cambridge. He thought he caught sight of the cream colored car. Willie pushed down the accelerator and after several miles downhill he caught sight of the Mercedes ahead of him.

"Fuckin' rich mother! Remote-starting bastard! Warm your fucking car up from the fuckin' kitchen while us poor boys have to play catch up. Son-of-a-bitch!" He shouted as if the hot words would warm him. The Musician needed more coffee.

They headed onto Storrow Drive and along the Charles, passing the early morning year-round scullers on the river, moving almost as fast as the traffic. The Mercedes headed on into Boston. The Musician dialed his wife to see if Jack had called. The wife said he had not. He left a message with the desk sergeant at Area A for Lt. Paris to call his cell phone number when she got in. Didn't she start this ball rolling?

The cars passed the Citgo sign by Fenway Park in Kenmore Square and cruised into Boston. Willie kept three cars back. He knew his van was not the best for a moving surveillance. It was the worst. The beat-up blue van stuck out and didn't have the quick response for city driving. But The Musician could drive with the reckless abandon of a lifelong city dweller.

They were passing by Charles Circle, past the "If You Lived Her, You'd Be Home Now" sign in front of the Leveritt Circle Apartments and up onto the Central Artery South. With the Fleet Center in the rear view mirror and the North End on the left, he drove past Fannieul Hall and the Marketplace on the right. Past the Aquarium on the left, the financial district on the right.

Then with Chinatown on the right, the Lawyer took a left at South Station and crossed over the Fort Point Channel towards Southie and Binford Street. The Musician followed, mumbling, "Southie, again."

The cell phone rang and he answered on the third ring.

"Hello."

"This is Jesse Paris, Willie. Where the hell is Jack Kelly? He didn't show up for the task force meeting and his credibility has sunk even lower, with the FBI, anyway."

"Jesse, nobody has heard from Jack for three days. Its' really not like him. I've checked with a few friends and they've left messages, too. His cell phone, I guess, is not working. His mail is piling up at the office. The used black Jeep Cherokee he got after the Provost Brother burnt his white Crown Vic is not where he would keep it in the lot across the street."

"What was the last thing he was going to do?" Jesse asked.

"I don't know. Work the case, basically, I guess. I don't know. But I'm behind Lindon Chase right now. I've followed him from his condo in Brighton."

"What's he doing?" Paris asked.

"We just crossed into Southie, looks like we're headin' to 44 Binford Street again."

"OK, Willie. Save my cell-phone number and check with me right away if something happens. I'm going to get a uniform unit to follow me over there. Unless you call me back within the next fifteen minutes and tell me it was just a dead end."

Chapter 29

Plan 9 From Outer Space

Jack Kelly had a plan. It wasn't much of a plan, but desperate times call for desperate measures. He would act drowsy and unconscious the next time the Brothers drag him out onto the dirty warehouse floor. Maybe they would let their guard down and Jack could make a run for it. If he could walk, he might be able to run.

It wasn't much of a plan.

"Suzanne!" Jack shouted into the wall. And again, "Suzy!"

"Yes Mr.… ah, Jack." Suzanne's feeble voice could barely be heard.

"If they come back to feed you, or whatever, tell them you think I'm sick, OK?"

"Yes, Jack. I will. I can smell them cooking, chicken I think. They'll eat first and then bring me something. I'll tell them."

Jack took his left boot off, then his sock, and put the boot back on. Jack felt around and gathered some hard coal lumps and filled the end of his sock with them. He tied a knot in the sock and then smacked the wall a couple of times to test the weapon.

He tucked the business end up his sleeve and held the knot in his fist.

It wasn't much of a plan.

The Musician followed Chase to the old factory where Kelly had found Bucky in the window seat and the girl's hair. Chase parked his car in front of the building next door and Willie parked around the corner. Willie watched as the Lawyer looked around to see if anybody was observing him. Chase walked past the old factory and slipped around the corner, leaving Willie wondering where he was going. Lawyers don't sneak around corners to take a quick piss, do they?

By the time Willie was able to peak around the corner of the old brick factory, the Lawyer was nowhere in sight. "What the...?" Willie mused as he scratched his chin and peered at the junk cars piled up along the railroad tracks. The Musician was looking for fresh tracks in the snow or some kind of a sign when he heard the sound of footsteps behind him. His blood ran cold and sweat popped out on his forehead as he turned.

"Look. It's the crazy joker here again." One of the Soul Brothers said.

Willie was relieved to see the five rag-tag, juvenile, black gang members that he had spoke with before. "What up, my fine dark dudes?"

"You slummin' again Whitebread? Or you trying to plant some weed down here in the snow?" one brother said while two others howled with delight, slapping high-fives all-around.

The tension in Willie's shoulders was releasing as he smiled and nodded with respect to the leader of the pack. Then he realized he was relaxing a little too much when he saw the main-man pull what looked like a folded switchblade from the back of his waistband. Willie was starting to say something but a stuttering sound was all that came out of his mouth as his eyes grew wider and wider, staring at the stainless steel knife handle.

Soul Brother number one lifted the folded blade up in front of his own face and Willie's eyes followed it up until the two men stared ahead at each other. Willie felt helplessly trapped with no avenue of escape. The Brother made a sweeping motion across the top of his head as he pressed the button on the switchblade and a four-inch comb popped out. Once again the Brothers howled with laughter at Willie's expense.

"I'm gonna have to check my shorts for skid-marks on that one, Brothers," Willie said as his shoulders slumped and the air he was holding in his lungs was allowed to escape. The Soul Brothers were falling out with laughter. High-fives all-around, again.

The Musician stared at the fake switchblade, smiled, and held out his fist to Soul Brother Number One. The Brother punched it back lightly and smiled. As Willie settled down he realized he had seen the stainless steel appearing knife handle before.

"Where'd you get that, man? I seen that before. The stainless steel handle, man."

"Nah, man, its plastic."

"Yeah. I seen that when I dropped off Jack Kelly's car. The guy I'm looking for. It was in the Jeep"

"I didn't steal no knife, you crack head!"

"Look, man. I need to know where you got that! My friend has turned up missing, he might have been in this area and he had a comb like that in the center console of his Jeep! I ain't looking to bust you. Keep the fuckin' comb."

The Brothers looked vacant, the little standoff was over, and The Musician was about to call it a day and began to move around the gang, saying, "Sorry, man. I suppose there are thousands of those around. Its' just that my friends' in trouble, I know he is. And there was one of those in his ride. Sorry."

As Willie started walking and took a last look back to where the Lawyer seemed to disappear, Soul Brother Number One said, sheepishly, "Hey Whitebread? Was it a black Jeep Cherokee with tinted windows?"

The Musician stopped, turned and smiled and the Brother pointed to the distinct grill of Kelly's black Jeep parked among the junks by the rail tracks two hundred yards away.

When Jack heard the voices coming down the hall, he knew it was strike now or forever hold your peace. Skinny Provost opened the girl's bin door holding a plate of food and Suzanne yelled, "He's sick! He been coughin' and puking!"

Skinny yelled for his portly brother but there was no response. "Shit!" Skinny yelled down the hall and mumbled something about having to do everything himself. He put Suzanne's plate of food down in front of her and turned away. Suzanne crawled out onto the dirty wooden floor and started to pick at the food. Skinny looked down the hall and yelled, "Gino?"

Skinny begrudgingly lifted the cast-iron handle up and pulled open the coal bin door with a grating creak that gave him a shudder. He peered into the darkness, straining to see. As his eyes became accustomed to the dim light Skinny saw the lifeless form of Jack Kelly.

The thin man took hold of Kelly's hand and began pulling him out onto the dirty basement floor. "Gino!" he yelled again.

Provost let go of Jack's hand and Kelly's battered body slumped down onto the brick floor with his legs still stuck in the bin. "I don't think he's breathing," Suzanne said, peeking out from behind the open door of her oven-like coal bin.

It was easy for Jack to fake being half-conscious. He was about at the halfway point. He felt like a wounded animal lying by the side of the road.

Skinny bent over and looked into Kelly's face for some kind of sign. He saw a slight twitch in Jack's temple, Kelly's eyes popped open, and then thud! Skinny felt a crunching smack on the side of his head from the homemade black jack that Kelly had made from a sock filled with hard Bituminous coal. Jack hit him again.

Dazed and confused, Skinny wobbled to his feet just as the Lawyer, Lindon Chase, came through the factory's back door. Skinny took a step forward and his lower jaw dropped. Then Skinny fell forward and he hit the floor like a bag of shit.

The slight, wispy, Lawyer recoiled in fear, backing into the doorframe as Jack struggled to his feet, barely able to walk, and staggered toward the Lawyer.

"Gino! Gino?" the Lawyer squealed and screamed. Gino finally responded to the commotion. His heavy footsteps were heard coming down the hallway.

"Can't a guy even take a shi..." his voiced trailed off as he saw his brother laying facedown on the dirty cellar floor.

Jack Kelly, in his weakened state, attempted to grab the Lawyer, but instead fell back to the floor.

"Shit!" Gino yelled as he closed the distance, drawing Jack's .45 caliber from his waistband. Jack didn't have time to crawl away. He looked up at Gino in horror and covered his face with his arms as the Provost Brother pointed the gun at his head. The young girl screamed. The Lawyer stood in the doorframe's corner and screamed like a white lady seeing a mouse.

It wasn't much of a plan. No. And that point was driven home by the toe of Gino's boot as it made contact with Jack's side and then again on the side of his head.

Suzanne screamed again.

Jack looked at the girl, exhaled and mumbled a brave "Don't worry." He attempted to get back up onto his feet, turned toward Gino and said, just before losing consciousness, "The last time I got beat up, they put me in a hospital for a week with a morphine drip and cable TV right over my bed. Best vacation I ever had. So take your best shot."

Then Jack fell to his knees and fell forward with his face down on the floor.

Attorney Chase stepped forward, looking down on Kelly as Jack lost his struggle to regain consciousness. Blood trickled from Kelly's mouth onto the dirty factory floor.

"Billie took a digga, help me with him!" Gino screamed at Chase. They pulled Skinny up the three stairs and into the kitchen area. Then returned to drag Kelly up. Gino waved Suzanne on with the pistol and she walked haltingly up the few stairs to the kitchen area. The eight-year-olds' long blond hair was limp and full of coal dust. She wore what must have been a white dress, but it was now covered with coal dirt as was her white ankle sox and black leather shoes. She sat on the kitchen floor with her back to the wall. Her thin arms and dirty little hands clutched at the red scarf around her neck.

Gino had hurt his foot kicking Jack in the head and limped along in pain, dropping Kelly in the middle of the room. The 110-pound weakling, Chase, wasn't much help as Gino propped up his brother against the leg of a kitchen chair and sat down in it. He gently slapped Skinny's face trying to wake him. Gino walked back to where Kelly was stirring and trying to open his eyes and the Provost Brother pointed the gun at Kelly's head.

"You fucking bastard! You got Ray. And don't you keep calling him Bob. His real name was Ricardo-Ray, shit head."

Sleep When I'm Dead

"Ricardo-Ray Shit Head? What a pretty name." Jack mumbled in mock admiration.

"You smacked Billie with this fucking rock-sock," he said throwing the coal-filled sock at Kelly's face. The rocks hit the floor and scattered. "You got our cousin Bucky hooked up on attempted murder and kidnapping."

"Cousin Bucky Buxton-Smythe. Another mutant." Kelly offered.

"Why the fuck do you think Big Ray was following you, asshole?"

"Oh. You talkin' to me. Ah… I don't know… I mean I wasn't sure it was your brother. So, that whole thing with Bucky was to set me up?"

"Yeah, after what you did to us and Uncle Thaddeus. You just ain't too fucking bright, are ya dick head?" Skinny piped in, regaining his senses. "Maybe we should kill you right now. Shove you under one of those trains out there. Beat you to death with that shovel. Lock you in that freezer 'til you turn to hard vanilla ice cream."

Jack winked a swollen eyelid at Suzanne and said, "You scream. I scream. We all scream for ice cream."

"You are a plague on my family," Gino said taking a step toward Kelly. "If I had shot you the first time I wanted to, years ago, I'd be out of jail by now. I'll kill your ass right now, son of a bitch!" His fingers tightened on the gun as he took aim.

"No, Gino! Let's think for a minute! Let's do this right!" Chase said with a thick lisp.

"You don't want to do it, Gino." Kelly added.

"I've done it. I'll do it. I'll do it again." Gino yelled at Jack.

"Yeah," Jack said after a pause.

"I will if I want and if I want, I will." Gino said.

"What are you? The fucking Cat In The Hat?" Kelly wisecracked in the face of death.

Skinny, failing at an attempt to stand, asked his brother what happened, and moaned in pain and discomfort. Gino stepped back, sat down and held his brother, wiping the trickle of blood from the bump on the side of Skinny's head.

"This mother-fucking dick hit you with that sock filled with coal. The asshole!"

"Keep it together, Gino. Lets put these folks back in the bins." the Lawyer said.

"These folks? These fuckin' 'folks' just tried to whack my brother! Go ahead, Chase." The Lawyer looked at Jack Kelly and Suzanne Stanton and back at Gino, realizing that more was out in the open then he had intended.

"We could use a hand around here, you know?" continued Gino. "Don't forget who rolled the power window up on the girl's driver's neck and helped hold his head under water in that fuckin' duck pond in Belmont."

Suzanne screamed, "No!" and began to cry, rocking from side-to-side.

The Lawyer looked disgusted as he spoke to Gino.

"Look, Gino. I wish you wouldn't talk right now. We can discuss this down the road. Maybe there will be a little more money."

"*More* money? When do we get *any* of our fuckin' money? I was supposed to get seed money! I been payin' for the fuckin' food she's eatin'. What fucking money? What the fuck is going on? You were supposed to poison her or drive her nuts with all that fuckin' LSD, speed, and the mushrooms. You didn't even pay me for the drugs. This is *not* the way things were supposed to fucking go!" Gino yelled at Chase as he held his brother.

"There's not a shred of evidence on that!" Chase held his hands if front of him and said with a lisp as he pleaded his case to Jack Kelly.

Chapter 30

You Can't Stop the Rain

It was after sunset and it was one of those days when the temperature hovered right around 32 degrees. If it went under thirty-two it snowed and if it went above, it rained. It looked like rain. As soon as night fell so did the cold December rain. Paris pulled up to the front of 44 Binford St. in her gold unmarked Ford Taurus. Right behind her was a cruiser with two young, male, uniformed officers in it. As they exited their vehicles they caught sight of Willie and the Soul Brothers standing at the corner of the factory. The Soul Brothers began to scatter.

"Wait, my Brothers. These are friendlies." Willie pleaded. But the Soul Brothers only slowed to a moderate dispersal and would have continued to exit the scene, if it weren't for the rapid ascension of the biggest gang in the city. The Boston Police.

The two uniforms moved quickly with their hands on the butts of their holstered .40 caliber semi-automatic Glocks. No match for a comb.

It looked like a standoff. The Musician, with his long greasy hair and Jimi Hendrix T-shirt, with the five Soul Brothers and the three Boston Police officers. It was a tense moment as the rain began to pour down but it wasn't anything the BPD didn't routinely deal with during a shift.

Lt. Paris stepped forward in-between the two uniforms.

"What's going on Willie?" she asked The Musician.

"Its all good, L.T. My retro friends, here, have located what might be Jack's Jeep. Its right over there," he said pointing toward the tracks.

"Let's have a look." Paris began walking toward the Jeep with one uniform behind her. Willie and the Soul Brothers fell in behind her with an officer at the rear.

The black Jeep with its' tinted windows sat solemnly parked between a twisted yellow and black checkerboard wreck that was once a Checker taxicab and a faded, black, junk Dodge fish truck. As the divergent group approached, Lt. Paris experienced the familiar fear, based on experience, that an ordinary vehicle can often become a crime scene. They walked toward the black Jeep. The rain came down in sheets as Jesse tried to peer through the blacked-out windows. She silently prayed that the man she cared for, the man she had shared a bed with just over a week ago, was not a cold corpse within.

"We were supposed to get the money from you. From the estate. You're her fucking lawyer. Can't you just cut a check?" Gino was still agitated but wanted to cut and run.

"Cut a check? Oh, god, no! You sent the ransom note two days late. They are processing it at the Mass State Police Laboratory out in Jamaica Plain. Then the District Attorney and the police will let me write a check on the estate. Then we can convert it to cash. Now the banks are closed for the weekend. Maybe on Monday you and I can make the exchange. The girl for the cash. And nobody gets hurt." The Lawyer slowly explained again to Gino.

Gino, still cradling Billie, looked incredulously at the Lawyer.

"Nobody gets hurt? What about Billie, here? The dead fucking chauffeur? The girl has seen us now." Gino's voice grew louder perhaps as he realized just how deep in this he was getting. He continued, louder and louder.

"Nobody gets hurt? What about cousin Bucky? The cops took him out of Kelly's office and he was going to make a deal with the cops. He couldn't stand up. Not with his drug habit. He would have started spilling his guts just like he did when we were kids. He would have told them everything. Now, we lost the bail money on him and we had to snuff him. Mama's gonna kill us if she finds out we killed Bucky. What about the fucking Quaaludes, acid, Ecstasy, Bella-Donna strychnine, and the other shit you were putting in the kid's food? We can't just turn her over to the cops. She will pick my photo out of a line-up. Me and Billie will have to leave the country. And this private detective, he's going to have to be taken care of. He fucking executed my older brother."

"Bob? Bob-Ray, or Ricardo? That would be Bob, right? Big Bobby Boy, right?" Jack Kelly said almost reflexively through a mouth half-filled with blood.

"Shut the fuck up!" Gino screamed as a clap of thunder boomed through out the canyons of old deserted factory buildings.

Kelly coughed, spit, and continued as the lights flickered.

"Oh yeah. My boy Bob. Big boy Bob. Bob's big boy Bobby Bobby boy.

Bibbidy, Bobby-dee, Boo."

"Shut up! I'll kill you right now, motherfucker!" Gino screamed, his eyes popping as he dropped Skinny Billie on the floor and tugged wildly at the gun tucked in his waistband. He was now officially out of control. He yanked at the gun as he stepped toward Jack.

The bang from the gun sent a sick feeling through Jack and he tried to crawl toward the door expecting to feel a piercing pain.

The gunshot echoed loudly off the factory's cellar walls rendering everyone momentarily deaf. The acrid gun smoke filled the room as Jack, Chase, Skinny, and Suzanne looked around trying to see where the bullet went. As they looked back at Gino they realized that the gun had discharged while still in Gino's waistband. He looked startled and the menacing glare directed toward Jack Kelly soon gave way to shock. Gino realized the trajectory of the bullet may have headed downward to his own southern regions.

"Uh, oh…" Gino uttered like a four year old that had spilled his milk as blood began to run down his left leg and out across the toe of his black work boot. He looked downward, startled, and he turned pale. He groaned in pain and hopped a few feet sideways, sitting down on the creaky old wooden kitchen chair.

"Gino?" Skinny said getting up to his knees and then to his feet. "Are you hit, brother?"

"It's my little Willie Johnson!" Gino cried out, looking at his brother forlornly.

Chapter 31

Dead Wood

As the ragtag group of Willie and The Soul Brothers, Lt. Paris, and the two young officers walked behind the factory, toward the rail yard, and surrounded the Jeep, Willie said, "That's Jack's, alright."

The loud and grating sound of locomotives backing freight cars into the yard muffled the gunshot from the factory.

But one of the Soul Brothers stopped in his tracks.

"Was that a gat?" he said.

"I heard it, too. Sounded like a gun, for sure." One of the rookie cops said, pointing toward the old factory's back door. Paris instructed the young officer to get a couple of units started their way as she pulled her .38 revolver out from a shoulder holster under her jacket. The younger officer spoke into his microphone, the radio squawked back, and the two Uniforms drew their .40 caliber Glocks. The three cops crossed the thirty or forty yards to positions along the brick wall on either side of the rear door of the old factory. The Soul Brothers and Willie hung back by Kelly's Jeep looking at each other and at the cops as they alternately sought cover.

Sleep When I'm Dead

Both Provost brothers, Jack, Suzanne, and Chase looked down at the pooling blood beneath Gino Provost's left jean cuff, running across his boot and out onto the floor.

Muffled footsteps could be heard outside.

"Somebody is shuffling around outside," Chase said dramatically in an affectedly hoarse voice.

"Gimme the gun, Gino." Skinny said grabbing at the weapon. The two struggled briefly but Gino held on to the gun.

Skinny Provost jumped up on the kitchen table against the wall and peeked out a small window.

"There's some black gang-bangers out there. With a white hippie. And a chick. She's got a gun. She's by the back door. And two five-o fuckin' cops. Let's get the fuck out of here," Skinny said, jumping back onto the kitchen floor.

Skinny and the Lawyer started moving toward a door in the rear of the kitchen.

"Where does this go?" Chase asked Skinny.

"Wait!" Gino yelled, "What are you fucking crazy. You can't leave me here. You have two witnesses who can ID us!"

"Sshhh! What do you want to do? Shoot them now and the cops will come in and we're toast!" Skinny said.

Gino pointed the gun at Jack Kelly, who was still lying on the floor, and then at Suzanne sitting in the corner and then back at Jack.

"Don't! Not now." Chase said in that low, hoarse voice, and added, "Come on, Billie. Lets get him up and start moving!"

But Gino wanted to plug Kelly with a bullet, badly. He stared at Kelly and lined up the sights with Jack's head. Then he pointed the gun again at the girl, Suzanne.

"Hey! Some Christmas, huh, Pudgy?" Jack said, and Gino pointed the gun back at him. "Don't shoot. Just go! Go... I'll count to twenty before I let the cops in," Jack said.

"Make it thirty!" Gino screamed in pain as they shuffled through the rear kitchen door.

The cops outside must have heard the commotion and Paris knocked loudly, announcing, "Police, open the door!"

Jack wearily looked at Suzanne Stanton and counted aloud, "One. Two, three, four. Thirty!" and tried to get to his feet. Jack yelled in the direction of Paris's voice, "Kick it in! We need help."

Suzanne yelled even louder than Jack, "Help us!" and ran over to Jack and jumped into his arms. Jack fell back on the floor from the weight of the eight-year-old.

The factory door burst open and the two uniformed officers jumped through what tactical forces call the fatal funnel of the doorway with guns drawn. They began their systematic sweep of the rooms. Lt. Paris entered cautiously until she saw Kelly and Suzanne on the floor in the middle of the makeshift kitchen. They were momentarily unrecognizable. Their white teeth and blinking white eyes stared out at Paris.

"Jack! Suzanne!" she screamed bounding up the stairs and running over to them. The two uniforms had finished checking the coal bin area at the end of the factory and had come up the few stairs to the kitchen. As they moved toward the door that Skinny, Gino, and Attorney Chase had exited through, Jack spoke up.

"Chase, Skinny Billy, and Gino Provost just went through that door. Gino has a gun. A .45. And he's been shot." The detective reported as the young officers stopped and looked back at the Lieutenant.

"Jack, did you shoot another Provost Brother?" the Lt. suggested, trying to wrap her arms around Suzanne Stanton. Suzanne pulled away and put her arms around Kelly.

"No, Lieutenant. He shot himself." Jack answered.

"Oh, right. Shot himself," said the Lt. while she pushed back the hair off of Ms. Stanton's forehead.

"Really!" Suzanne said excitedly. "That man had the gun down his pants, and it went off. He said he shot his 'Willie.'"

"Hey! I resent that!" Willie Crawford, The Musician said from the doorway with the five Soul Brothers peering in from behind him.

"Mr. Kelly got him so mad, he was spitting, and swearing, and screaming." Suzanne said.

"Oh, I'm sure. Mr. Kelly can do that. And I know the feeling." Paris nodded, looking at Jack with a smile as she squeezed his dirty black hand.

The two uniformed officers were going through the back door from the kitchen into the factory when Lt. Paris said, "Call it in, Murphy. And lets' get medical and back up on the way before you go rushing through that door. Let's get the perimeter secured, Jones. Go back out and take the front outside corner of the building. You can see the street and two sides of the building from there. And guide the responding units in," the Lt. yelled as the younger officer took off like a gazelle. Murphy's police radio crackled and tweaked as the officer advised dispatch of the situation and asked for available additional units.

"Murphy, who's the shift super?"

"Sgt. Donavan, Lieutenant."

"Of course. Ask Area D to give Sgt. Donavan the heads up."

Jesse pulled a five-shot Charter Arms Bulldog .44 Magnum revolver from her jacket pocket and gave it to Jack.

"C'mon Murphy. You got the big flashlight, let's go." Jessica Paris and Patrolman Murphy went into the factory through the back kitchen door. Kelly thought she was a hell of a cop.

Jack opened the cylinder of the Bulldog. It was fully loaded. He looked at the girl sitting on his leg. She was still shaking.

"Its almost over little doll. You have been through so much. You are so brave!"

Kelly and Suzanne were still holding on to each other. As they looked into each other's eyes, Suzanne's lower lip trembled. Tears began to well up in the eyes of the girl and the detective. Jack wiped his eyes with a filthy sleeve and said, "You're so brave..." He hugged her and then held her at arms length. "And so dirty!" They both began to laugh through the tears and hugged again. The two were completely black, covered from head to toe with coal dust. Jack's face was swollen and bloody on one side and there was an oblong shaped goose egg on Jack's forehead.

Willie came over and helped Jack and Suzanne, who would not take her arms from around Jack, up onto an old wooden chair at the kitchen table. The Soul Brothers filtered in, smelled the acrid gun smoke, and looked around at the bloody spots on the floor. The smallest turned to the tallest and said, "Let's beat it."

The Musician stood up and said something meant to be a Muslim salute, "Allah Salaam Alaikum, my brothers," and put a fist to his chest, then shot it out in a peace sign. The Soul Brothers made faces at one another and one dismissed him with a wave, saying "Yeah, whatever," as they filed out the door.

"Let's all get out of this rat hole." Jack Kelly said, helping the girl off his knee and to her feet. Suzanne would not let go of his hand as the Musician helped Jack get up from the rickety wooden chair. Kelly walked like an 85-year-old with Rheumatism.

"I'm so glad I found you Suzy. We're both gonna check in at a hospital, then I'm going to take you to any restaurant you want, and then I'm going to take you back to your home." Jack said, looking down at the eight-year-old. She looked like a five-foot pile of soot with very dirty blond hair but with a smile shining through like a star in the night.

"I want to stay with you, Jack. I've been counting the days and tomorrow night is Christmas Eve. I've got nobody else, now. Please," she said, as she looked up at Jack, happily unafraid. Oh, the indomitable spirit of youth.

"I've got nobody too, Suzanne. And I'd love to be with you right through Christmas."

Chapter 32

Cut To the Chase

The Provost Brothers and the Lawyer had stumbled through the warehouse, the book repository, and into the old shoe factory. They went up a set of creaky stairs to the street level doorway. Gino was bleeding badly and they stopped just before stepping out onto the sidewalk to wrap a sweater around his waist. Gino slumped against the wall.

"Fuck this!" Gino said after repeated attempts, stuffing the whole sweater down the front of his bloody blue jeans. "Get me up. Lets' get to the car. Go start it up, Billy."

Skinny and Chase each took an arm and pulled Gino up onto his feet. Billy pushed open the door and ran out onto the snow as the icy New England rain came down in waves. Skinny Billy ran down the alley between the buildings at 44 Binford and 42, to where he had moved the Cadillac the day before. He got the keys out, jumped into the Caddy, and started it up. The wipers knocked the accumulated snow off the windshield as the engine roared to life. Skinny jammed the car in drive and headed for the front doors on Binford St.

Chase and Gino heard the approaching footsteps of the cops making their way, as stealthily as they could, through the building. Gino leaned on Chase as he hopped out through the front doors and the Caddy pulled up. Lt. Paris's lookout, Officer Jones, observed the front end of the Caddy and signaled Murphy by radio.

"Got a black Cadillac pulling up at the front doors, Murphy. Where are you?"

"We are almost through the building and I just heard a door shut."

Lt. Paris grabbed Murphy's shoulder mike and said quietly, "Start sliding down the side of the building, Jonesy. Use caution, go slow."

As Paris and Murphy approached the old wooden double doors, Chase and Gino were visible out on the porch through the glass. Murphy stepped out first with his gun drawn. The Lawyer, Lindon Chase, saw him first and said, "There they are officer!" pointing to Gino and then Skinny behind the wheel. "Arrest them!"

Gino turned and whacked the Lawyer in the head with the side of the gun, knocking him to the ground. Then Gino turned the gun toward Patrolman Murphy discharging one round that pierced the cop's leather jacket below his right shoulder. Murphy's Glock.40 flew into the air and clattered on the stone stairs. Murphy spun around and fell against the door, closing it on Lt. Paris and pushing her back in. As the cold rain poured down Gino leveled the gun on Paris through the windows of the factory door. Just as Gino began squeezing the trigger he was hit from the side by three rounds from the gun of Patrolman Jones, a few feet away on the side of the building's stairs. Lt. Paris then shot twice through the glass in the door, the first bullet shattering glass over the stairs and the second finding the side of Gino's head.

Skinny Billy looked up from the Caddy at the lifeless expression on his brother's face as Gino turned and slumped to the ground. Billy felt the blood draining from his own head. He stomped on the Caddy's gas pedal but the car sat for a few moments before the rear end swung around on the hard-packed snow. The big car fishtailed out of the alley, grinding against the wall and then the brick stairs. As the tail end cleared the building Officer Jones was knocked back onto the street. The car headed up Binford St, spraying snow, sand, and water in its wake.

Jones got back up to his feet and he and Paris met at the center of the street, running and stopping to aim at the back of the speeding car. For a moment they were censored by protocol, unable to shoot at the fleeing felon. Then Lt. Paris said, "Bullshit!" and discharged one round and Jones popped off five quick shots. The officers looked around helplessly. Lt. Paris yelled, "Where's the goddamned back up?"

Jack, Willie, and Suzanne turned the back corner of the brick warehouse and they had begun walking up the middle of the street. Jack was looking up into the street light and feeling the cold rain wash away the filth that covered him when the first shots were fired. As they looked up Binford Street they saw Skinny swing the Caddy around, knocking Jones on his back, and speed up the cobblestone street.

Lt. Paris screamed into her portable radio, "Shots fired, officer down! Suspect fleeing from Binford Street in a black Cadillac!"

Then they saw the big equipment van with "The Soul Brothers" written on the side swing down from A Street and pull across the top of Binford Street blocking any exit. Skinny hit the brakes but slid into the side of the van. He gunned the engine, trying to push the Soul Brothers equipment van but the Caddy's tires just spun faster and faster and began to smoke as they melted away the snow and found the cobblestone beneath.

Paris and Jones began to move toward the collision. Skinny put the car in reverse and the car spun back around toward the dead end of Binford St. then he hit the gas and the large and heavy car began moving forward faster and faster toward Paris and Jones. The two cops fired two shots each through the windshield but did not hit the thin man. The officers dove headfirst to either side of the car as it passed within inches. The car gained momentum and was heading straight ahead, toward Suzanne, Willie, and Jack Kelly.

Jack pushed Suzanne toward the Musician and said, "Take her, Willie."

The Musician clutched the eight-year-old and moved quickly back to the corner of the brick building. The Cadillac gained more and more speed as Skinny gripped the steering wheel and his knuckles turned white. Jack could see the menacing grin on Billy Provost's face. He could see the anguish and desperation of a man inevidibly trapped by the circumstances of his own actions. Billie screamed, "Say hello to my brothers in Heaven!"

Jack could see the windshield wipers splash the rain up over the roof and he thought of the gasoline "Bob" Provost had poured over Jack's car, and on Jack. And Kelly said quietly, "Good boys go to Heaven," Jack Kelly pulled the .44 Magnum Bulldog from the blood and charcoal covered waistband of his black pants and cocked the revolver's hammer back. The Caddy flew towards him and he took aim, lining up the barrel of the revolver with Skinny's head. Jack said, "Say Hi to My Boy Bob in Hell."

Jack squeezed the trigger with a steady pull and the hammer released striking the firing pin, which hit the cartridge on the center primer. The primer ignited and the tiny explosion propelled the projectile forward at an extreme velocity. The spinning .44 Magnum slug exploded from the gun's barrel, transversed the distance, and cut through the windshield, forming a spider webbed shatter pattern, and soon thereafter the bullet hit Skinny in the right shoulder shattering the bones in his upper arm.

The thin man cried out in pain and he slumped forward against the wheel as his foot pushed the accelerator to the floor. The Caddy passed Jack Kelly hitting 82 miles-per-hour before it got to the end of the dead end street. The car hit the ramp at the loading dock and was propelled twenty feet up into the air and out onto the train tracks. There, a freight train locomotive, in search of a coupling, struck it and pushed it along the tracks into a freight car, crushing it and its driver.

Chapter 33

The Scales of Justice

Murphy and Jones were on their feet and assessing the damage. A bullet had passed through Murphy's leather and through the fleshy part of his right tricep but he didn't want to be taken out of the game. And although Jones had been knocked back by the fishtailing Caddy, he was OK. Paris finally realized that the Lawyer was no longer present at the proceedings.

"Where is that fucking rat bastard barrister?" Paris asked as additional units began pulling into the dead end.

"That's kind of harsh, Lieutenant? You're giving rats a bad name," Jack said, sarcastically as he, Suzanne, and the Musician walked up to the front stairs of the warehouse, getting out of the rain. Suzanne was hugging Jack again. She would have stood on top of his shoes like little girls do when they dance with their fathers, if she could have.

"How do you save a drowning lawyer, Jack?" the Lt. said and continued with the answer, "Take your foot off his neck."

Murphy leaned in close to Lt. Paris and whispered something to her.

"Jesus Christ! He's got your fucking Glock?" Jesse yelled at Murphy.

Jack quickly went over to the bullet-riddled body of Gino Provost and retrieved his own Colt .45. He handed Lt. Paris's .44 Bulldog to Murphy telling him there were four shots left.

The little Soul Brother stepped forward and pointed to the doors of the factory, saying, "The little guy picked up the gun and went in there."

"C'mon Jonesy. Let's hunt down this varmint. Wanna come, Jack? You used to do the negotiator thing didn't you? Yeah, FBI training, right?"

"Yes, Lieutenant. But that was with people. This is a lawyer."

"You're right, Jack. They're not right in the head. You can tell him it's in his best interest to surrender but he'll find some argument," the Lt. agreed, handing Jack the flashlight that Murphy had given her.

"Murphy, get the shotgun from my trunk, brief the incoming units to cover the outside perimeter, lets go down to channel three on the radios, and hold all non-essential talk. Also, until we can secure and get her medical attention, get that shivering girl and those other civilians into warm cars," Paris instructed as the three went cautiously through the front doors of the factory.

"Anybody see a light switch?" Jones asked.

Kelly, Paris, and Jones moved slowly and quietly along the walls of the dark warehouse into the enormous, long closed down, shoe factory with all its assembly lines. As they moved toward the book repository entrance they heard the sound of a falling book and exchanged glances. Only darkness filled the skylights and the huge room was almost pitch black. As Jack, Jones, and Paris separated, the Boston Police officers moved along the walls, and Jack walked among the stacks and ceiling-high shelves heading towards the room's center. It was the elephant's graveyard of books. The warehouse was huge, with old, dusty, out-dated books bought and sold by the ton. Like an enormous library of dead books, the massive shelves went from floor to high ceiling in every direction.

"Hey, Chase?" Jack yelled out into the room. "It was so cold Monday I saw several lawyers outside the courthouse with their hands in their *own* pockets."

Paris chimed in, "Attorney Chase, you know what's black and brown and looks good on a lawyer? A pack of Dobermans." And she continued with "Jones. What's the difference between a dead dog in the road and a dead lawyer in the road?"

"There are skid marks in front of the dog," Murphy answered and continued, "Lieutenant? What do lawyers and sperm have in common?"

"Only one in three million have a chance of becoming human." all three answered.

At the center of the warehouse, this graveyard for over a hundred thousand outdated books, and up at the top of a double column, sat Lindon Chase, Esquire. His arm was resting on a huge industrial-size scale for weighing books by the hundred pound lot, perched at the top of the shelf. He was shaking his head, thoroughly confused for the first time since childhood, and fretting, wondering what to do, which way to turn. From Chase's twenty-five foot perch he could see the flashlights of the three moving in, surrounding him. He pulled out the .40 caliber Glock automatic and pointed it at Jack walking through the bookshelves below him. The attorney shook and began to whimper. Kelly heard him, looked up and saw that Chase had the drop on him. Jack wondered if this would be the last thing he saw. He began to talk quietly to Chase.

"Hi Lindon. We were just looking for you. We want to straighten this all out. Lets go in and see just what we got here. You haven't killed anybody, Lindon. Well, maybe not. Well, maybe you did, but that hasn't been proven. I think you'll work something out. You're not a bad person."

"I'm not a punk kid, Kelly! Don't patronize me. I am quite familiar with the laws that have been broken and what crimes I have committed."

"Well, you should know that you have the right to remain silent. Anything you say can or will be used against you in court. You have the right to an attorney…"

"Shut up! Shut up! Shut up! I don't want *you* giving me Miranda!" the Lawyer screamed, pointing Murphy's gun at Jack.

"Take it easy, Chase. One of these officers is going to think you're threatening and shoot you. We can still walk out of here."

Chase began to sniffle and shake his head in disbelief. He moved the muzzle of the gun up to his own temple and held it tight against the side of his head.

"I went to Yale!" the Lawyer screamed.

"Should have gone to Harvard." Jack said quietly, remembering fondly his years at the Harvard University Extension School. Lt. Paris took aim from around the corner of a bookshelf.

"I graduated at the top of my class! What happened? I didn't need that much money. My lover was going to get some plastic surgery. But we could have made ends meet." Jack wasn't going to touch that line as Chase carried on with his lisp in full service, "I don't even know how to shoot this ugly, ugly gun."

"Come to the edge and start climbing down. I'll help you. Leave the gun," Jack said sincerely and he moved under the bookshelves with his hand extended upwards.

But Chase tried to rock the big book scale balanced on top of the shelves to make it fall on top of Jack Kelly. But when he couldn't get it to fall over, he pointed the gun at Kelly and pulled the trigger repeatedly. The shots rang out and the acrid gun smoke filled the air. After four or five shots, all of them missing Kelly as he ducked behind a bookshelf, Chase lost his balance and tried to clutch onto the heavy scale. Jesse and Officer Jones tried to get a clear shot from behind the shelves. Several books tumbled off the top of the shelf, hitting other books and falling to the floor below. And then as the big scale began to rock, Chase lost his grip and tumbled down onto the pile of books on the floor below.

Chase hit the floor hard but sat up still clutching the gun as Jack Kelly stood before him. The frail lawyer seemed surprised that he didn't get hurt and smiled at Kelly. Chase pointed the gun at Jack's stomach as they both heard the metal and wood creak as the top shelf splintered. They looked up to see the heavy book scale falling over the top edge of the bookshelf. The Lawyer's eyes grew wide and he was frozen. The scale turned slowly in the air as it fell off the top and its cast iron mass was pulled downward. It landed directly on top of Chase. It crushed the top of his skull and pushed his head down into the frame of his upper body. Jack heard the crunching and snapping of facial and neck bones from the weight of the big scale.

As the dust began to settle Jack could see, in the pile of books, the blood oozing out of the top of Chase's forehead and hear the air escaping from his lungs. He heard the gurgling sound of the bubbles of blood as they oozed out from his open face. First a half-dozen and then more and more books from the broken top shelves poured down onto Chase. Hundreds of old books rained down on the dying counselor until he was completely covered and could no longer be seen. Lt. Paris and Patrolman Jones walked over and stood by Jack as the three stunned cops looked at the pile of books and rubble that had buried Chase. The dust and smoke settled as the three looked down in shock at the sight.

Jack picked up a particularly large and heavy book that was lying on top of the pile and read the tittle.

"M.G.L. Chapters 268A to 274, Crime and Punishment, Massachusetts General Laws."

The End

Epilogue

Christmas Eve's cold night had turned into a sunny Christmas Day. A light snow had covered everything with a fluffy inch. Jack and Jesse had stayed overnight at the Stanton Mansion in Belmont with Suzanne Stanton. Jesse and Jack had given Suzanne a six-foot high fuzzy brown Vermont teddy bear. Suzanne gave Jesse some perfume and a red and green scarf. She gave Jack a beautifully framed gold leafed copy of Invictus, the hundred-year-old poem by William Ernest Henley that Jack had so much trouble remembering.

Cooper and Ed had arrived at noon; their heads covered with bright red and white Santa Claus knit caps. In the early afternoon The Musician and the five Soul Brothers came out in Willie's old beat up blue van. There were turkey sandwiches, lasagna, fruit, coffee, pumpkin pie, Christmas snacks and eggnog on the dining room table but most gathered in the living room by the warm and glowing fireplace. Jack had found a Christmas jazz program on the radio. They were playing a few tunes by Thelonious Monk and the Jazz Giants and launching into John Coltrane's 23 minute version of "A Love Supreme." Jack was at peace, even though he knew he could never really leave the dark side of life and regain the innocence of an eight-year-old child.

As Suzanne Stanton, Jack, and Jesse sat together on the couch, Jesse leaned over, gave Kelly a kiss and said, "Now you can finally get that long rest you've been needing, Jack."

"That's what its going to say on my tombstone. 'Now I can finally get some sleep.'"

"Jack, you are my shining knight. My savior. You are a good man," Suzanne Stanton told Kelly, hugging his arm and looking up at him. Jack couldn't help but be touched. Tears *almost* began to well up in his eyes.

Jack looked at Jesse and then at Suzanne with a dream in his eye and a smile on his lips and said, "Virtue is its own punishment."

Printed in the United States
154103LV00016B/73/A